UNTIL
SHILOH
COMES

UNTIL SHILOH COMES

A Civil War Novel

THE SHILOH TRILOGY BOOK 1

KARL A. BACON

Historical Chronicles Press

Until Shiloh Comes
Copyright © 2015 by Karl A. Bacon

Historical Chronicles Press

ISBN 978-0-9863244-0-6 soft cover
ISBN 978-0-9863244-1-3 EPUB
ISBN 978-0-9863244-2-0 PDF-merchant

Editor: David Lambert
Cover design: Andy Meyer
Interior design: Beth Shagene

Printed in the United States of America

15 16 17 18 19 20 21 • 10 9 8 7 6 5 4 3 2 1

My son, if thou wilt receive my words, and hide my commandments with thee; so that thou incline thine ear unto wisdom, and apply thine heart to understanding; yea, if thou criest after knowledge, and liftest up thy voice for understanding; if thou seekest her as silver, and searchest for her as for hid treasures; then shalt thou understand the fear of the LORD, and find the knowledge of God.

PROVERBS 2:1–5

A CIVIL WAR NOVEL

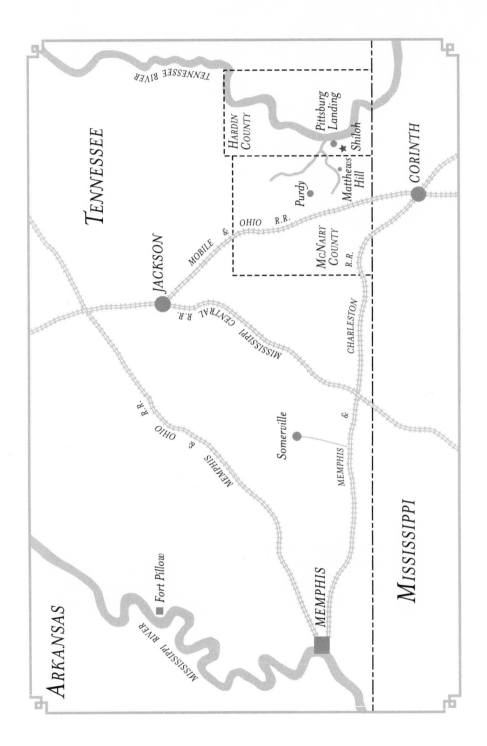

CHAPTER 1

———·—

*D*AVINA MATTHEWS STOOD AT THE EAST WINDOW OF HER bedroom as daylight broke upon her sleeping farm. Her eyes slowly traced the split-rail fence that separated pastureland from woodland. Yankee patrols had appeared now and again to graze their mounts in her pastures. Levi said they had stolen a couple of hogs from the woods a week past, but thus far they hadn't bothered the small flock of sheep or the few grazing beef steers and milk cows.

A time to be born, and a time to die; a time to plant, and a time to pluck up that which is planted; a time to kill, and a time to heal; a time to break down, and a time to build up; a time to weep, and a time to laugh; a time to mourn, and a time to dance. She had learned those verses from her father back in South Carolina, as well as many other passages of Scripture through the years, but now those words of King Solomon plagued her nearly every day.

"'All is vanity and vexation of spirit.'" Davina's whispered words created small breath puffs upon the window pane. *Vexation of spirit. Yes, indeed, ever since her husband, Ben, rode away to join Forrest's cavalry corps.*

The war had seemed so distant then, except for Ben's absence. Sometimes it almost seemed to be someone else's war. Until that cold, blustery day in late February when a single soldier on horseback, Hank Fowler from over near Selmer, had ridden up the lane with the terrible news of Ben's death at Donelson, a place Davina had never heard of before. Pastor Blackwell told her it was God's will, and he told her good would come from her loss, even *showers of blessing*. His words still felt hard and cold like midwinter earth.

Now she was surrounded by Yankees. The first of their large steamboats had arrived at Pittsburg Landing just three Sabbaths before. The Yankees—Sherman's men, most of them—had pitched their tents around the little church that her own Ben and their slave Levi had helped build. Their humble Shiloh Church was now the enemy's headquarters, and again today, April 6, no preaching of the Prince of Peace would be heard within those simple log walls, only the deadly schemes of war.

It was our hands that built your house, Lord, and Ben and Levi done a lot of it. Now it's only a stinking, muddy city of filthy men and filthy beasts. Just ain't no place to take the little ones for preaching, Lord.

Davina sighed and wiped the window pane with the cuff of her nightgown. A few days ago several riders in gray had dashed across her pastureland to the cover of the trees beyond. And on Friday afternoon, a Tennessee cavalry patrol had stopped at the farm to water their horses. The captain of the patrol confirmed what Davina already suspected—the army was coming up quickly from Corinth and there would soon be a great battle. But yesterday all was quiet, and this morning was just as peaceful.

If the army was close, then Aaron was close, too. Very close.

I'm empty, Lord. Is this what you want? Is this why you took Ben? Because I was leaning too much on him and not on you? I'm only a woman, Lord, and without Ben my heart is broke. You say you can put it together again, Lord, but can you even find all the pieces? And today, Lord, I'm afraid for Aaron. Keep him safe, please. He's only eighteen, and I can't lose him, too.

Davina dabbed at her eyes with her kerchief.

A soft knock on her door broke the silence. "Mama?"

It was Luke, her fourteen-year-old son. "Come in, dear."

The boy entered and came to Davina's side at the window. "Will it be today, Mama?"

Davina put her arm around Luke's shoulders and drew him close. "Only God knows for sure. I was just standing here thinking about your brother, and praying, too. We haven't seen him in more than six months, and it's hard on a mother to know her boy's so close, maybe in danger. I'd give anything to hold him just like this."

"I wish I could go and fight, Mama. Just think of it, me and Aaron fighting them Yankees side by side."

"Ain't your time, my dear. Besides, this family's already given so much." Davina hugged her son a little closer. "It's a hard thing, your papa never coming home, but I need you here with me."

"I know, Mama." Luke gave his mother a peck on the cheek. "Wish Aaron was here. Why can't it be like it was?"

Davina had asked that same question countless times. Things would never be like they were before, not without Ben. And it was ever so hard for her to know how things ought to be, now that he was gone.

"I hate them Yankees, for what they did to Papa." Luke's words were hard and terse. "Every last one of them."

Davina turned from the window to look at Luke. He tried so hard to be a man, sometimes, but so much of the boy remained, and that boy was tussling with the same hard things she was. So different from her grown-up Aaron, who was so much like Ben. But Luke was growing fast, now; another year and she'd be looking up at him.

"Hating ain't good, Luke. 'Love your enemies,' that's what Jesus said." But the words sounded hollow and left a bitter taste.

"Oh, Mama, I can't—"

A low rumble like distant thunder rolled across the farm. Davina's breath caught in her throat. Luke stiffened beside her. Then there was a second report, more distinct this time, and another that Davina felt in her feet. The window glass in front of her face vibrated a raspy note within its frame.

"It's started, Mama."

"Yes. Now leave so I can dress. And pray for your brother."

"Yes, Mama." Luke paused at the door. "I'll pray that Aaron kills lots of Yankees."

Davina dressed quickly—not her pale blue Sunday dress with the frills at the hem and sleeves and bodice, but rather loose-fitting, workday attire: faded brown duck trousers with leather braces and a plaid cotton flannel shirt. She went to the front door, drew on her boots, and walked out onto the veranda.

"Missus Davina." Min Jackson stepped up onto the veranda, breathless from running up the lane from her family's cabin. "Did you hear, missus? Did you hear?"

"I heard, Min. Wish I hadn't, but I heard." Davina looked over the line of trees beyond the fields to the east. "Seems a big fight's started down near the church."

Davina and Min stood at the railing of the veranda, listening intently as the thump of artillery grew more constant. Waves of clattering musket fire filled the gaps between cannon blasts, and soon the noise of pitched battle became a steady clamor from which there was no escape.

"Oh my," Min said every so often. "Oh my."

Davina's children appeared one by one on the veranda, still dressed in their bedclothes. She hardly noted their presence until six-year-old Davy, the youngest, began to scream. Ruthie, his ten-year-old sister, took his hand and tried to quiet the boy.

Davina was about to gather Davy into her arms when Anna, her fifteen-year-old daughter, came rushing out of the house, as did Luke. "Anna, look after your little brother, please."

Anna picked the boy up. "Don't cry, Li'l Davy. You remember them bad Yankees we seen? Well, Aaron's down there, and he's giving them Yankees a whipping and we won't see them no more. Then Aaron'll come home, and everything'll be good again." Davy screamed all the louder.

Davina fixed her gaze on the wisps of battle smoke rising over the trees. Aaron *was* down there somewhere, down near the Corinth Road maybe, with all the rest of the Thirteenth Tennessee. She knew her eldest son would go into battle and do his duty, just as his father had done. His courage warmed her a little, but it frightened her more, and she wished only to take the buckboard and dash down the lane and bring Aaron home to Matthews Hill.

Still, it was the Sabbath, and she would try to observe it as best she could. The family would gather, and Luke would read from the Bible, and maybe Willy would remember some verses, and she would pray for the little flock—her flock. They would do these things just as they had done them last Sunday, and the Sunday before that. But first, her flock needed to be fed.

"Min." The black woman moved not at all. Davina turned and laid a gentle hand on the short, stout woman's shoulder. "Minny."

Min jumped at the touch. "Yes, missus?"

"Go fix breakfast for this hungry gang. Do up some ham and eggs, and griddle cakes. Make plenty for all yours too."

"Yes, missus." Min tore her gaze away and disappeared into the house just as her husband, Levi, came running across the yard from the barn.

"Excuse me, Missus Davina," Levi said, bounding up onto the veranda, his brown eyes dark, wide, and darting. "You need me doing anything, missus?" He ran a large hand over the top of his nearly bald scalp and down the side of his stubble-roughened face to his chin. "I mean, not the usual, missus, already done it, me and my boys. Anything, Missus Davina, with the fighting and all?"

"Settle down, Levi," Davina said, trying hard to settle her own voice. It had been a long time since she'd seen Levi in such distress. "There might be work to do later, but right now, I just need a clear head."

Davina turned her back to the battle sounds. "Anna, Luke, come here, please." Anna, still holding Davy in her arms, seemed every day to grow a little more toward a beautiful young woman and a little farther from the gangly child she used to be, and it pleased Davina deeply. Luke, just thirteen months younger than his sister, tried hard to look the man of the house, but the fear in his eyes was unmistakable.

"There's no way of guessing what the Lord's set on our table today," Davina said, "but I think it best we be prepared. First, we're all going to have breakfast. Levi, bring your little ones up here to the house. We'll find room. It's chilly here on the veranda, so maybe in the living room by the fire."

"Yes, missus," Levi said.

Luke didn't look pleased. Several times during the recent months, he'd made it clear that, in his judgment, his mother was too good to the Jacksons.

"It's the Sabbath, so after breakfast we'll have Bible reading," Davina said. "Luke will read for us, won't you, Luke?"

Luke's face brightened a little. "Yes, ma'am."

"Anna, I need you to look after Ruthie and Li'l Davy today. That'll be two less things I need to worry about. And, Levi, I'm thinking that, win or lose—and I pray God to smile on us and we beat them Yankees to kingdom come—Aaron and his friends will need anything we can take them. You and your boys go look around and figure what we can spare—hams, bread, butter, corn-meal. Look at all our hidings too. Get a heap together, and if we get an opportunity, we'll load up the wagon and get on down there."

"Yes, missus."

"No matter which way the fight goes, they'll need whatever we can spare."

Davina felt a soft tug at her elbow. It was eleven-year-old Willy, his blue eyes the exact image of her own.

"What can I do, Mama? I want to help Aaron, too."

Davina got down on one knee. She cupped Willy's face in her hands and kissed him lightly on the forehead. "You got the most important job of all, my boy. We'll all be doing lots of praying today—for Aaron to be safe, and us here, too, and for beating them Yankees, and for this wicked war to end so we can have peace again. Remember what St. Paul said to do?"

Willy nodded. "You mean pray without ceasing?"

Davina hugged Willy close. "That's what we need today, my dear."

Willy's voice was barely a whisper. "I will, Mama. You know I will."

CHAPTER 2

MIN JACKSON WAS WASHING A LARGE IRON SKILLET WHEN Levi stepped quietly into their cabin. She didn't pause and threw him only a brief glance, but Levi knew exactly what that glance meant. It was a look Levi had seen cross his wife's face only a few times since they first met twenty years before. There was no hint of the usual bright and often playful smile that showed twin rows of even teeth that she whitened regularly with vinegar and savory herbs. And her deep brown eyes that usually spoke softly of the love and joy in her heart were crying out in fear. It was the same terrified look she had thrown at him when he told her Mistuh Ben was taking him to Memphis, and it had been all Levi could do to convince her that their master had no intention of selling him. They were simply going to the city to buy a pair of horses.

Levi walked slowly across the small cabin toward Min. She was always the cheerful one, the only person who could always lift his spirits when he was discouraged. But when something got to bothering her, he knew the best approach was to stay away and let her stew for a while. Now, there was no choice. "You know I got to, Min."

Min set the skillet on the table beside the washtub. "I know you got to, because we're slaves, and we always do what we're told." She stood facing him, hands on her wide hips. "But there's more, ain't there?"

Levi stood mute before Min's worried gaze. He nodded slowly.

"You could get killed down there, and then what's me and the young'uns to do? And you still want to go, don't you? You always thinking they's your family, but they ain't, and we ain't their family neither."

"But you loves them young'uns like your own, I seen it, Min. And they call you Aunty Min."

"Oh, I'm friendly with them, sure enough, and they friendly with me 'cause I feed them so good, but—"

Levi lifted his right hand toward Min, palm forward, a gesture they had both used in the past, a silent plea for peace between them. "But whites and blacks cain't never be family. That's what you was saying."

This time it was Min's turn to nod. She picked up the skillet and hung it on a nail on the wall.

"Minerva." Min froze at the sound of her given name. It was Levi's secret way of telling her, whenever their paths crossed during a busy day, that he loved her and nothing could change that fact. "You and me are slaves, Min, and our young'uns too. But Mistuh Ben and Missus Davina—it's been good here, ain't it? And we been happy more than not. And Aaron's a good, Christian boy and you're right, Min, I do feel real kindly toward that boy, and I do want to go with Missus Davina and help that boy, if I can. It's something I got to do for them. Ain't nobody else."

Min walked slowly toward Levi. Her tenderness had returned; her eyes were once again soft and warm. "But it'll be a danger," she said, poking a strong finger in his chest, "you chasing off down the lowgrounds where they all fighting, and I'll fret 'til you come back."

Min lifted her face to Levi's and kissed him, as gentle and pleasant a kiss as he could remember.

"And you'll likely get your head blowed off, Mr. Jackson," she called after him as he stepped out the door of the cabin. But Levi smiled all the way up the lane to the barn, because Min's *Mr. Jackson* was the same as his *Minerva*.

———•———

Aaron clutched at the sudden agony in his belly and fell to the ground. He drew his bayonet, sliced off as much of the tail of his shirt as he could—the red shirt Mama had sewn for him—and stuffed the wadded cloth into the wound to stem the flow.

It was the last blast of the Yankee battery that had got him, fired even as the gunners were leaving their pieces and starting for the rear. His own screams mingled with the whooping, joyful cries of his infantry brigade as they celebrated their conquest before surging past the guns and continuing to drive the Yankees back.

A dozen or more of Aaron's comrades from the Thirteenth Tennessee turned back to offer help, but the looks on their faces when they saw his wound told him what he already knew—there was no cure for a canister ball in the gut. "Tell Captain Wright I'll not be up for roll call," Aaron called after them.

He was done—he knew that too—and there was only one place for him to spend his final moments, or hours, however long the Lord gave him. He had known this ground since he was a child, the grove of trees beside the creek that wound its way down the little vale behind the church. He rolled onto his knees and struggled to his feet, his left hand pressing against his wound, his right holding his musket like a crutch. Then he staggered down the slope toward the creek, the weakness inside him spreading. His legs grew heavy like the iron ball that had pierced him.

At the water's edge he sat and leaned against the trunk of the large oak he and Mary McBride had carved their initials into one Sunday afternoon when they were thirteen. She was pretty enough, and he thought she might make a good wife one day. One day that he didn't have.

Blood oozed through the shirttail bandage. Aaron pressed the cloth deeper into the wound, clenching his teeth against the pain until he could bear it no longer. Then he leaned back against the tree and soon lost consciousness. When Aaron awoke, the pocket watch his father had given him read just after two. It had been three hours. Would there be three more? Or three minutes? Other wounded soldiers gathered near the creek to drink the cool water. Several lay unmoving within a yard or two of the creek. Some of the dead and wounded wore Federal blue, but many more wore Confederate gray or butternut.

A slight movement across the stream caught Aaron's eye, a raised hand attached to a sleeve of dark blue about thirty yards away. *The Yankee boy is still alive. Looks about my age, maybe younger, and scared to death. My last kind deed on earth was to fetch that boy some water before we charged those guns.* Aaron waved a feeble hand in return. *Is this what loving your enemy means, Lord? That boy won't last the night. Does he know you? Be merciful to him.*

Aaron reached into his jacket pocket and took out his Bible, a gift from his father, Captain Benjamin K. Matthews, on the day he had ridden off to the war. Aaron opened to the Psalms, intending to read, but his eyes were heavy and closed against his will. *O death, where is thy sting?* Pastor Blackwell had told him that death held no power over him, but he sure felt that sting now. *O grave, where is thy victory?* How much longer would it be? Just four miles from home. Would Mama ever know?

Shiloh, the place of peace. Good ground to die on. Holy ground.

CHAPTER 3

⸻

*T*HERE HAD BEEN SO MUCH TO DO AFTER THE READING AND praying was ended—slop the hogs, milk the cows, feed the horses and mules and chickens, gather the goods, load the wagon, hitch the team—but Levi knew Missus Davina, and when she said something needed doing, it got done one way or another.

Everyone had pitched in, and Levi had kept each of his young'uns busy at this and that. And when Luke told his mama it was a silly idea to go looking for Aaron's regiment, and that he refused to work alongside Levi and his boys, the missus just looked him in the eye and said, "Get to it, Luke, and don't give me none of your sass." That made Levi smile, just on the inside, though. Levi usually tried to avoid Luke as much as he could, because for a boy of only fourteen, he had grown-up meanness. It had mostly come on after his papa went away to the war.

"There's no way of knowing for sure, but it sounds like our boys have pushed the Yankees back, maybe a long way back toward the river." Missus Davina stood next to the loaded buckboard that Levi had driven into the center of the yard between the house and the barn. She was surrounded by her five anxious children. "It's now or never. Two hours 'til sunset. Now pray—all of you pray for us and for Aaron. Come give your mama a hug." Anna, Willy, Ruthie, and Davy surrounded her and were gathered into her embrace, but Luke retreated to the veranda.

Missus Davina turned and took hold of Levi's arm, as she usually did, to climb up to the seat of the wagon. As she put her foot on the wheel hub, she paused and turned to Levi. "What's this for?" she asked, pointing at her husband's scattergun, which Levi had stowed underneath the seat.

"Don't never know what's down the road, Missus Davina."

The ride eastward down the gradual slope of Matthews Hill was almost effortless for Lily and Penny, the team of seven-year-old mules. The road was still damp from the heavy rains of previous days and even quite muddy in several places, but Levi steered both team and wagon around the few deep wheel ruts that still remained.

Levi knew the road. He had driven it every week to Shiloh Church, sometimes two or three times if there was a trip to the market or the landing. There were times he'd felt a little jealous of Mistuh Ben and Missus Davina riding up ahead in the carriage with Luke and Anna, because the carriage had seats and springs that softened the hard and rutted lanes, and a canvas covering to protect the family from rain and sun. Mistuh Ben had always driven Duke and Earl, the matched team of draft horses he'd bought in Memphis, and that made Levi a little jealous, too, because Levi always drove the mule team and the buckboard.

But such a sweet ride it always was in spite of its roughness, with Levi and Min sitting side by side and the young'uns in the back, white and black children laughing and playing and singing their Bible songs, or with Willy saying his verses. And if storm clouds threatened, or if the sun was too hot, Levi would put up the wooden hoops and lash the weathered canvas cover over the wagon, just as he'd done for this ride, which, he knew, had little chance of being as sweet and joyful.

"That boy just don't understand," Missus Davina said.

"Missus?"

"Luke. He thinks I'm a fool going out like this, that we ain't never going to find Aaron."

Levi didn't hear a question, so he remained silent.

"He just don't understand I have to do this. If it was Luke out there fighting, I'd do the same. Am I a fool, Levi?"

There it was, a question he had to answer. "Oh, no, missus. You ain't no fool, but Mastuh Luke, now he a fool, if I may say, 'cause he think only about hisself. You ain't no fool, 'cause it's a hard thing you're doing, and frightful, too, and that's 'cause you got love for your boy, and you cain't stay put and do nothing."

Missus Davina and Levi traveled in silence for a while down the tree-lined lane. Levi listened closely to the clamor of battle, and whenever the overhanging trees parted, he studied the clouds of light gray smoke that hung above the trees down toward the landing. Dreading what awaited them at Shiloh Church, if they were able to get there at all, Levi tried to determine the ebb and flow of the battle. Missus Davina looked like she was troubled, too.

When they reached the Pittsburg-Corinth Road, it was deeply rutted from the passage of thousands of Confederate soldiers and hundreds of wheeled vehicles drawn by teams of horses or mules. When Levi turned the wagon north toward the landing, he had no choice but to slow the pace of the team and follow the sun-hardened ruts.

Each turn of the wheels drew them closer to the fighting. They began to pass wounded men, one or two at a time, then by the half dozen or dozen, walking, shuffling, stumbling southward away from the battle. Shirts and trousers were stained darkest red. Heads and faces were bloodied and bandaged. Some sat or lay at the roadside in their weariness; a few lay stone-still in the sleep of death.

"Oh, what a horror," Missus Davina said. "These are our boys. God help them." She turned this way and that, and Levi found himself searching every forlorn face for that of Mastuh Aaron too.

"What of the Thirteenth Regiment?" she asked whenever a soldier raised his head. "Any news of the Thirteenth Tennessee?"

Most simply shook their heads and continued to plod south-ward, but a few mustered the strength to tell what they knew.

"...across a field..."

"...through the Yankee camp..."

"...Russell's Brigade...a rough go of it...shot to pieces..."

"...took a battery...hill behind the log church..."

A sudden clatter of hooves up ahead startled Levi. A troop of horsemen came into view, trotting down the center of the road, causing men on both sides to shuffle out of the way.

"Gee, Lil. Gee, Pen." Levi steered the team to the right side, almost off the road. "Whoa, girls, whoa."

A smartly attired officer led the small column. "Make way for the commanding general," he shouted as he rode by, followed by a half-dozen cavalrymen. The riders were escorting a box-like cart draped with white canvas on all sides and drawn by a team of two gray horses. All heads followed the wagon as it passed.

"The commanding general." Missus Davina repeated, her words barely audible to Levi. "Either wounded or killed. General Johnston? I heard he was in command down at Corinth."

"Giddap, Lil. Giddap, Pen." Levi steered the team of mules back onto the road. "Less than a mile now, missus."

No sooner had Levi spoken than he was enveloped by a strange and sickening smell. Every breath combined the odors of war—smoke of musket and cannon, upturned earth, splintered trees with their leaves just budding, blood spilt in abundance, bodies of hale and hearty men blown to the four winds. Round-ing the next bend brought everything into view.

The fields to the left and right of the road were strewn with all the ruin of pitched battle—wagons of war, artillery pieces, and ammunition chests blasted to splinters, horses and mules lying in hideous heaps beside the bodies of the fallen, some clothed in blue, some in shades of brown and gray. Many of the bodies still moved. Droning voices begged for relief from pain or thirst. Others, straining with the effort, pleaded for aid from anyone at hand. And here and there, Levi heard the words of a mournful prayer—for loved ones at home, or for eternal salvation.

Tears welled in Levi's eyes and he yielded to them willingly, thankful for the blurring of the scene that tormented him from all sides. *They say if the Yankees win, then I be free, me and Min and my young'uns. All us slaves be free. But does it got to be like this, Lord?*

Beside him Missus Davina heaved with sobs, and he knew her sorrow must be much greater than his own. *Peace, Lord. Now.* Levi dried his tears with his shirtsleeve, and fixed his gaze on Lily's hindquarters.

"Could anyone survive this?" Missus Davina asked. "There must be hundreds, Levi, hundreds, and Aaron could be one of them lying out there. Is there no end to it?"

"Prob'ly not, Missus Davina, not 'til it be dark." Levi looked toward the western sky. The sun had been hidden by a lowering bank of clouds. "About another hour, I think."

Missus Davina grabbed Levi's arm. "We must stop and look for him before it's dark."

"Yes, missus, but there ain't no knowing where he be, missus. A lot of boys on that field, missus."

Davina looked sideways at Levi for what seemed to him a long time. Then she turned away and her shoulders heaved under the weight of a great sigh. "You're right, Levi. Like the needle in the haystack. I'll have to trust the Lord to take care of Aaron and to help me find him. Drive on."

———

A pair of sentries stepped to the center of the road. They were grimy and disheveled, and they wore no uniforms as far as Davina could tell, at least not like the Yankees. "Halt," said the taller of the two, his voice heavy and tired. "What's your business here, ma'am?"

"My son is with the Thirteenth Tennessee and they've been in the fight. Do you know where they are?"

"Well, ma'am—" The shorter man was silenced by a sharp elbow in the ribs.

"Maybe...maybe not," said the tall man.

"Which is it?" said Davina. "It's simple as yes or no, unless you're simple yourself, boy."

"Not me, ma'am, I'm just thinking there oughta be a price for that kinda information."

A soft answer turneth away wrath. Davina tried for all the sweetness and respect she could muster. "So what's your price, sir?"

The shorter man howled with laughter. "Hey, Emmett, she called you 'sir.' Ain't that a hoot?"

Emmett's elbow struck home again. "Shut up, Billy. Now, ma'am, just what're you hauling down thataway?"

Levi was suddenly tense and alert. Davina laid a hand on his arm to make sure he didn't do anything rash. Time was passing too quickly. "We're taking food to my son's regiment. Please, tell us where they are."

"Well, ma'am, we need food, too. We been fighting and we're hungry like them, and your boy ain't getting that food without us helping. Seems kinda fair, don't it, ma'am?"

"All right," she said, "there's bread near the back. Take one loaf each and cut off a piece of that fatback."

The two men ran to the back of the wagon and rummaged around. Davina heard them muttering back and forth. She watched them out of the corner of her eye until they started forward, loaves and pork in hand.

"Uh...ma'am?" Emmett said, as he approached Davina. "I'm thinking we should have one of those hams back there 'cause—"

Davina leveled the scattergun at the man's head. "And *I'm thinking,*" she said, her voice high and disdainful, "that you best tell me what I want to know, and then you boys just clear out."

Emmett stared at the barrel of the gun, suddenly at a loss for words.

"Up...up the road, ma'am, there's a little church," Billy said.

"I know it well."

"That's headquarters. Anyone know where's your boy, that be the place."

"Giddap, girls." Levi's sharp words carried the force of a whipcrack and the wagon jumped forward.

Davina looked sideways at Levi. His face was fixed in a wry smile. "That be fine, missus," he said, keeping his gaze fixed on the road ahead. "That be right fine." And with a few soft words to Lil and Pen, he urged the team down the road toward a little stream known as Shiloh Branch.

CHAPTER 4

THRONGS OF REBEL SOLDIERS STOOD IN THE ROAD AHEAD. Levi slowed the team and steered the rig carefully. As Davina had heard, the Confederate soldiers had won the day. "We done whipped them Yanks today," they were saying as the wagon rolled slowly through. "Finish them Yankees tomorrow, we will —drive the whole mess of 'em into the river, yes-sir-ree." But Davina sensed weariness in their joy. It was all they could do to shuffle out of the way when the mules drew too close.

Levi urged the team up the last rise toward Shiloh Church. Some of the soldiers followed the wagon, perhaps curious to see what vital mission brought this wild-eyed, gun-brandishing woman among them. *Good, let them wonder*. But Davina knew she had to be on guard. A moment's carelessness, and a dozen men could empty the wagon in no time at all. *Sit tall. Look like you belong here and know what you're about. And, Lord, don't let them trifle with me.*

The scene at the little log church was one nothing in Davina's forty years had prepared her for. The Federal camps around the church were marked by scores of tents, some so trampled into the muddy earth they almost became one with it, while others still stood their ground, bloodied and torn. Wounded men of both armies lay intermingled with the dead. No one passed among them to offer aid; no one stooped to give a sip of cool water, but

Davina saw many a southern soldier enter those Federal tents and emerge moments later with an armload of meaningless plunder.

"Look, Levi," she cried, "look what them Yankees done to our church." Lamplight from within glowed through several large holes made by cannon shot. "Closer, Levi. Draw up the closest you can."

Davina stood, gun in hand, even before Levi drew the wagon to a halt. "An officer!" A hundred heads turned toward her. "I've got to talk to an officer!"

A tall soldier with a bushy red beard stepped forward. He removed his black slouch hat and bowed gracefully. "Captain Bennett, ma'am, at your service."

Davina lowered the scattergun and cradled it in her arm. "Sir, I'm Mrs. Davina Matthews from McNairy County. My husband was a captain in Colonel Forrest's cavalry. He was killed at Donelson."

"I'm truly sorry, ma'am," Bennett said. "What's your business here?"

"I'm looking for my son's regiment, the Thirteenth Tennessee. He's one of Captain Wright's Boys. I've got food for them. Can you help me, sir?"

The captain's eyes widened. "Ma'am, I'm mightily amazed you've come here at all—just ain't safe. The Yankees are sending shells over this way now and again. Maybe you should just go back home."

Davina pointed at the small log church. "This is *my* church and *my* home, captain. Where else should I look for my son?"

"Well, ma'am, the church is now General Beauregard's headquarters. I'll inquire after the Thirteenth." The captain summoned a half dozen of his men and ordered them to guard the wagon. Then he disappeared inside the church.

He returned a few minutes later. "Ma'am? Colonel Russell commands the brigade the Thirteenth is part of. The general's already sent for him, so he's expected shortly, ma'am. You need anything else, ma'am?"

"Did the battle go well, captain?"

A wide smile formed on the captain's face. "Yes, indeed, ma'am. The Yankees fought hard, but we pushed them back all along the line. As you see, we've taken their camps, and up the road a piece we captured a whole entire division, general and all. Another two hours of daylight and I dare say we'd have finished those devils for good. But..."

"But what, captain?"

"Well, ma'am, General Johnston's dead—shot this afternoon. They brought his body here, laid him out on a bench for a while, then took him south not an hour ago."

"What a shame. We seen his ambulance, didn't we, Levi?"

Levi nodded silently.

"We lost a lot of good men. See them torches there under the trees where the light's getting dim? Our sawbones are trying to save as many as they can."

Davina had seen the blazing torches but hadn't guessed their purpose. She looked around and saw dozens more. A high-pitched scream rose above the multitude of voices and commotion around the church.

Captain Bennett shook his head slowly. "Begging your pardon, ma'am. No woman should witness such bad unpleasantness. Please excuse me, ma'am." Again he removed his hat and bowed. Then he turned on his heel and disappeared into the throng of men around the church.

"Maybe Luke was right. Maybe it's a fool's errand we're on, Levi."

"What you mean, missus?"

"Will I really find Aaron? He could be anywhere, maybe dead, or wounded. For all I know, that could've been him screaming. Maybe Luke was right saying this was a stupid idea. What was I thinking?"

Levi's soft chuckle soothed her a little. "Sometimes mothering ain't about thinking, Missus Davina, just loving and doing, and sometimes you cain't do nothing but your mothering, and that ain't never stupid."

Several horsemen rode down the road from the north. They turned into the clearing around the church, dismounted, and went into the church. A few minutes later, a young officer walked out of the church and approached Davina, hat in hand. He appeared not a day older than Aaron had the last time she'd seen him, six months ago.

"Ma'am? I'm Lieutenant Cook, Colonel Russell's aide. The colonel presents his compliments and asks if you will allow me to represent him while he attends to other matters."

"Yes, of course," said Davina, impressed by the young man's manners and pleasant speech.

"Then how might I be of assistance, ma'am?"

Davina repeated what she had told Captain Bennett.

The young lieutenant smiled and nodded. "It's indeed a pleasure to make your acquaintance, Mrs. Matthews. I'm an officer of the Thirteenth currently assigned to brigade staff. The Thirteenth is about two miles from here, close by the river, but I cannot allow you any farther up this road. They are encamped this evening in the camp of the enemy and they are well provisioned with the enemy's own victuals. Your son's friends have plenty while others near at hand have little or no food. Might I ask that you leave these supplies here under my care? I assure you they will feed true men of the south most in need."

"All right, lieutenant, I'll trust you in that. Levi, take the canvas off and help with the unloading."

Lieutenant Cook barked several rapid orders to the soldiers guarding the wagon. The wagon's cargo was soon stacked neatly against the hewn log wall of the church and another guard was set.

"What of Aaron, lieutenant? Have you seen him?"

"I have regularly seen your son's name in the roll of the regiment, but I can't say I know him personally. Is there something by way of appearance that might distinguish him?"

"Yes. I made a shirt from a pair of red-checked window curtains. He wears it a great deal. He also wore a brown cloth jacket and a small straw hat. The army hasn't gone and issued uniforms, has it?"

Lieutenant Cook chuckled. "No, ma'am. I stand before you in the only uniform I own, bought with money my uncle sent me. You know, Mrs. Matthews, now that I think of it, I do know that shirt and the hat, so I do know your boy by sight. Saw him this morning, as a matter of fact, when the fighting started, but I don't recall seeing him since."

"Are you sure?"

"As much as I can be, ma'am. It's been a muddled and tiring day, but the colonel inspected the Thirteenth's position just before he was summoned here. Come to think of it, we were there when they were calling the roll." The lieutenant paused, seemingly uncertain or unwilling to say more.

"Go on, lieutenant, tell me everything you know about my son."

"Well, ma'am, only about half the men answered when called, and ma'am, I can't say this for certain, but I don't recall hearing anything when 'Matthews' was called out."

Davina sighed in dismay. "You got any notion where he could be, sir?"

"The brigade swept over the enemy camp in a field just south of here. There were many tents. Then we crossed a small stream and charged up the hill, just behind the church here, I think it was. We charged a battery and took it. The men fought gloriously today."

Just like Ben had done. "What should I do, lieutenant?"

"That's hard for me to say, ma'am. As I said, I can't allow you to go any farther, so if you're determined to search for your son, it will have to be back the way you came. If a man's wounded, he'll more than likely try to find fresh water. The only water close by is that little creek we crossed."

"Shiloh Branch is what we call it, sir. I know it well."

"Then, ma'am, I guess that's where I'd start my search, but be careful. Do you have torches?"

"A pair of lamps. I knew it'd be dark for the ride home."

"Good. Make sure that scattergun is loaded and keep it close. The field of battle at night can be a desperate place."

Lieutenant Cook bowed to Davina and then addressed Levi. "Your mistress is a good woman."

"Yessuh, I know."

"Then take care that no one harms her."

CHAPTER 5

ANY WARM MEMORIES DAVINA MATTHEWS MIGHT HAVE had of Shiloh Branch quickly vanished when Levi steered the team off the road to follow the course of the creek. The ground was indeed familiar. On many a bright and warm Sunday afternoon, the groves along this branch of Owl Creek became a favorite setting for the people of Shiloh Church to gather for a time of sweet fellowship after the worship service. Every family brought food enough to share, and there was always an abundance in both quantity and variety. The white folk ate their meal on one side of the grove, while the slaves and their families ate on the other side of the grove. Afterward, both groups gathered to hear the pastor read Scripture, the white folk standing in front and the black folk behind. Finally, all voices rose together in several hymns.

But that Sunday evening it was nearly dark. The two oil lamps, one hanging on each side of the wagon, lit the way. Progress was achingly slow as Levi cautiously maneuvered the rig around the dark forms that littered the ground. The cool flow of the creek had drawn scores of wounded men from both sides.

Soon Levi brought the team to a halt. There was no way for the wagon to approach the creek without crushing one or more of the unfortunates under hooves or wheels. He climbed down and came to help Davina. "Don't be afeared, missus," he said, handing a lamp to Davina and grabbing the scattergun for himself. "I be right here."

Davina walked slowly among the wounded. "Has anyone seen a boy with a red-checked shirt?" she called out, swinging the lamp to the right and to the left. "My son's one of the Wright Boys with the Thirteenth Tennessee. Has anyone seen him?"

Davina made her way slowly toward the creek with Levi close behind. On either side, as far as she could see in the dim lamplight, the southern and northern soldiers lay nearly side by side, pitiful in their common wretchedness. Here and there across the field she saw the torches of Confederate ambulance orderlies trying to tend to their own wounded, but there were far too few of them. Many of the wounded would pass the night in their own private struggles against death, and for the wounded Yankees there would be no help at all until the fighting ceased.

Davina's heart ached at what she saw, but she couldn't pause even for a moment to offer help or to speak a kind word, not even to pray for those caught in the throes of death.

"Here, I've got a red shirt."

Davina turned in the direction of the voice, unfamiliar and with too many years in it to be Aaron. "I'm sure you do, sir, but I'm not your mama, so I'll thank you to not call out again."

Davina and Levi paralleled the creek for about a hundred yards. Again and again Davina called out. Hundreds, perhaps a thousand or more heard her pleading: "My son had a red-checked shirt. He's only eighteen, light hair—has anyone seen him?"

"I'm afraid it's no use, Levi," she said after a long search. "Maybe the lieutenant was mistaken." She bowed her head and fell slowly to her knees. "Oh, Lord, where is my boy?" Then she wept. Tears of frustration and sorrow flowed freely, dampening her shirt, until Levi's strong hand took her by the arm.

Davina stood slowly. Not sure of her knees, she leaned heavily against him. "Let's go home," she said. With a final sigh, she turned and began to retrace her steps to the wagon.

"Wait…wait." A voice, feeble and raspy, came out of the darkness. It seemed to come from a short distance to the right, back near the creek.

"Who's that?" Davina called. "Have you seen my son?"

"Yes…here…over here."

Levi leveled the gun and pointed toward the voice. "Thataway, missus, about thirty yards out, I'm thinking. Step careful, missus."

The feeble voice called again; now it was very close.

Davina lifted the lamp as high as she could. "Who is it saw my boy?"

About twenty feet away, a hand rose toward the light.

Davina rushed toward the outstretched hand, stepping carefully around the bodies. "You saw my boy?"

"Yes, ma'am…maybe." Brass buttons gleamed in the lamplight—brass buttons on a dark jacket, now bloodied and stained with mud.

"But you're Yankee." Davina's last hope of finding Aaron faded away.

The Yankee nodded. "From Ohio, ma'am."

His face was streaked with blood, obscuring his features, but his eyes blazed in the lamplight, and his rasping voice was that of a young man, perhaps very young, like Aaron.

"How is it you seen my boy?"

"I was hit early…about an hour before. He almost fell over me…young, about my age." The Yankee paused for a long wheezing breath of fresh air. "He filled my canteen at the creek."

"What did he look like?"

"Red shirt—"

"Plain or checked?"

"Checked, ma'am."

Davina's spirits rose again. "Yes, I made it for him."

"Brown jacket."

"Yes, that's him."

"Odd straw hat…narrow brim."

"That's my Aaron." Davina fell to her knees beside the Yankee. "Thank you, Lord." She seized the boy by the shoulder, but his pitiful cries caused her to release her hold. "Where is he? Please."

"I'll tell you, ma'am, but…"

Davina sat upright, bewildered. "You fixing to pass words with me, boy? Tell me before I have Levi here—"

"I will…but first…"

"What? You want water? Levi, run and fill this boy's canteen."

"No, ma'am."

"Then what, boy?"

The boy wheezed another strained breath. "Put me in your wagon there."

"What!" Davina shook her head in frustration. "Don't you see? I just want to find my son." *Please, God, make this boy tell the truth so I can find Aaron.*

Levi stepped closer and stood over the boy, the scattergun aimed at the boy's chest.

"That's my only way out. I can't move…leg's broke. Been shot in the chest. Arm, too…maybe my stomach. I'm dead by morning…unless you take me, ma'am."

"You Yankee rascal. So you want me to put you in that wagon and take you home with me?"

The boy nodded. "And you'll thank me…when I tell you."

Levi cocked both hammers on the scattergun and lowered it to within a few inches of the boy's face. "I heared lots about you Yankees. Some say we be free if you win, but we ain't doing no bargain with the devil, and I ain't going to take you sassing the missus. Best speak now, or die now, no matter to me."

"Just as well," the boy said, his eyes wide and fixed on the barrel of the gun. "I'm good as dead anyway…but then you'll never know."

Davina looked at the boy's face—so young and so scared. She knew what had to be done, and the boy had said himself that he wouldn't last the night.

She laid her hand gently on Levi's arm and pushed the gun barrel away from the Yankee's face. "I've got no choice, Levi. He says he knows where Aaron is, and he knowed all Aaron's clothes. I've got to do it."

Levi carefully released both hammers and shouldered the weapon. "Yes, missus, but I don't like it, not at all."

Between them Davina and Levi hoisted the boy up. He was tall, better than six feet, and well-muscled, at least two hundred pounds. With Davina under the boy's right arm and Levi under the left, the boy carried most of his own weight on his right leg while the left dangled helplessly. The boy howled in agony with every hobbling step toward the wagon. Davina shuddered a little at each of his cries; perhaps Aaron was in such torment too. Finally, the two of them heaved the Yankee into the back of the empty wagon and laid him down flat.

"Now, where's my Aaron?" Davina asked the boy, who was still quivering with pain. "Talk straight now, or Levi *will* shoot you, and with my blessing."

"Wait...wait." The boy spoke through clenched teeth. "Just one more thing, ma'am."

"What's that, boy? Get to it."

"Don't let me die, ma'am. Please...don't let me die. Promise. Promise me you'll try to save me, ma'am. I beg you...promise."

When Davina spoke, the hard edge of her words was gone. "How old are you, boy?"

"Sixteen."

Davina's breath caught in her throat. He was younger than Aaron. Too young to enlist, too young to...to be here like this. Some other mother's son lay before her, still a boy, not yet a man. Did that mother even know where her boy was? "I give you my word," she said. "I promise."

"Saw him just at sundown...by a big tree across the creek... think he was shot...might be dead...hope not." The boy's strength was spent. His head thudded heavily against the floor of the wagon.

Davina hesitated for but a moment to see that the boy was still breathing. Then she and Levi headed toward the creek as fast as the lamplight allowed.

They found Aaron just as the Yankee had said, across the creek beside the large oak tree. Davina put her hand on his forehead; he was still warm. He stirred at her touch.

"Mama?"

"Yes, my darling boy, I'm here." She cradled her son's head against her breast and gently rubbed her tears into his matted hair.

"They've killed me, Mama."

His soft, murmured words pierced her through, and she knew he was right. She had seen his red-checked shirt stained almost black in the amber glow of the lamp. "Hush now, we're going to take you home."

"That would be real fine, Mama."

When Levi's strong arms slid under him and lifted him gently from the earth, Aaron groaned heavily, from within, but during the short journey across the creek and up the incline toward the wagon, he made no other sound. Davina climbed into the back and helped Levi lift Aaron headfirst into the wagon beside the Yankee.

"Home, Levi, fast as you can." Davina sat on the floor of the wagon and cradled her son in her arms. Levi wheeled the team of mules around and carefully navigated his way back to the Corinth Road.

"Don't cry, Mama."

Davina saw that some of her own tears had fallen on Aaron's face.

"A mother shouldn't never see her son like this," he said. "But we did it, Mama...we beat them Yankees...charged that hill...took their guns, too." His eyes were bright and lively in the torchlight.

"You sound just like your papa. I'm so proud of you."

38

"I wish Papa was here. I know I'm dying...canister ball got me. I fought for our land, Mama. I saved our home...but I'll see Papa soon, and Jesus too."

Aaron struggled to turn so he could look his mother in the face. His arm brushed against the Yankee lying beside him. "Who's that?"

"Yankee boy we found. Said you got water for him and he told us where to find you."

At the Corinth Road, Levi turned Lily and Penny southward toward Matthews Hill and gave each mule a quick flick with the whip.

Aaron and Davina gazed at each other for some time, until Aaron's head rolled slowly downward, as if it had become too heavy for him. He tried to raise his head again, but could not.

Davina gently cradled her son's head in her arm and raised his face to her own. "Don't leave me yet, my boy. We'll be home soon."

"Remember when Jesus was dying...on the cross...what he said to his mother?"

"What did he say, dear?"

"He said...'Woman, behold thy son.'"

Horror wrenched Davina's insides. "That boy? He's a stranger —and a Yankee. You can't ask me to do that."

Aaron stared into her eyes. "I'm not the one asking, Mama. Just like you always told us, 'The Lord gave and the Lord hath taken away...'"

"'Blessed be the name of the Lord.' Yes, I know it well."

"So maybe God's giving you this boy, 'cause he's taking me."

"No! I can't bless the Lord for taking your papa—or you. How could I ever bless him for this Yankee boy?" Davina began to stroke Aaron's face lightly with her hand. "Hush now, my dear. Let me rock you to sleep like I used to."

Aaron fell asleep in his mother's arms. She looked down at him and brushed her fingers through his matted hair. Her eyes closed. She fought to open them, but the day like none other had drained her strength. Her head drooped lower and lower between her shoulders.

A short time later, when Levi turned the team onto the lane that led to Matthews Hill, the wagon lurched suddenly in a wheel rut. Davina woke with a start. The Yankee boy had awakened, too, and moaned with every jostling of the wagon, but Aaron slept on, his face now tranquil, slightly smiling, free of pain, and cool to her touch.

Her son was gone and she had missed it. With weary, weeping eyes Davina searched the sky through the trees over the lane for a star, any star, any faint sign of heavenly light, but there was none. The clouds Levi had seen earlier had thickened and lowered. Davina bowed her head and rested it against Aaron's still face.

Why him, Lord? He loved you. Why do you punish me like this? Why not kill me and let Ben and Aaron alone? And why don't you just kill off this Yankee while you're at it?

Curse God and die, Job's wife had told him, and Davina thought maybe she should, too. The weight would be gone; the terrible, grieving days ahead would be gone; the war would be gone; she wouldn't have to bury her son or deal with the Yankee. But there were Li'l Davy, and Ruthie, and dear Willy, and Luke with all his troubles, and Anna too. Her children were the heritage of the Lord. She had known that from her own childhood.

And there was Aaron too. There was only one more thing that she could do for him, and she would not rest until it was done. Then she would leave him to the Lord.

Davina felt weak, drained of all life. Every breath was a struggle. As the wagon emerged from the tree line and began to pass the familiar fields of Matthews Farm, one more saying of the Savior echoed within her—*Follow me, and let the dead bury their dead.*

CHAPTER 6

*L*UKE HAD BEEN ON EDGE ALL DAY. SUNDAY EVENING WAS usually the most peaceful time of the week, but the Matthews home was anything but tranquil that Sunday evening. Minutes dragged like hours as Luke stood shoulder to shoulder with his sister, Anna, at the railing on the east end of the veranda that ran along the south side of the two-story house.

The Matthews children had often greeted the rising sun or taken shelter from pouring rain or blazing afternoon heat on that veranda. Now young eyes scanned the dim outline of the trees at the edge of the pasture for any sign of the buckboard coming up the lane from Chambers Road. Davy stood atop the railing securely wrapped in Anna's arms. Ruthie wandered back and forth along the veranda or sat on the red-cedar bench beside the front door of the house or stood fidgeting at the railing beside Anna, while Willy just sat quietly on the bench.

The lowering bank of heavy clouds that had moved in with the setting of the sun turned balmy evening quickly to night. The regular thump-thump-thump of artillery had quieted, but every ten minutes or so, the long glowing trail of a shell arced high above the tree line before it plunged earthward to end its flight in a dull flare of light down among the forest or fields of the lowgrounds near the river. Seconds later, usually twenty-two or twenty-three by Luke's count, the waiting children both heard and felt the sharp report of the explosion rumble over the farm.

"There they are." Of all the children, Anna's eyes were the sharpest. "Levi's driving them right along, like Mama's in a hurry or something."

"Wagon's empty," Luke said. "Just Mama and Levi. Prob'ly just beating the rain."

"See it, Li'l Davy?" Anna pointed carefully at the faint points of light. "Down there where the lane goes into the woods."

"I see it! Mama's home."

"How about you, Willy?"

Willy stood, approached the railing, and squinted into the darkness. "Not yet. They got to be closer."

Luke struck a match and lit the pitch torch he'd brought.

A few minutes later, Levi drew the panting team to a halt in front of the house. On many previous occasions when Levi had returned home from driving Mama here or there, Luke had seen Levi set the brake, jump to the ground, and run around the back of the wagon to help Mama down. But this night, Levi ran across the yard toward the barn.

Mama sat motionless in the back of the wagon. Something was wrong. Luke and the other children started down the steps.

"Luke, bring the torch!" Mama called out. "You others stay put."

Anna set Davy down on the veranda. "Why, Mama?"

"Stay put, I say." Anna and the other children froze where they were. "Now, Luke, the torch!"

Luke approached the back of the wagon, holding the torch high. Two corpses lay shoulder to shoulder. His upraised arm sagged slowly downward, weakened, the torch now too heavy for him. "Mama?" His voice croaked with fear.

"Yes, Luke, it's Aaron," Mama said, her voice hushed so the other children wouldn't hear.

Aaron's face was bloodied and barely visible in the torchlight, but his red-checked shirt, the shirt Mama had so lovingly labored over, was unmistakable. "Is he—?"

"Yes, Luke, he's dead."

Luke leaned heavily against the side of the wagon and closed his eyes.

"Luke?" Mama's voice was insistent. "Luke!"

Luke raised his head and turned toward his mother.

"Help me down, Luke."

With tears filling his eyes, Luke took hold of Aaron's legs and lifted some of his lifeless weight off Mama so she could slide off the back of the wagon. Then he looked at the other body. Revulsion twisted his bowels. "He's a Yankee, Mama. You brought home a dead Yankee?"

"He ain't dead."

Luke looked again. Yes, the Yankee was still breathing, barely noticeable in the dim light, but to Luke he was as good as dead. His hand closed around the hilt of the knife that always hung from his belt.

Mama's strong, callused hand closed over Luke's before he could draw the knife from its sheath. "No, Luke!" It was the quiet, commanding voice Mama saved for those times she required absolute and instant obedience. "I'll have none of that. If the Lord takes him, so be it, but we'll not be doing it."

"But a Yankee? In our house? I won't, Mama."

"Yes, you will, Luke. This here's a Christian home and Christian charity don't know Yankee from Rebel. I didn't go looking for this boy, but the Lord put him in my way, so I got to do what I can."

For several moments Luke didn't move a muscle while his mother glared at him. Then he relaxed his grip on the knife.

"Good, Luke. We've got work to do, and fast, if he's to live."

Levi returned from the barn carrying a wooden plank about a foot wide and six feet long. "I got it, missus, and the rope, too, just like you said."

"Good," Mama said. "Slide it under the boy and tie him to it." Levi jumped up into the wagon.

Luke didn't move. "No, Mama, not until we see to Aaron."

Mama stepped in close to him, her movements heavy and awkward as if she could barely move for exhaustion. She smelled heavily of sweat; her shirt was stained dark with blood—Aaron's or the Yankee's, Luke dared not ask. Her eyes burned fiercely in the torchlight. "I know you love your brother, Luke," she said, her voice hard and yet soft at the same time. "Do I love him any less? There's nothing I'd rather do than tend to Aaron, but my boy's dead and the other one's alive. I know it's hard, but please do as I say, and no back talk." She took Luke by the elbow and steered him toward the back of the wagon. "Now, get up there with Levi. Turn the boy on his side and slide the plank under. Take care of that left leg—looks broke bad. Then slide the ropes under and tie him down. Can't have him falling off."

Levi had already moved Aaron's body to the side, clearing just enough space on the floor of the wagon to lay the plank next to the Yankee. The boy groaned as soon as Levi and Luke laid hands on him. "Aawugh! This devil stinks bad," Luke said. "I figured all Yankees reeked, but this bad?"

A dreadful shriek pierced Luke through. Unseen, Anna had approached the wagon and peered over the sideboard.

"He's dead, Mama? Aaron's dead?"

Mama nodded slowly.

Anna's wailing echoed through the yard between the house and the barn. "The Yankees killed my Aaron, Mama! The best boy ever…they just killed him!"

Luke and Levi stopped their work. On the veranda, Willy began to cry while Ruthie and Davy hugged each other and began to sob as well.

Anna went on, shrill and accusing. "And you brought a Yankee home? How could you, Mama? Maybe he was the one killed my Aaron. I hate the day Aaron went to the army…ain't been

44

right around here since. I hate all them Yankees, too, and I wish God would—"

"Enough!" cried Mama. "All of you! Stop your wailing. We got work to do. Take the Yankee boy upstairs, Luke. Lay him on Aaron's bed. And for heaven's sake, be careful."

Luke opened his mouth to protest, but before he could say a word Anna said, "Aaron's bed? Mama!" She glared. "How could you ever?"

"Aaron's dead. He's resting with God now, so he won't be needing that bed, will he?"

Anna threw herself to the ground beside the wagon and wept loudly.

"Now, Luke!" Mama said. "Levi, get to it."

Levi's usual "yes, missus" was the only audible response.

It was all Luke and Levi could do to lift the heavy Yankee, and Luke was more than happy to allow Levi, broader across the shoulders and much more powerful, to bear most of the groaning, unwashed burden. After ten torturous minutes of huffing and struggling up onto the veranda—past the terrified faces of Willy, Ruthie, and Li'l Davy (who, suddenly curious, turned and followed)—into the house and up the twelve steep steps, Luke and Levi finally deposited that bloody, filthy, Yankee heap on the clean whiteness of Aaron's bed.

After removing the ropes and the plank, Levi shepherded the children back down the stairs, leaving Luke alone with the Yankee.

The intruder groaned low and deep; his eyes were open, wet with tears.

Luke stood over the Yankee. "You hear me, Yank?"

The Yankee nodded slightly.

"You in a lot of pain?"

The Yankee nodded again.

"Good. The way it oughta be—more pain the better for you. What shouldn't be is, that's my brother's bed you're in. Ain't right. He was a Matthews, my brother—him and me did every-thing...everything. And you're nothing but a lousy, stinking Yan-kee. Ain't right him being dead and you being alive. Only one way to make it right, and we both know what that is." Luke's hand once again closed around the hilt of his knife.

"Luke, you leave him be!"

Luke froze at the sound of Mama's voice. It was all right. There would be plenty of time to do what had to be done. He turned to face his mother. Dust and sweat and tears had etched weary trails upon her face.

Mama drew him into a tight embrace. Then she took his face in her hands and looked into his eyes, as if searching for some-thing. She had done that several times since Papa had been killed, but she never said if she found what she was looking for.

Mama ran her fingers through his hair. "Min will be along to help me clean this boy up and bind his wounds. It's starting to rain now, so there's nothing to do 'til morning. You and Willy and Li'l Davy go bed down in the girls' room. Take your own bed in there, if there's room. Anna and Ruthie will sleep downstairs with me. First light, go help Levi in the barn."

Luke started to shake his head, but Mama's gentle hand stilled him. "Don't give him no trouble, just do as he says. You'll be helping me and Aaron too."

CHAPTER 7

*L*ATE IN THE NIGHT, ALMOST AT THE APPROACH OF DAWN, Stanley Mitchell awakened. He tried to open first one eye, then the other, but even this small effort pained him. It was quiet, but if he listened carefully he could hear the occasional tread of footsteps on wooden floors or the patterned tones of muffled voices. He knew he lay in a warm, soft bed in a house, but whose house it was, or where exactly it was, he didn't know.

A few minutes later he willed his eyes to open. At first he couldn't tell whether they were open; all he saw was total darkness. No, not quite total. As his eyes became accustomed to the gloom, he perceived the dim outline of a door to his right and perhaps a window to his left. He was uncomfortable lying on his back. He tried to move and was rewarded with stabbing, searing pain, and something else—a tightness, a sense of being bound. He lay still. Uneasiness gnawed him. Dreadful images captured his thoughts. There had been a battle—many men dead, all around him. He had been shot—was it once or twice? Why couldn't he remember?

He closed his eyes again and tried to think of the time before. Was it only this morning that the enemy had rushed screaming and shooting out of the woods and into their camp just as Gilbert Goode had been fixing their morning coffee? Or had it been yesterday morning or the day before that? They had seen lots of the

47

enemy when they were out on patrol just one day earlier. Why hadn't the officers raised the alarm? Why had they been left out in the field like sheep to be slaughtered?

The sound of a door latch caused him to start. A warm glow suddenly bathed the inside of Stanley's eyelids, but he kept them shut, feigning sleep. The door closed, the light grew brighter. Its bearer came near and stood over him.

Whoever it was moved around to the left side of the bed, took hold of the coverlet, and drew it down, exposing his chest. The light grew brighter still. A hand probed his left arm and shoulder, causing pain that was near agony. A moan formed in his throat, but he forced himself to neither move nor cry out.

"Good, the bleeding's stopped," a voice whispered.

It was the woman again, the one who had found him. This was her house, her own son's—her dead son's—bed he lay upon. It had been her whiskey she had forced him to drink earlier. "It'll quiet you," she'd said, "lessen the pain awhile." But it had only burned his throat and left him wishing for some of that cool water from the creek, or some of Gilbert Goode's good coffee. He almost chuckled at that, but checked himself—no use letting the woman know he was awake.

She laid her hand upon his chest and pressed gently with her fingertips. Dull, throbbing pain this time. He struggled inwardly to maintain his steady breathing. Couldn't she just leave him alone?

The woman grunted softly and drew the coverlet back up to his chin.

The light dimmed and Stanley opened his eyes. Holding a short candlestick in her right hand, the woman walked slowly across the room to a dresser against the far wall, about eight feet away, beneath the dim outline of a curtained window. She placed the candlestick in a holder atop the dresser.

The woman stood motionless with her back to Stanley for what seemed a long time, her hands hanging loosely at her sides.

Each of her deep and labored breaths seemed to echo within the room. Then she slowly raised her head, as if to gaze at the wooden beams above her. Her hands tightened into fists and rose slowly, and as they rose, they began to tremble. Higher and higher she raised them. By the time they, too, pointed toward the rafters, the trembling had spread throughout her body.

"Oh, Lord."

The soft whisper was gone. Her words now came in panting, raspy, guttural bursts. A few of the words were audible, most were not.

"First Ben, now Aaron…" The woman lowered her arms and head. Her fists opened. Her trembling ceased. She brought her hands to her face and covered her eyes.

"What have I done…your own son said, 'let this cup pass.'"

Prayer, he knew. But such prayer as he had never heard before —not like the quick, necessary blessing Uncle Charles always said before dinner, or even the prayer Reverend Higgins had said when Mrs. Macready was sick.

The woman grasped the pull of the top drawer and opened it. She paused as if to study the contents, then heaved a great sigh and removed a pair of dark trousers. She held them up to the candlelight for inspection. Then she carefully folded the trousers, smoothing out any creases, and placed them on the chair next to the chest.

The second item the woman removed from the drawer was a vest, also dark; it seemed to match the trousers. As before, the woman inspected and folded the vest, laying it atop the trousers.

Lastly, the woman removed a white shirt from the drawer. She held it up to the candlelight and examined it for what again seemed a long time before lowering the shirt and clenching it to her breast. "My dear, dear boy."

The woman leaned forward and rested her arms atop the chest of drawers. She pressed her face into the folds of the shirt. She breathed in deeply again and again—savoring, Stanley assumed, the familiar, living scent of her now-dead son. She trembled and appeared to sag against the dresser. Stanley thought she might fall to the floor, but there was nothing he could do but watch—and feel something of the weight of her grief, grief such as he had never before witnessed.

The woman felt blindly for the edge of the chest, then stumbled the few steps toward the chair, gathered the folded trousers and vest in her arms, and sat down heavily.

For several long minutes, Stanley listened with closed eyes as the woman's grief poured from her. Then, when her wracking sobs had subsided, she spoke again: "Lord, give me strength to bear this. Keep me from being angry and help me do good."

She stood, went to the door, and left Stanley once again to the darkness.

This much he knew: the woman dearly loved her son, and with such a love as he had never known, and likely never would. Who would mourn for him if he died? Who would miss him and seek to find him? Who would shed even one tear for him? Who would so lovingly choose his burial clothes?

Stanley knew pain and grief and loss and tears, but his were different. And if by chance his life did not end within the next few hours or days, he would likely find more of the same.

CHAPTER 8

*T*HE FIRST GRAY-PINK STREAKS OF DAWN FOUND LEVI WALK-
ing slowly through the wet grasses and weeds that bordered
the narrow lane from his cabin to the barn. Steady rain overnight had drenched everything and turned the lane to mud, and
Levi much preferred soggy shoes to mud-caked ones. Heavy, cold
drops from the trees that arched over the lane fell on him, causing
him to shiver. He tugged the broad brim of his straw hat a little
lower and turned up the collar of his dark-blue jacket.

Wood was always true, never false. It would never be anything other than what it already was. Sure, a man could come
along and saw it and plane it and shape it and make it look a lot
different, but that wood was still the same as it had been when
it was a tree. There was warmth in wood, warmth all its own,
just waiting for the right man to come along and uncover it. No
matter what kind—pine, ash, maple, oak, or walnut—the right
man was all that was needed to find that warmth and turn it into
beauty, and Levi knew he was the right man for the job at hand.

But this morning his choices were few. There was no time to
select a particularly beautiful piece of timber, no time to saw it
into planks, no hours to spend smoothing it with the draw knife
and plane. He would have preferred oak, strong and fragrant, or
even maple for its strength, but pine was all he had.

He arrived at the barn and lit a lamp. Then he climbed the

ladder to the loft where the wooden planking was racked just below the rafters, one-inch thick planks for floorboards and two-inch thick for framing.

A twisted and warped board wouldn't do. The grain and knots had to be the best of the lot. Levi carefully examined each piece from end to end and finally chose five planks, along with several pieces of framing lumber, which he carried one at a time across the loft and placed beside the ladder.

"Oh, there you are," a voice grumbled from below, harsh with the belittling tone that always tainted Luke's words whenever he spoke to anyone of lesser importance. "Mama told me to help. I don't want to, but I got to."

"Well, that's fine, Mastuh Luke. How about I hand these boards down and you stand them next the ladder?"

"How about I come up there and you come down here and I hand them boards down?"

"That's fine, too, Mastuh Luke." And it truly was fine with Levi—that was exactly how he had wanted it, because he wanted to stack the planks properly so as not to mar or scratch them.

As Luke handed the five planks down, Levi carried each of them into the tool room at the rear of the barn. "I done up a drawing in my head, Mastuh Luke."

Luke opened his mouth as if to speak, but Levi knew the boy would only grumble if given the chance, so he forged ahead: "Got to do the cutting first, then the building. Got to ripsaw every board. They twelve inch wide now, and we need eight and ten."

Levi carefully measured and scribed a line along the entire length of each of the five planks, two at ten inches and three at eight inches. When he finished scribing, he measured each plank again.

"What're you doing that for?" Luke asked, clearly annoyed. "You already done that."

"Cain't be too careful, Mastuh Luke. Got to be right first

time. Do it wrong and then you got to do it again, and ain't no time for that."

Luke steadied each board on the long workbench while Levi's powerful shoulders and arms did the sawing. As he bent to the work, he would now and again comment on the what and the why of the task at hand: "It always easier sawing with the grain than cross." "A sharp saw's like a good friend that never let you down." "I cut this wood for something common, prob'ly just walking on, but it been called to a better thing now."

"I don't know what you keep going on about," Luke said as they set the last plank on the workbench. "Like an old man rambling on about things I don't need to know. You being so careful and all, and I don't see why. It's just a coffin, and it's going in the ground today and nobody'll ever see it again."

"Yes, Mastuh Luke, but me and you, we'll see it, and your mama and your family, too. And the Lawd. Cain't forget him. He's going to see it and I got to do everything for the glory of God."

From the corner of his eye, Levi saw Luke's head wagging back and forth. "How's making my brother's coffin for the glory of God?" The boy's words were more snickered than spoken.

Levi finished the last long cut and returned the ripsaw to its place on the wall of the barn. Then he took down the finer-toothed crosscut saw and returned to the bench. "Now, Mastuh Luke, we got to cut them planks in half, and it got to be right, 'cause all them pieces got to line up, nice and even like, all the same length. It ain't so nice if they ain't even or if they ain't straight as we can do it, and the Lawd give me the learning to do it good, so if I don't do it good, I ain't giving the Lawd the best of what he give me."

Levi sawed through one of the boards. Then he laid one piece atop the other on the bench and nodded with satisfaction. "This coffin, it the last thing I'm doing for your brother, and I mean to do it right, Mastuh Luke. That the best I can give him too."

Levi set to work again, and was soon completely lost in his task. After a while, he noticed that Luke seemed greatly annoyed about something—coughing when he didn't need to cough, stamping his feet, fidgeting with Levi's tools. Levi paused his cutting midstroke, wondering what had bothered the boy—and then realized that, while he worked, he had been mindlessly humming the same familiar hymn tune, over and over again. He smiled inwardly, returned to his work, and kept humming.

By nine o'clock the coffin was almost finished. The design was simple, for Levi had avoided the popular toe-crusher style, with its angled sides, in favor of a rectangular pine box, about six feet in length, twenty inches wide, and sixteen inches high. Its corner joints were reinforced with short lengths of framing lumber. The long seams in the top, bottom, and sides where the two ripsawn planks abutted each other were likewise strengthened with four pieces of framing lumber nailed across the seam. To finish, Levi nailed to the reinforcing blocks on each side of the coffin one of the narrow pieces that he had sawn from the wide planks. These were the two carrying rails. He used eight carefully driven nails for each rail, the only nails visible from the outside of the coffin.

Levi stood back to look at his work. "It done, Mastuh Luke. As fine a piece as I can make. But one more thing."

"What's that?"

"Me and my boys needs to be digging the grave. Lot of digging to do and not much time now, Mastuh Luke, and I been thinking your brother's coffin needs some linseed oil. Got some up on the shelf there. Just need to take this cloth and rub it all over inside and out. Maybe you want to do that while me and my boys get to digging, Mastuh Luke?"

———

Luke's job was simple enough—just slathering the pungent oil on the wood, making sure it got into every corner, then wiping off any excess. The wood drank up the oil that instantly darkened it, both beautifying and preserving it. Soon, very soon, the box would consume Aaron's body as well. He would be carried from the wagon in the stable behind the barn where he had lain all night. That was Mama's idea—didn't think it proper for the little ones to see their brother like that. And it let her make Aaron ready in private.

The body—that's what he was now—would be laid out inside the cold, hard box, and the lid would be nailed securely. There would be a slow, agonizing walk to the graveyard. There would be a prayer, maybe more than one, and holy words would be spoken, and then the coffin would be lowered into the ground. The body would never be seen again. The flesh would rot away or be eaten by—Luke wasn't sure what would do the eating, but imagined beetles and worms and the like—and all that would remain of his beloved brother would be his bones. But even that much Luke wasn't sure of.

Luke began to rub the oiled wood to an even sheen. Faster and faster he rubbed, over and over the pine box that so soon would confine his brother for eternity. *Mama must have been addled in the brain, bringing that blue-belly home, thinking we'd all just take him in and show that...that varmint what charitable Christians we could all be. Things can't stay as they are. Got to be sorted out and set right. There's got to be a reckoning for all that's happened. That's what's needed, all right—a reckoning.*

A heavy tear fell on the oiled bottom of the coffin. A dozen tiny droplets scattered in every direction, which Luke immediately and furiously rubbed and rubbed and rubbed until each droplet had become a part of his brother's coffin.

Then another heavy tear fell and shattered.

CHAPTER 9

THE DAY WAS ALTOGETHER TOO BEAUTIFUL FOR DAVINA. THE rains had stopped, the clouds had parted, and warm sunshine beamed down upon the forlorn procession making its way slowly out of the yard between the house and the barn. The lane to the burial ground led up a gentle slope across a hayfield, cut short for the winter but awakened and greening in the springtime warmth. It was about two hundred yards to the crest of the low hill. Years ago Ben and Davina had chosen that plot of ground beneath the spreading boughs of a large oak tree to serve the necessary-though-somber purpose as the family's burial ground. A single white cross stood within the low white picket fence that guarded the ground.

The fighting down near Shiloh had grown louder and closer as the morning wore on, so that now, still an hour before noon, Davina knew that the Yankees had not been thrown into the river. The tide had been reversed, and the billowing battle smoke that rose over the trees to the east revealed, as clearly as if the news had been shouted from those same treetops, that the Yankees were driving the Confederates back across the same ground that had been so dearly won the day before. Aaron's life had held such promise; his death had been in vain.

Much too fine a day for this.

Davina had asked Levi to lead the procession. He walked

slowly, head bowed, holding Duke's bridle. Davina walked a few paces behind the wagon with one arm around Ruthie, the other around Davy and Willy. Luke stumbled along the left edge of the lane, sometimes in the grass beside it, while Anna walked in front of Davina and the young children, directly behind the wagon. Her head was bowed, and her right hand held onto the end of Aaron's coffin, her knuckles white with the effort. Min Jackson and her children brought up the rear of the procession.

Not an hour before, Davina and Levi had wrapped Aaron in a white bedsheet and laid him carefully in the coffin. His love for her boy was obvious; she had seen his tears, and he had seen hers. "I'll be near," he had said, just before leaving her alone in the barn.

Davina began at Aaron's feet, using a large curved needle and heavy thread to sew the edges of the sheet together. Her hands worked mechanically, inch by inch closing the seam with neat, regular stitches no one would ever see, shrouding her son forever from her view. And when only Aaron's face remained uncovered, Davina put the needle and thread aside. She gazed for a long time at her son's already cherished features, committing them to memory—from his fine, sand-colored hair to the several days' growth of stubble on his chin. She wet his face and the surrounding cloth with her tears and kissed him over and over until she knew the time had come.

Davina dried her face with a fold of the sheet and quickly stitched the shroud closed.

"Levi?"

She had hardly spoken his name and he was at her side. She helped him lay the oil-darkened lid on the coffin. Davina noted how perfectly the edges lined up. But when Levi reached for his hammer, her tears flowed once again. Each nail pierced her through. Each echoing blow of the hammer confirmed the truth and finality of it all. Aaron was gone.

Levi led Duke alongside the open grave. Without a word,

Luke and Levi's two eldest sons, Jeremiah and Micah, stepped forward to help Levi lift the coffin from the wagon and lay it upon the grass next to the gaping hole in the earth that Levi and his boys had dug.

If only she could have sent for Pastor Blackwell. But whom could she send? Luke? No, she couldn't put another child in danger. Levi? She couldn't spare him. And there wasn't time to wait for the fighting to end and the smoke to clear. Aaron had to be buried soon, before he started to...

"Let's all gather around," Davina said while she unfolded a page of notes she had written. She had not slept at all during the night, plagued by weariness and weighed down by sorrow. But it was her obligation, as head of the family, to say what needed to be said and do what needed to be done.

Just fifteen minutes, maybe twenty, and then rest. She paused to steady herself. She looked around at each face. She listened to the din of battle, so close and threatening. Then she quieted herself before the God of Heaven. *Not my words, but yours, O Lord.*

Mama suddenly looked like an old woman, with her eyes red and puffy and weepy, and Luke knew he had to be strong. The time for sniveling like Willy or Ruthie, or even Mama for that matter, was past.

"'The Lord gave,'" Mama said, "'and the Lord hath taken away; blessed be the name of the Lord.'"

"Amen, missus. Amen." It was Levi's soft, but firm voice. He always said "Amen" whenever he heard the Bible, but Luke wished that for once, just this once, the slave would keep quiet.

"Aaron reminded me of those words of Job just before he died," Mama said, "and we all know the Lord has taken much from us. We all know grief. Your father and I buried baby Robert just after Aaron was born, and scarce a month ago we met at

Shiloh Church to mourn your father. Now here we are again to bury your brother Aaron."

Anna began to sob quietly. Luke stepped close beside her. She was a couple of inches taller than Luke, but he draped his right arm around her trembling shoulders and hugged her close, as he had seen Papa do.

"My own sorrow is so deep I don't know where it ends," Mama went on, "and I can't put it in words. I'm sure you feel the same. As a wife and mother, I know there are many perils in this life. I thought that years from now, maybe many years, I might have to bury my husband, but I don't even know where he is buried. And no mother thinks she'll bury one child, let alone two."

Mama seemed about to cry again. Anna lay her head against Luke's, wetting the front of his shirt and vest with her tears. Davy just looked confused. His head turned from Mama to Anna to Luke to Willy, and then to Ruthie, who was trying her best to act the big sister. All the while the boy appeared as if he might start bawling, but he never quite got to it.

Mama had control of herself once again. "Job said, 'Blessed be the name of the Lord.' I don't know how to do that, not now. For eighteen years I saw my second baby boy grow into a fine young man. But God had a different plan, and I don't know what it is. I just know that he's got one, and it's good and perfect, even if I don't think so. I have to trust him. Maybe he's testing my faith. Sometimes I think I don't know much, but I do know this —hard things make us stronger. In the book of Revelation, Jesus said, 'Be thou faithful unto death, and I will give thee a crown of life.'"

"Amen, missus, amen."

Couldn't he just hold his tongue for once?

"Aaron was faithful unto death, and now he wears that crown of life," Mama said. She smiled a weak, tight smile, and even Luke had to admit to himself how hard that had been for her. "I know that sure as I know his body's here in this coffin. For

Aaron and for your father, and for baby Robert, death was the last enemy, but death is also the last enemy for us too. Willy, please say those verses from First Corinthians I asked you to remember."

"Yes, Mama," Willy said. He raised his arm to dab his eyes with his shirtsleeve, then spoke in a high, clear voice. "'Behold, I shew you a mystery; we shall not all sleep, but we shall all be changed, in a moment, in the twinkling of an eye, at the last trump: for the trumpet shall sound, and the dead shall be raised incorruptible, and we shall be changed. For this corruptible must put on incorruption, and this mortal must put on immortality.'"

"Amen, Mastuh Willy, amen."

Luke fought to keep his annoyance from showing, because Mama was quick to spot those things.

"Aaron's soul is already with God," Mama said, her voice now hushed and wavering, "and in a few moments, his body will be buried in the earth, as will all of ours when we die." Mama paused a few moments to look at each of her children. "But that ain't the end, 'cause just as Willy spoke, our bodies will rise from their graves never to die again. That's the promise of God and we must believe it."

Mama looked down at the crumpled page in her hand. She took a slow, deep breath, then started again.

"The Lord has taken Aaron and your father from us, and it might seem all the Lord's done is take. The prophet Isaiah wrote, 'If thou draw out thy soul to the hungry, and satisfy the afflicted soul, then shall thy light rise in obscurity and thy darkness be as the noon day.'"

Luke was puzzled—what did she mean? He hardly noticed Levi's "Amen, missus."

"There is now one among us who is even more afflicted than we are."

His head snapped upward now. He stared at Mama with all the contempt and fury he thought he could get away with. "No, never," he said under his breath. Anna lifted her head to look at Luke.

"Yes." Mama held Luke's gaze. "I'm talking about that Yankee boy. When Aaron was dying he didn't think about himself. He had pity on that boy, and the last thing Aaron asked me was to take care of that boy. I mean to do it. And I expect every one of you to help me do it. You've all heard the words of Jesus, "For I was an hungred, and ye gave me meat: I was thirsty, and ye gave me drink: I was a stranger, and ye took me in.'"

Levi's response was now but a soft whisper, "Amen, missus, amen."

Mama's gaze never left Luke's. "I don't know why, and I don't like it either. But whatever his reasons, I think the Lord's brought this Yankee boy here, so there won't be any arguing about it."

Luke lowered his head and studied the open grave before him. How sweet it would be to put that Yankee in the ground too.

"Let me say that again," Mama added. "There will be no arguing. We call ourselves Christians. Is that just when things are nice and pleasant, or is it also when hard things come to us? This is going to be a very hard thing, and I mean to do it and ask God's blessing on it."

Mama again looked around at each one gathered at the gravesite. All stood with their heads lowered, except Willy, who stared lovingly up at his mother, slowly nodding his head.

"Then in hope of the resurrection of the dead," Mama finally said, "we now commit our beloved Aaron's body to the earth. 'For dust thou art, and unto dust shalt thou return,' and again from the fifteenth chapter of First Corinthians, 'It is sown in dishonour; it is raised in glory: it is sown in weakness; it is raised in power: it is sown a natural body; it is raised a spiritual body.'"

"Amen, missus, amen," Levi said.

"Amen, indeed," Mama said.

Davina turned away to gaze out over the fields of greening hay grass and corn stubble, sparing herself the sight of her son's coffin being lowered into the earth. There had been many joyful days, days when Ben and Aaron had ridden whooping and laughing through those fields, days of hard labor, father and son working side by side, and long midsummer days of picnicking, fishing, and frolicking along the meandering, shaded Owl Creek. But those days were past, never to be seen again.

Davina's tears should have come in abundance, but there were no more. For now, all she yearned for was rest from the profound heaviness of both body and soul.

CHAPTER 10

*D*AVINA'S ATTEMPT AT A NAP HAD FAILED MISERABLY. AS she lay on her bed in the stillness of her bedroom, her broken heart had pounded in her chest. Sorrow had weighed heavily upon her soul, and dark, worrisome thoughts had driven all else from her mind. After more than an hour of fitful tossing, she rose and went outside to sit on the red-cedar bench on the veranda. The bench had been Davina's favorite resting place from the moment Levi had placed it against the wall of the house next to the front door.

As the afternoon wore slowly on, the din of battle subsided. Faint staccato echoes of musketry echoed across the fields from time to time, and there was still the occasional rumble of cannon fire.

Anna came out of the house and slumped heavily against her mother. "It's all over, ain't it, Mama?"

"I'm afraid it ain't been a good day for our boys." Davina held Anna closely and brushed a few long strands of honey-brown hair away from the girl's face. "Sounds like they're heading south, back to Corinth, maybe."

"They'll come up again, even stronger next time. They'll throw them Yankees off our land, I just know it."

"Maybe, my dear, but if our boys have been beat, I think the Yankees will be staying awhile."

"No, Mama! We can't let them stay here."

"*We*, Anna? What can one small family do against an army? I'm just hoping they move along, and take all their tents and animals too, so we can live normal again. In a few days, I'll take a ride down to the church with Levi—see what needs cleaning and fixing. Maybe our people can have services again."

Movement down the lane caught Davina's eye. "Looks like Luke's back with the doctor. Good, this day's been the hardest of my life—but it's far from over, and I'm ready to have supper and be done with it."

Anna leaned forward, watching Luke's approach, and seemed to hesitate. "I know you said no arguing, and I ain't arguing, Mama—but Luke don't like you bringing Dr. Comstock for that Yankee, and I say he's right. Him being here just ain't right, Mama."

"All right, dear, you said what you needed to. Now, sit up and look at me." Davina looked into her daughter's beautiful hazel eyes. "Fact is, I don't like it any more than you. But like I said up the hill there, it mightn't seem right to us, but it's what the good Lord's given us, so that makes it right. Now, go fetch Min while I take the doctor upstairs."

———

Heavy footfalls upon the pinewood floorboards should have forewarned Davina that Dr. Comstock had finished examining the boy, but both she and Min, who were standing just outside the bedroom door, jumped with a start when the doctor flung the door open.

"Mrs. Matthews, where are this man's clothes?"

Dr. Comstock, the only medical authority in McNairy County, was respected by all as knowledgeable in the medical arts and skilled in the treatment of diverse ailments. More than once Davina had known the blessing of having such a healer within an hour's hard ride, but she had never found anything likeable about the man, in either appearance or manner. He was cursed with the unkindest voice Davina had ever heard, high pitched and harsh, and she had rarely heard him speak in anything other than a brusque, almost rude fashion. A small, wiry man with unruly hair, formerly a curly light brown and now gone almost entirely gray, he possessed a pair of dark, keen eyes that darted everywhere at once and seemed to miss nothing. "Where are his clothes?" he said again. The nostrils of his small, beak-like nose flared wide. "I must see his clothes."

"Yes, Doctor, right away. I was thinking to burn them, but I'll have them brought right away. Anything else you need, Doctor?"

"Yes, bandages, lots of them, and cotton—you must have cotton—and I may need an apparatus made of wood."

"My man Levi can—"

"Send for him."

"Yes, Doctor," Davina said, turning to Min, who was already halfway down the stairs.

"Come in, Mrs. Matthews. I'm done with my examination for now, but I need to examine his clothing to be sure."

The Yankee boy lay flat on the bed, entirely unclothed but for a folded white linen cloth laid discreetly to satisfy the demands of propriety. Davina closed the door against the young and inquiring eyes that would be sure to pry if she didn't.

"He says his name is Stanley," Comstock said, "Stanley Mitchell. I gave him a large dose of laudanum, because he's in a lot of pain, so he'll be quiet for a while. You did right to bandage him tightly. It kept him from moving and causing further injury to himself. When I removed those bandages I discovered four distinct wounds."

Davina drew near to the bedside and listened closely.

"The first wound is here in his chest, and it is most unusual." Comstock probed the place with his learned fingertips. "It's about five inches to the left of center, and it seems not to have caused any mortal damage. The area is most painful and I heard a grating sound while he was breathing, so it seems one or two of his rib bones are fractured. I had him sit up so I could see his back—terribly painful for him, but I found a slight bump on the right side of his back, just above the lowest rib. I believe a musket ball punctured the skin here, struck the rib, not straight on, mind you, but at an angle, thus changing its course, so that the ball traveled all the way around his rib cage until it came to rest in his back. When I looked closely I saw this faint blue line tracing just such a path."

"Yes, I see it too," Davina said. "Can anything help such a wound?"

"There's not much to do in this case. There's hardly any bleeding, but with any open wound the main enemy is putrefaction. I'll clean the wound in his chest as best I can. Turpentine can be helpful in such cases, but I think grain alcohol may be better for a penetrating wound like this. I brought a bottle with me, and you will need to keep the bandage moist by pouring a bit of alcohol on the bandage every couple of hours. If you run out of alcohol, use clean water."

"How many days should I do that, Doctor?"

"Five, I think, not more than a week, just until the wound closes. I'll also bind his chest rather tightly to allow the ribs to heal, and when I return a week from today to remove the ball from his back, perhaps I can remove the bindings.

"This second wound, here in the abdomen, just beside the umbilicus, is also most curious—severe bruising, perhaps a little bleeding from skin contusions, but there's no significant penetration. It seems he was struck a rather severe blow, but the exact nature of it is a mystery to me until I see this man's clothing.

"As you can see I've already bandaged the wound to his left arm. He must have had his arms raised, like this, in the shooting position, because the ball passed through the flesh on the underside of his arm, just below the armpit. He suffered significant blood loss, and had he not bandaged it himself, he surely would have died. Try to keep this bandage moist as well."

"Yes, Doctor," Davina said.

"The left leg is this boy's most serious wound," Comstock said, gesturing toward the leg. "His femur—his thigh bone—is broken a few inches above the knee. There's no bullet wound, just this large contusion in the shape of an arc."

"Looks like something gave him a wallop, Doctor."

"Yes indeed. The boy couldn't remember what happened, or he didn't wish to say, so I didn't ask further, he was in such pain. I've seen two or three cases like this, and it's always a most difficult injury to recover from. The area is swollen and very sore, and look here," Comstock said, pointing toward Stanley's feet, "his left foot is turned outward more than the right, and his left leg is now visibly shorter than the right. The best thing I can do is saw it off."

"Oh my, that's dreadful." Davina felt her face flush with heat as she remembered the ghastly scene beside the church the previous evening. She reached out to grasp the footboard of the bed, steadying herself. "Can't you save it, Doctor?"

"It would be most difficult, and he'll never walk right." The doctor stroked his closely trimmed goatee. "If I do attempt it, I will need your man to make me a wooden brace. Where is this boy's clothing, Mrs. Matthews?"

A soft knock on the door signaled Min's return. Davina went to the door, glad for the interruption.

"Missus Davina," Min said, her voice low and hesitant, "I fetched the clothes, an' Levi's coming quick-like, now I'm gone to fetch the bandages."

"No need to whisper, woman, he can't hear you." Comstock snatched the boy's mud- and blood-stained shirt and jacket from Min, whereupon she dropped the trousers on the floor and fled to complete the rest of her mission.

Comstock stared at the shiny brass buttons embossed with the Federal war eagle, then looked in wonder at Stanley. "He's a Yankee?" Comstock's voice was as shrill as Davina had ever heard it. "You just buried your boy Aaron this morning, and now this half-dead Yankee is in your boy's bed? And you're thinking I'm going to save his life and you're going to nurse him back to health?"

Davina looked Comstock in the eye. "I mean to, yes, if the Lord wills it."

"And if I don't will it? You know the penalty for aiding the enemy."

"An enemy? Really? Somehow I don't think he'll ever fight again, not with that bad leg. And there was no one else, for pity's sake. It was either I help this boy or leave him die. My conscience burdened me and I had no choice. Call me a fool, if you must, Dr. Comstock, but that boy is some northern woman's Aaron."

Comstock's small eyes grew smaller still; he seemed to stare clear through Davina. "Your compassion for Yankees is noted. I'll do only what I must."

His words were more hissed than spoken, but Davina didn't care. She even felt a smile warm her face as he slid the chair loudly across the floor, kicking it like an unruly child, until it was next to the bed. He sat down with a huff.

The doctor examined the shirt, paying particular attention to the hole made by the bullet. He pressed the frayed edges together with his fingers. Then he peered intently at Stanley's chest wound. "Just a few pieces..." he said, opening his medical bag to retrieve a magnifying glass and a small forceps. Then he spent a few minutes intently probing the wound, extracting several bits of the coarse shirt cloth that had been carried into the wound by the musket ball.

"Now the trousers," he said, without looking up at Davina.

Comstock bent to his examination once again. "Humph... makes sense...of course."

Finally, Comstock sat back and looked up at Davina. "Mrs. Matthews, I think I've got it." The anger seemed gone, replaced by the excitement of discovery. "Look here. He was struck squarely on the belt buckle—would have killed him outright but for the buckle—and that's what caused that ugly bruise. A shot like that might have knocked him over onto a rock or a log, thus breaking the leg. We won't know for sure until he wakes up and tells us."

A few minutes later Levi announced his presence with a solid rap on the door. "Here I is, missus."

"Good," Comstock said, beckoning Levi to his side. "I need to brace this boy's leg. It's got to be held stock-still while it heals." The doctor drew a simple plan for Levi and told him how to construct the brace. Two pieces of wood, each about six inches in width and three feet in length, were to be fixed at a right angle to each other along their entire length, resulting in a V-shaped channel.

"Do that with hide glue and nails," Levi said, "and it stronger if I nail a wood piece across the foot end of it, Mistuh Doctah."

"Yes, that would maintain the angle and make it stronger. Get to it."

An hour later, shortly after the sun had set, Stanley's chest had been bandaged, the brace had been made, and Stanley had been clothed in a large white nightshirt. Anna and Luke, along with Levi and Min, gathered in that upper room, now alight in the warm glow of several candles, to take part in the saving of Stanley's leg. His own belt was forced between his teeth. His left leg was raised. The wooden brace was slid underneath and a thick blanket roll was forced under the brace to keep the leg elevated. Though now awake, Stanley suffered all this in silence, perhaps due to the liberal use of the laudanum and, perhaps even more, his settled determination not to cry out. But when Dr. Comstock tied his ankle tightly to the bedpost, he groaned deeply and began to weep. With Davina and Luke at one bedpost, and Levi and Min at the other, the foot of the bed was hoisted off the floor while Anna placed thick wooden blocks under the bedposts for support, all under the direction of Dr. Comstock.

Stanley's own weight began to pull against his constricted thigh muscles, the fractured bones began to grind their way back into place, and Stanley could no longer restrain the screams of agony.

Dr. Comstock went to the head of the bed and motioned Levi to do the same. "Grab him under the armpit, like this. Now, on my count, pull him sharply toward you, toward the head of the bed. One. Two. Three!"

Stanley's screams died suddenly and mercifully as he passed into oblivion. "Hold him there," Comstock told Levi. The doctor probed Stanley's leg carefully with his fingertips. He made one adjustment to the angle of the boy's foot and checked the length of the left leg against the right.

"It feels like it's set," Comstock said. "Now, the bandages."

Ten minutes later, Stanley's entire leg was securely bandaged from foot to hip and strapped to Levi's wooden brace. Then all except the doctor helped lower the foot of the bed to the floor. Luke and Anna nearly ran down the stairs without waiting to be dismissed.

The doctor looked around the room; exhaustion lined his face. "Now, Mrs. Matthews, don't move that leg for three weeks. I'll leave you some opium pills. The pain will get worse, so give him one if he starts to get restless. And he'll get hot with a fever, already is, I think, but it should break in a couple of days—send for me if it doesn't."

"You'll stay for dinner, Doctor?" Davina said.

"Yes, thank you, and then I must return to Purdy. I'll come again next Monday. One last thing, Mrs. Matthews—I treated that Yankee only for your sake and at your request, and not for his sake. I trust you will bear that in mind."

CHAPTER 11

B LACKNESS, UTTER BLACKNESS—AND SILENCE, UTTER silence. Searching the blackness, probing its farthest reaches with as much of his mind as he could muster, he found nothing, absolutely nothing. This must be death, he thought, the everlasting nothingness so many believed awaited at the end of every human life. But why was the nothing not nothing? Why did he still sense? Why did he still think? Why did he still perceive, or at least believe that he did?

Again he peered into the void. A fine point of light appeared, small as a speck of dust, then another, and a third, each widely scattered from the other. A few more specks of light dotted the blackness, then it seemed an entire host, as numerous as the stars in the heavens, and all seeming to draw gradually closer to him— or was he being drawn closer to them? Perhaps the specks would soon merge and the blackness would be gone and he could enjoy the light in its fullness. But the specks began to move back and forth across the blackness, in straight, streaking lines, or darting here and there in swirling circles and figures. Closer, ever closer they came until there arose the sound of a mighty rush of wind on a stormy night. And yet he felt not even the faintest breeze, only sudden warmth that built quickly to searing heat upon his flesh.

Out of the storm a single speck approached so near to his

face that he reached out with what he thought was his hand to touch it, but it dodged sideways and lunged straight for his face. The speck of gleaming, welcoming light he thought he had seen was a single sharp, flashing, metallic tooth, glowing white with heat like embers from the hottest fire. Terror seized him, terror the likes of which he had never known, as the dreadful knowledge of what was about to happen fell upon him. Instead of being enveloped in the brilliant glow of glorious light, he was being surrounded by an army of grinding, flashing, burning teeth, their keen edges shining brightly like well-honed barbers' razors, each attached to some small, vicious creature still hidden in the hot darkness that seemed all the more black in spite of the multitude of flashing teeth.

The creatures flew all around him. They danced before him, up and down, round and round, nearer and nearer, a horde of voracious teeth, hot and evil, surging hungrily forward to lance his skin and spill his blood. The incessant beating of their wings and gnashing of their teeth composed a chorus of dissonance that, now that he heard its fullness, was not a storm-driven gale, but a pitiful, plaintive refrain of boundless woe accompanied by the sound of rushing waters, a thunderous cascading river of tears.

Stanley awoke with such a scream that a short, round black woman, who was sitting in attendance upon him during the mid-morning hours, jumped up and ran from the room, screaming even louder than he was.

"The fever's broke," Davina said. "Could be a bad dream made him yell like that, don't you think, Min?"

"Yes, missus," Min said, frozen in the doorway, still wild-eyed, "but the devil be in it, so I'm thinking to stay right here, missus."

"But he's sleeping quiet now, probably will for hours."

"I'd likes be gone just the same, missus."

"All right, Min, as you will. I'll get Willy, but I'll need you to help wash him again this evening."

"Yes, missus," Min said, already halfway down the stairs.

CHAPTER 12

_S_TANLEY AWOKE. HE THOUGHT HIS EYES WERE OPEN AND yet he saw nothing, not even that terrible black void. He still lived, of that much he was sure, but where was he? Was it a night so dark that nothing at all could be seen? Had he been blinded? He'd been able to see before…before whatever had happened to him had happened. He remembered seeing the woman that first night, and the screaming black woman sometime after, but now he couldn't see.

Were his eyes really open or did he just think they were? They felt somehow cool and moist. He arched his eyebrows, thinking surely they were open, but still he saw nothing. He tried to raise his right hand to his face, but he was still tightly bound. To himself? To the bed? It didn't matter. What if he called out? Would anyone hear? Would anyone come?

Stanley quieted his thoughts and began to take stock of himself. He still breathed and his chest throbbed in pain with every breath and his leg ached most of all, so he knew he was alive. There was also a smell, an odor that seemed familiar, but he was unable to identify it. He inhaled slowly, as if savoring for the first time the enticing aroma of some sweet confection or another fresh from the oven, but this odor, while not overpowering, was more offensive than pleasurable.

And then it came to him, like the sudden lifting of a veil,

that his eyes had been covered by a cool, moist cloth, that he still remained in the very same bed in the very same room where he had been placed and where the doctor had treated him in a most rough and even brutal manner, all of which could only mean that the odor that assailed him he could now identify as that of swine —hog manure to be precise.

Stanley turned his head slowly to the side. The cloth fell part way off; light glowed around the edges. Another turn of his head and the cloth slid down the side of his face. Brilliant sunshine streaming into the room made him squint against the glare. He quickly gave up and closed his eyes altogether. What was there to see anyway? Just the rafters and roof boards above and—he opened his eyes again and strained to lift his head a few inches —a glorious view of the dresser and the window with its plain white curtains hanging loosely on either side. The muscles in his neck screamed for relief, and his head fell back heavily upon the thin pillow.

How long had he lain there? A day? A week? How could he know? And what of the battle? He listened for sounds of musketry and cannon fire, but there were none. Had the North won or lost? And what had become of his friends? Were they off fighting another battle? Were they even still alive—Gilbert Goode and John Miller, and Sergeant Morehouse? He was a good man, tough, but fair. And where had the colonel run off to at the first sign of the enemy?

Stanley opened his eyes again and stared at the rough timbers above him. Why was he still alive? The woman hadn't seemed to care much when he whimpered and groaned as she and the slave woman undressed him, washed him clean, and wrapped his wounds. He could have died right then, whenever then was. And during the long night hours, when he had been stupid with whiskey or opium, there had been opportunity aplenty for the woman's son to slit his throat. What could he have done to defend himself, bound as he was? Perhaps he still would die.

A sound, soft and lyrical, almost musical, and within the room itself caught Stanley's ear. A voice. Yes, a child's voice, small, soft, gentle. Stanley lay perfectly still, captivated by the soothing tones of the voice, and he soon found himself straining to hear the words.

"'...as a root out of a dry ground: he hath no form nor comeliness; and when we shall see him, there is no beauty that we should desire him. He is despised and rejected of men; a man of sorrows, and acquainted with grief: and we hid as it were our faces from him; he was despised, and we esteemed him not.'"

Despised, rejected, a man of sorrows, acquainted with grief—that sums it up. Stanley turned his head toward the voice. A small figure sat on the chair beside the dresser. "Who are you?" Stanley's voice was strained and hoarse to his own ears, and it startled the boy.

"I...I'm Willy. Thought you was asleep. So—the Yankee can talk?"

"Yeah, I can talk," Stanley said. "You have water?"

"Yeah."

Stanley followed Willy with his eyes as the boy stood. Something about the boy's movements seemed measured and deliberate; he took great care in pouring the water from the large earthen pitcher into the small tin cup.

"Need any help?" Willy said, as he approached the bedside.

"Loosen my right arm, and I can make do."

"I guess Mama won't mind." Willy worked at the rope with both hands, and a few minutes later placed the cup in Stanley's free hand.

Stanley raised his head as much as he could and gulped the water down. "Thank you," he said, handing the cup back to Willy and laying his head down again. "What's the wet cloth for?"

"Cover your eyes 'cause of the light and so they don't get dry. Mama said you might wake up. I'll go fetch her."

"No—wait, Willy."

"Want more water?"

"Maybe later. What day is it?"

"Friday. You been here since Sunday. Doc was here Monday. He didn't want to doctor no Yankee boy, but did it just the same."

"My name's Stanley."

Willy's head bobbed slightly. "I know. Mama told us."

"So, I've been asleep four days?"

"Yeah, if that's what you want to call it. Mama's been giving you opium pills. They kept you quiet, but you been in a fever, and you been talking strange, scary even."

"What did I say?"

"Sometimes no words at all and sometimes words I ain't never heard before, but I think you don't like Uncle Charles much."

"No, not much." It pleased Stanley that the sound of that name brought no vision of that dreadful man to mind. "What were you reading?"

"Oh, I don't read," said Willy. "Used to read—can't no more—eyes been getting bad. So I try and remember what I used to read. From the Bible, that is. Most other things I read before, I forgot. They ain't important anyway."

"So you're blind?"

"Not yet. Things are just kinda blurry and dim. I can see where's your face, and I can see you got dark hair, kinda curly maybe, but your eyes is just darker spots where I know your eyes gotta be."

"That must be hard."

"No, not too hard. Mama says I got a gift. If Mama or Luke or Anna—or Aaron, when he was here—if they read something from the Bible, maybe two, maybe three times, I can remember it."

"That wasn't my doing, Willy."

"What?"

"Your brother Aaron."

"I know. Mama told us that, too. Said you was hurt before Aaron was there."

"That's right. But I'm sorry, just the same." Stanley waited for Willy to respond, but the boy's gaze seemed fixed on the empty tin cup in his hand. "It must have been good to have a brother like him. I never had a brother, or a sister, for that matter."

"That's too bad," Willy said. "He used to look after me real good, 'specially after my eyes started getting bad, but he's with God now. Can't get no better for him than that."

"So what was it?" Stanley asked.

"What was what?"

"Those words you were saying when I woke up."

"Fifty-third chapter of Isaiah the prophet."

"Fifty-third? That's my regiment, the Fifty-third Ohio."

"Ohio? That's where you're from? Don't know where that is."

"A long way from here, Willy, and it seems even farther now." Ohio was where he was from, but he couldn't think of it as home. Nothing drew Stanley back to Ohio—no fond memories, no bright prospects, no one near and dear, and that saddened him. "I'll take more water now."

Stanley drained the tin cup for the second time, and laid his head back on the pillow. He knew he should sleep again soon, but it was good to be awake, and he was enjoying talking with Willy. "So, can you remember the other fifty-two chapters?"

Willy's laughter was high and shrill. "Can't nobody do that, Stanley, even with good eyes. It's just the important parts I remember, the parts Mama says I got to remember."

Then, just as suddenly as it had begun, the laughter ended. Willy turned and went to the door. "Ain't right," the boy said, "me laughing and Aaron dead. Got no business carrying on. I'll go fetch Mama."

CHAPTER 13

WILLY'S MOTHER BEGAN TO SPEAK THE MOMENT SHE entered the bedroom, and in the same strident tone Stanley had heard on the field of battle. "Our little church is gone, nothing but a burnt-up heap now. Heard it from Mr. Sharpe just passing through on his way to Purdy. Your Yankee friends must have done it, 'cause our boys know to honor the house of the Lord, but I suppose you don't care a whit about that."

"I'm sorry, ma'am."

"Being sorry don't mean a thing, 'cause the good people hereabouts got no place for meeting now, and I can't take my children to hear the preaching. Just have to do what I can here when Sundays come. Wasn't enough you Yankees chased us off the place for your camps, you just had to fire it."

"Yes, ma'am."

She glared at Stanley. "Yes, ma'am? That's all you have to say, boy? And I'll expect you to call me Mrs. Matthews from now on."

"Yes, Mrs. Matthews."

She turned and walked across the room to the dresser. "The good Lord said, 'Love your enemies, do good to them which hate you, bless them that curse you, and pray for them which despitefully use you.' That's the meaning of Christian charity."

But Stanley heard nothing charitable in her words. "Mrs. Matthews?"

"What, boy?" She continued to gaze out the window before her.

"My name is St—"

"I know your name."

"But I didn't do what you said. I don't hate you and I've never cursed you."

"But you did *despitefully use me*." Mrs. Matthews turned to face Stanley again. "Now listen to me, Stanley. I'll say this once and then I'll not speak of it again. It was wrong for you to bargain with me over my Aaron's life."

"That may be, Mrs. Matthews," said Stanley, trying his best to sound sincere, "but then you wouldn't be speaking to me now. You were my last hope. I had to do it."

"Then you understand if I can't but feel ill toward you?"

Stanley nodded.

"You said I'd thank you for what you did. Remember?"

"Yes, Mrs. Matthews. I'm sorry for that too."

"Then I'll say this just once too. I—" Suddenly, Mrs. Matthews seemed uncertain of her words. Looking directly at Stanley, her stern face softened and her blue eyes seemed a little warmer, a little sadder. "I've been thinking a lot about that night. It pains me to admit this, but without your help, I'd never have found my Aaron and I'd never have been able to..."

Mrs. Matthews turned quickly away, and returned to the window. "So," she said, so quietly that Stanley held his breath to hear the words, "I find I *must* thank you."

Stanley couldn't guess Mrs. Matthews' age, but she seemed old now. Her golden, shoulder-length hair showed no sign of graying, but the vitality he had witnessed on the field of battle seemed to have drained away. Her shoulders were rounded, stooped even, as if under some heavy burden. But then, almost as if she sensed Stanley's eyes upon her, Mrs. Matthews stood a little taller, squared her shoulders, and ran a hand quickly through her hair. Then she turned and walked slowly back to the side of the bed.

"Now—I'm a Christian woman," she said, "but a woman and a mother just the same, and I can't find love in my heart for you, and I can't bring myself to bless you, so I can only do good by you and pray you'll heal up so you can be on your way. That's as much charity as I can put out for a Yankee rascal. But I done gave my word as a Christian woman and I mean to abide by it."

She looked down at Stanley, shaking her finger at him to emphasize her words. "But this I'll also say, you'll get no mollycoddling here, just what you need to get you up and on your feet again and out of my house, nothing more. And I expect you to pitch in and do whatever I tell you, 'cause 'if any would not work, neither should he eat.'"

"Yes, Mrs. Matthews."

"You fond of cussing, boy?"

"Not generally, Mrs. Matthews."

"There's no cussing in my house, and no taking the Lord's name in vain neither. You got that, boy?"

"Yes, Mrs. Matthews. I never had much use for swearing."

Mrs. Matthews stood looking down at him, arms folded in front of her, and apparently not convinced.

"My uncle would cane me hard if I let one slip," Stanley explained, "but he could swear up the bluest streak you ever heard. They didn't allow it at school, either. Only in the army was swearing mostly tolerated, but I don't think my short stay was long enough to do much damage."

"And just how long was that?"

"I left home the first of December last, Mrs. Matthews."

"All right, then, no cussing at all, and no drinking spirits neither."

"Yes, Mrs. Matthews. The whiskey you gave me was the first I ever had."

"Good. Now, let's see if we can raise you up in that bed some, so's you're kinda sitting. Doc said it would help against the pneumony and them other bad humors." Mrs. Matthews slid her arm under Stanley's shoulders and helped him to sit up. Then she placed a thick blanket roll and a second pillow on the bed. Stanley leaned back against them.

"When you had the fever you was confused," Mrs. Matthews said as she walked across the room toward the dresser again. "You'd only take a spoon or two of broth, and sometimes swat my hand away, so we need to start feeding you proper and getting you strong again so you can be on your way."

She picked up the chair next to the chest, set it next to the bed, and sat down with a heavy sigh. "I'll have Min bring something up in a bit. Now we're clear of those matters, who's it the Lord brung under my roof? Willy says you're from Ohio."

"Yes, Mrs. Matthews."

"And that's where your mama and papa are?"

"No, Mrs. Matthews."

"How's that?"

"I have no mother."

Mrs. Matthews looked at Stanley for a moment. "No mama?"

Stanley shook his head.

"Why not?"

"She died before I was three years old."

"Oh my. And your papa?"

Stanley shook his head again.

"Is he dead too?"

"I don't know. He might as well be. He left me with my aunt Bess and uncle Charles and I haven't seen him since."

"Oh my," Mrs. Matthews said again, shaking her head. "So you're an orphan?"

"Yes, Mrs. Matthews."

Mrs. Matthews nodded slowly. "Now I see why your uncle caned you for cussing. Your aunt and uncle done your rearing. You'll need to write a letter and let them know you're alive."

"I don't think so, Mrs. Matthews. In their house it was never 'Uncle Charles' and 'Aunt Bess,' only 'sir' and 'ma'am,' or 'Mr.

and Mrs. Haggerty' when we were out in public. Aunt Bess was a mean and plain woman and Uncle Charles was just plain mean, so I think it was good that they had no children of their own. I joined the army to be done with them, and I'm sure they're just as glad to be done with me."

"But you're too young to enlist."

"They never blinked an eye when I said I was nineteen. I'm big, and they wanted to fill up the ranks."

"Yes, you're a big one for sure. Are they church folk?"

"Oh, Aunt Bess would attend the Episcopal church once in a while, but I never saw Uncle Charles go to church."

Mrs. Matthews raised an eyebrow. "Never?"

"Not even for a wedding or a funeral, Mrs. Matthews."

"Well, it'll be different in my house. When you're able you'll meet with me and my children for our reading and praying times. If you're in my house you'll learn about God."

"I don't see what God has to do with any of this, Mrs. Matthews. You said before that the Lord brought me here, but all my life God's been absent, just like my father, so I don't see why he'd be taking an interest in me now."

"Oh, you poor boy," Mrs. Matthews said, and Stanley thought she meant it. "Still, I won't have you leaving here not hearing the Word of the Lord. I said before I aim to do good by you, Stanley, and that means both your body and your soul."

CHAPTER 14

TIME SEEMED TO OCCUPY MOST OF STANLEY'S THOUGHTS when he was awake. Daytime could be told from night, of course, and on a sunny day he could tell morning from afternoon, but the hour could never be determined with any certainty. Worst of all was when the sense-dulling and time-suspending effects of the evening opium pill wore off in the long night hours, and the pain took hold of him once again, while he was unable to discern late night from early morning.

He lay still, hoping this night would be different and the pain wouldn't be so bad, but within a very short time, the first spasm seized the long sinews of his left leg. He tried to twist himself away from the pain, but restraints and the leg brace prevented nearly all movement. His breathing turned into a deep and tremulous panting, and as he had done the night before, and the night before that, he fought the cries his body demanded of him, so as not to waken the rest of the house.

The spasm passed, and Stanley's body gradually released its tension. His breathing slowed and became regular once again.

Time. He still lived, but was unable to tell one day from the next. He did recall the day before, or was it two days before, because that was when the sawbones had appeared and cut the musket ball out of his back. The doctor had again been uncaring and merciless, and Stanley was glad when he heard the man tell

Mrs. Matthews, as he dropped the bloody ball into her hand, that he'd done all he could and that he would not return again to treat the Yankee.

Stanley contemplated the candle burning warmly on the dresser. Someone, at some time of the night, had struck a match and held it to the wick. Each of the last few evenings, Stanley had tried to remain awake to see who this someone was, but try as he might, his eyes grew heavy as the opium took effect and the room dimmed with the setting of the sun. How many hours might that candle burn until it died of its own consumption? Eight hours maybe, or ten. The shorter the candle, the later the hour, and if the flame had died entirely, could dawn be long in coming? And with the dawn, perhaps more opium and then release, although Mrs. Matthews seemed to be giving it to him less often.

It was quiet in the house, and in the room where Stanley lay, it was so quiet that Stanley thought perhaps he was alone. He stilled himself and listened to the silence to learn if someone was occupying the sitter's chair—for that is how he had come to think of the chair in the corner next to the dresser—and he thought he heard the regular and deep, albeit hushed, breathing of someone sleeping. He turned his head and strained to see, hoping it was the boy Willy. He saw only the dim form of some-one almost entirely hidden in the shadow of the dresser cast by the candle flame. The only part not in shadow was the top of the person's head—light hair, blonde possibly, and straight like Mrs. Matthews' hair, whereas Willy's was dark brown and rather curly.

Stanley counted the four other persons he knew in the house-hold. Mrs. Matthews came twice during the day to clean him and feed him—a small bowl of broth with a piece of bread now that he was sitting up some, but nothing more. She spoke little, just checked his bandages and gave him another opium pill if he was in much pain. And the strong black man who had held the gun to his face—he hadn't seen him since the doctor was there the first time. The large black woman must be his wife. She fed him too, and never said so much as one word, but she always seemed to be humming a tune. Stanley also had a vague recollection of another boy, probably Willy's older brother, but he had dark hair too. The boy had said something Stanley couldn't recall exactly, but he thought it best to stay clear of him, if he could.

But there was someone else, he thought—someone he had seen that first night when his head lolled to the side as they lifted him from the wagon bound to that wooden plank—a girl, most likely, from the long hair that had hidden her face and her high, wailing voice.

———·—

Anna awoke from her dozing. She hated that chair—hard, straight-backed, no cushion. Waiting. Every third night—first Min, then Willy, then herself. Waiting for sleep to come, waiting for the seconds to pass one by one, wasted seconds, sixty in every wasted minute. Waiting for the clock in the dining room below to chime merrily that another three thousand six hundred seconds had passed, another hour of watching that candle flicker, another hour of listening. No, not listening, just hearing, for listening might imply she wished to hear the various revolting sounds the Yankee made—the snoring, the heavy breathing, irregular at times, sometimes punctuated with sharp gasps for breath. And of course there were the sighs, and the whimpering and, her favorite of all, the groans.

An abomination, that's what it was. Aaron belonged; he had Mama's looks—fair skin, blue eyes, and straw-colored hair. That boy didn't belong, with his dark, wavy hair all scruffy and matted. What was that word Luke had used? Interloper. Yes, that was it. *Ain't there any justice left in the world?* If it was Aaron lying there, she'd more than happily sit as long as it took. *Why won't that Yankee just get up and get out of here, then get on his way back to his kind? Or better yet, why won't he just up and die?*

86

When Stanley awakened again the candle flame had gone out. It seemed the new day was dawning, but he wasn't entirely sure. Several minutes passed before he decided that more light was filtering into the room from the window by the dresser; it was growing lighter, not darker.

The same unfamiliar form still occupied the sitter's chair, no longer sleeping but rather sitting motionless, staring at him. At least that's how Stanley perceived it in the dim light. But he could see clearly now that the person had long, light-colored hair. It appeared to be the girl he had seen in his agony while being borne into the house.

"Good morning." Stanley's voice scratched in his throat. He swallowed hard against the dryness.

"Nothing good about it," the girl said, still staring, not moving.

"What's your name?"

"Don't matter."

"Well, Miss Don't Matter, thank you for—"

"Idiot! Don't bother thanking me, 'cause I'd rather not be setting here, but Mama says I got to, says you can't be left alone, says she's afraid of what my brother Luke'll do to you. Says he wants to kill you, you know, and I say, that's fine with me."

Luke—that was the other boy's name. "What day is it?"

"Don't matter what day it is, but if you got to know, it's Wednesday."

"So I've been here about ten days?"

"Way too long for my liking."

The room had lightened a little more. "What color are your eyes?" he asked.

"What? Brown kinda, Mama says hazel, but that don't matter neither, 'cause you ain't nothing to me, nothing at all. Matter of fact, I say you're less than nothing. You know what creek muck is? Course you don't, 'cause you're a yellow-belly Yankee, and you all live in dirty cities. Well, Mr. Yankee, you're like that squishy, slimy stuff at the bottom of a slow creek in August, all nasty and smelly and makes your feet sink in and squishes between your toes and all."

Stanley chuckled in spite of himself. On many a summer's day he had crept out of the house and raced through the city streets to swim with Jimmy Atchison and Peter Gray at Storm Creek, so he knew very well what creek muck was. "You're probably right."

"I know I'm right, and Luke says much worser things about you, but I won't, 'cause Mama says such words ain't proper for a lady like me, but I sure will think 'em, and Luke says if it wasn't for Mama, you'd be dead already. He woulda stuck you in the ribs first chance."

"So he wants to finish me off?"

"Yep. Yankee cavalry came by twice since you been lying here. Looking for food and stuff they could steal. Me and Luke wanted to give you up, but Mama told us, 'Not a word,' and sent us inside. And then they searched all over, but couldn't find none of our hidings, but the rascals stole a couple of our hogs. Luke says he don't care what Mama says anymore. First chance he's riding up Purdy way to fetch the sheriff. He'll know what to do with a treed polecat like you."

"But you just said I was creek muck."

"Moron!"

Silence settled over the room for a time. The rising sun haloed the girl's hair in golden splendor. Finally, she stood and walked across the room toward the door. She wore a tan or light gray flannel shirt and suspendered trousers of a slightly darker shade, clothing more suited to a man or boy and rather too large for her slender frame, but Stanley watched her every step.

"My time's done," she said, "and I say none too soon." She

put her hand on the door handle, and turned back toward Stanley. "You in much pain?"

Perhaps it was the lingering effects of the opium, or the hours upon endless hours of pain and boredom, or perhaps his incessant thinking about his own desperate circumstances, but as the girl turned back toward the light of the sunlit window, Stanley saw the most remarkable creature he had ever seen. Fair skin, though somewhat reddened by the sun, framed with long tresses—not blonde as he had first thought, but light brown that caught the early morning light and shimmered like golden honey. "Brown kinda" eyes, she had said, but they were so rich in color, set aglow in the bright morning sun, revealing vivid hints of green. Stanley tried to imagine how those eyes might light up if the girl ever did smile. Surely such beauty must contain some compassion, some sympathy, some softness of heart, some joy.

"Yes," Stanley said, "but the pain seems less now."

"That's too bad, 'cause I say more pain the better for someone's done what you done."

"But I didn't kill your brother Aar—"

"Hush! Don't you never put his name in your mouth, you hear? Not ever! And Dr. Comstock says that leg of yours won't never heal proper—"

"And he whistled a merry tune all the while he was cutting that ball out."

"He says you'll be crippled all your life long, too. A wretched and crippled moron blue-belly, that's what you are now, and that's all you'll ever be, and I say it serves you right."

And with that Stanley's vision of loveliness vanished, slamming the door behind her.

CHAPTER 15

————

"WILLY SAYS YOU'RE WANTING TO ASK ME SOMETHING."
Davina knew her manner was abrupt, but she had been
working on the farm's accounts, and what she saw in the ledger wasn't encouraging. The last thing she needed was another
interruption.

"Yes, Mrs. Matthews, I am." Stanley seemed to be trying to
sit up straighter in the bed, but the heavy brace made it difficult
for him.

Davina didn't offer to help. "Well, what is it? Something
wrong with your breakfast? Willy didn't say."

"No, Mrs. Matthews, breakfast is always great and that Eas-
ter dinner yesterday? I guess that was Min's fried chicken. I hav-
en't had anything that good since I joined the army."

"I'm happy you have no complaints."

"No, but just lying here doing nothing is making me half-
crazy. How much longer will it be?"

"Another week, I should think. That's what you wanted?"

"No, Mrs. Matthews. I've been thinking about what you said
about me doing something to help."

Davina stood unmoving, arms crossed, looking at Stanley.
"It's enough you're feeding yourself now."

"But if you'll allow it, Mrs. Matthews, I'd like to read to
Willy."

That wasn't what Davina had expected when she climbed the stairs for the sixth time that morning. "Read for Willy? His Bible lessons? You'd do that?"

"Yes, ma'am. For ten years my uncle sent me to a boarding school. I think he and my aunt just wanted me out of their house, but it was a good school. Willy told me how he's going blind— that's got to be a tough thing for him—so someone needs to read for him, and although I can't do much else, I can do that."

"But you ain't a believer."

"It's just reading. I'm quite good at it."

"Your northern schooling, so you said."

"Reading was one thing I could enjoy without worrying what Uncle Charles might do to me. They had lots of books they never read. I would often go up to my room, open the window for a fresh breeze, and read about someplace far away."

It pained Davina to think the Yankee's proposal had merit. Reading to Willy had been added to the daily list of chores she assigned each morning to Anna or Luke, usually after an argument about who had the most to do that day.

Davina went to the door. "Willy, come in here." Willy appeared instantly, Bible in hand. "Let's see if this Yankee can read like he says. What verses are you memorizing now?"

"Last ones Anna read me was chapter eight in Matthew."

"Give Stanley your Bible."

Willy did as he was told, then went and stood beside his mother. Davina laid her hand gently on Willy's shoulder.

Stanley opened the Bible and began leafing through the pages.

"I don't think he can find it, Mama," Willy said.

"Is that true, Stanley?"

"Yes, Mrs. Matthews. We read the Bible some in school, but not a lot, and we read many other books."

"Willy, show him how you can find it, even with your bad eyes."

And not more than a minute later, Stanley's voice filled the small room: "'And when Jesus was come into Peter's house, he saw his wife's mother laid, and sick of a fever. And he touched her hand, and the fever left her: and she arose, and ministered unto them. When the even was come, they brought unto him many that were possessed with devils: and he cast out the spirits with his word, and healed all that were sick: That it might be fulfilled which was spoken by Esaias the prophet, saying, Himself took our infirmities, and bare our sicknesses.'"

Willy giggled a little when Stanley stumbled over the pronunciation of "Esaias," and was quick to correct Stanley when he finished reading. "It just means 'Isaiah,' like you heard me remembering before."

"Then why didn't they write 'Isaiah'?"

Willy looked up at his mother and shook his head.

"All right. You got a nice voice and you read real good. You can read for Willy." Davina wagged a finger at the Bible in Stanley's hands. "I said you'd hear the Word of God in this house, so maybe the reading will do you some good, too." She gave her smiling son a quick hug and turned to leave. "And you can start right now."

"May I ask just one more thing?"

"One *more* thing?" The edge in Davina's own words surprised her. "Well, I'm sorry, Stanley. You're just trying to help Willy. What do you need?"

"I'd like to be able to write down some of the things I learn, like 'Esaias' and such. May I have a pen or pencil, and some paper, please?"

Davina looked at Stanley. Something about the boy had changed. Or was it something within herself? Willy had taken to Stanley from the start, and he seemed sincere in his desire to help Willy.

She left the room and returned a few minutes later. "Pencils are hard to get way out here, so here's a quill pen and ink, some paper too. Just ask Willy if you need more." Davina placed the items on the small table next to Stanley's bed. "Willy, fetch that chair by the dresser and put it here next to the bed."

Davina watched Stanley arrange his pen and ink. He was still just a boy, trying to do a good thing, and she knew she should respond with good rather than evil. "Thank you," Davina said, laying a hand on Stanley's shoulder, much as she had done with Willy. "We're people of the Word here, and you'll be a big help for Willy, and maybe you'll learn some Scripture, too."

———

Stanley read the verses twice more to Willy and, just as Willy had proclaimed, he was able to recite them to Stanley flawlessly. Stanley was amazed and told the boy so.

"Like I said before, Mama says I got a gift. I can remember words I hear real fast. But my eyes is an infirmity, and just like the words say, Jesus will take my infirmity away."

"Infirmity means sickness or injury, Willy."

"Yep, Anna told me that, but it don't just mean what's bad with your body, like my bad eyes or your bad leg. It means anything that's bad on the inside of me, too. Like maybe I think bad things, or say bad things, or don't do what Mama says."

"When did you start losing your eyesight, Willy?"

"October 10th last."

"What? You know the exact day?"

Willy laughed heartily, and Stanley wondered if he would ever be able to laugh about his own injuries.

"Sure I do," Willy said. "That's the day Papa left for the war. Papa wore this brand-new uniform. He was a captain, and he had twisted gold stuff on his sleeves." Willy showed Stanley where by rubbing his right hand along his left forearm. "Anyway, he hugged Mama and me and the other kids good-bye. Then he got on his horse, and that's when I seen the gold stuff was kinda blurry."

"Couldn't the doctor do anything?"

Willy shook his head. "Dr. Comstock brought some spectacles, four or five I think. He told me to try them, but they wasn't no good. My eyes kept going badder."

"So, what's the worst part of it, Willy, the reading?"

Willy hesitated. "No. Like I said, I got a gift, and that helps a lot. Worst is not seeing nobody's face, Stanley. Can't never tell if you're smiling or not, or even if your eyes is open."

"Well, my eyes are open. I'm not smiling now because our talk is serious, but you do make me smile a lot, Willy. I like having you around."

Willy's wide grin brightened his entire face.

"There's something I don't understand though, Willy."

"What's that?"

"You've lost your father and your brother, and most of your sight, but you're still a happy boy. And Luke isn't. He seems mean and angry."

Willy's joyful appearance faded. He slumped in his chair. "Luke's always been a little that way, but more since Papa went away, and even more since Aaron died."

"Why aren't you like Luke?"

"Mama says it's part of the gift. She says God's taken my sight, but he gave me light. Don't know how that is, but if it's God's doing, I guess it's all right."

Willy went to the dresser and poured Stanley a cup of water. "We been talking a lot," Willy said as he placed the cup in Stanley hands. "Figure you need it."

"Thank you. I've been meaning to ask you something else too."

"What's that?"

"Your sister's been taking her turns sitting in here with me, but she won't tell me her name."

"That's Anna. She's a good sister, not mean like Luke, but she don't like Yankees and she don't like you. Can I ask you something?"

"Sure, anything," Stanley said.

"Are you my friend?"

"I am if you can stand having a Yankee for a friend."

Willy's face brightened again. "You ain't no Yankee at all, 'cause I ain't heard nothing but bad things about Yankees, and you ain't bad like they say."

"But I am a Yankee. Can you be a friend to this Yankee, Willy?"

"Yep. And seeing how it's me and Luke and Li'l Davy over there in the other room, I'll ask Mama if I can sleep in here so you ain't lonely."

"That's a good idea, Willy. Then nobody will have to sit in that chair all night long. And I haven't had a bad dream for more than a week, so I don't think I'll be scaring you half to death."

Willy laughed and laughed. "Oh, I near forgot. That's my Bible you been reading from, but you can have it."

"Thank you, Willy, but—"

"But nothing. It don't do me no good no more. Can't hardly see the 'Holy Bible' on the front." Willy went happily to the door. "Got to find Mama," he called out as he clumped down the stairs.

Stanley sat quietly for a while. He now had a friend. And something else had changed, too, but whether that something belonged to him or to the woman, he didn't know. His shoulder still felt Mrs. Matthews' warm touch, as if a trace of that warmth had penetrated deep within him.

Stanley looked down at the Bible still in his hands. He studied its worn black leather cover. He had always loved to read, and there must be other books in the house, perhaps volumes of the classics he hadn't yet read. He would have to ask Willy.

Then Stanley opened the Bible, turned to the Gospel of Matthew again, and began to read from the beginning.

CHAPTER 16

O N TUESDAY, APRIL 29, SHORTLY AFTER THE MIDDAY MEAL,
Stanley was surprised to hear the tramp of heavy feet upon
the stairs. Mrs. Matthews opened the door and entered, followed
by Levi and Min.

"Good news, Stanley. Your friends are leaving."

"My friends?"

"The Yankees." Mrs. Matthews was smiling broadly now.
"Levi saw this big cloud of dust this morning down toward the
Corinth Road, and I sent Luke off to see about it. He heard
them himself, and they said they're going down to take Corinth.
Seemed right proud saying it, too."

Stanley didn't know what to say.

"Losing Corinth would be real bad, though. We use them
railroads to get our crops and hogs to market. But within a few
days the way to Pittsburg should be clear. Maybe the boats'll start
running again. Anyway, folks can get back to their farms, and
maybe life can get back to normal, at least around here."

Levi held two wooden crutches in his hands while Min carried two bundles tied with rope—one contained straw, the other
several pieces of thick tree bark. They set these burdens down
beside the door.

"Well, Stanley," Mrs. Matthews said, "it seems like an age,
but you'll finally get up and on your feet today, and maybe one

day soon you can go down Corinth way and join your friends. Levi, untie the boy's foot and I'll set to cutting away the brace. This may hurt some, but there ain't no more opium. Besides, shouldn't be hard for a big, strapping boy like you."

Stanley steeled himself against the torture that was sure to come, but a few minutes later his ankle was free of the bedpost and the brace was gone. Much to his surprise, the pain he had dreaded was but mild compared to what he had known before.

"Dr. Comstock says we got to keep your leg from moving for three more weeks at least. We'll be undoing the wrappings and putting new ones on, but the wrappings ain't strong like the brace. You see that tree bark and straw?"

Stanley nodded. "Yes, Mrs. Matthews."

"First, we got to take off the old bandages and put on clean. Then we'll put some of that straw inside the tree bark, make it soft, you know, and then wrap your leg up in it, like another brace, but not heavy like the wood one, so you can get up and move some. With Levi's crutches, of course."

Stanley nodded again. All he could do was agree with whatever Mrs. Matthews decided to do to him, but in truth he did want to get up from the bed. He wanted to walk over to the dresser for a drink of water or to perform his own toilet for a change. He wanted to stand and gaze out the window.

It was a delicate operation. Mrs. Matthews replaced the bandages while Levi held Stanley's leg off the bed, then Mrs. Matthews and Min held Stanley's leg while Levi encased it in the straw-lined tree bark and bound the wrapping with a long length of leather lacing.

"Tight, but not too tight," Mrs. Matthews said as Levi tied the knot, "else his toes'll go blue. How's that feel?"

"A little tight, just as you said, Mrs. Matthews. I think it'll be all right. It aches some, but not too much."

"Then let's give it a try. The right's your good leg, so you got to get it on the floor first to help you up." Stanley eased himself over to the right side of the bed and found the floor with his right foot. Then, with Min supporting his left leg, Stanley slowly turned on the bed; his wrapped, immovable left leg swung out and Min lowered it gently to the floor.

Stanley sat on the edge of the bed breathing heavily. The effort to sit up and maneuver to the edge of the bed had been far more than he had expected.

"You ready, Stanley?"

"Yes, Mrs. Matthews." Stanley wiped the sleeve of his nightshirt across his brow.

"Levi, you get under his left arm; Min, you get under his right. I'll hold the crutches."

Under Mrs. Matthews' constant direction, and with much grunting and groaning, Stanley Mitchell finally rose from the bed that had held him prisoner for more than three weeks, and with the strong shoulders of both Levi and Min to lean on, Stanley slowly stood to nearly his full height—until his head struck a rafter just above.

"My, you are a tall one," Mrs. Matthews said. "Can you stand on your right leg? Min, stand away and let him try."

Stanley tried for all he was worth to put all his weight on his right leg, but found he could not. He wavered back and forth, and had Levi not been there to support him, Stanley would have fallen.

"That's 'cause your good leg's gone weak," Mrs. Matthews said. "A day or two and you'll be fine. Try the crutch under the right." A few minutes later, after Stanley had leaned heavily on the crutch and gotten a feel for it, she said, "Now the left. Help him, Levi."

"Yes, missus." Levi helped Stanley position the crutch under his left arm, then moved cautiously away. "Try it some, mastuh. They's strong crutches, made them with maple wood. If they's too long, I can cut them easy."

Stanley shifted his weight from side to side and front to back, finding out what he *could* do with the help of the crutches, and even more importantly, what he could not do. He had watched men walking with crutches at the army hospital back in Paducah, but try as he might, he couldn't remember what exactly he was supposed to do to go one step forward, let alone cross the room.

"You wanting to go a step, mastuh?"

Stanley nodded.

"It ain't hard once you done it, mastuh." Levi came close beside Stanley to show him how to use the crutches. "Got to hold tight with both hands, mastuh, they's what keep you from falling down. Lean on that good leg first—then move them crutches a little, just a little—good, mastuh—now lean forward on them crutches and slide your good leg up the middle of them—that be real good, mastuh."

"A lot of work for four inches," Stanley said.

"Sure is, mastuh, but you be doing a whole foot real soon, real soon."

Stanley "walked" another four inches, then another and another. He paused at the end of the bed to decide how he might turn left toward the window. Levi had remained at Stanley's side, ready to help. "How far is it to the window?"

"About eight foot, mastuh, no more."

"Twenty-four steps then?"

"Less, mastuh, if you step more, just a little more."

Ten minutes later Stanley stood before the window, only four panes, small in comparison to the large windows with twelve or sixteen panes in his uncle's house, and the glass was of inferior quality with waves and imperfections that distorted the view. A large barn stood perhaps thirty yards away. Except at its edges, where grasses and wildflowers were growing tall in the spring-time warmth, the yard between the house and the barn was almost devoid of vegetation, probably packed hard by wagon wheels, horse hooves, and countless boots dashing back and forth between the buildings.

Stanley strained to look as far to the right as he could, then all the way to the left, but except for a dozen or so chickens scurrying to and fro, no other living and breathing creatures were visible, and this both surprised and disappointed him. Even more disappointing was that there was no sign of the creature he most hoped to see, the beautiful, honey-haired Anna.

Stanley half turned from the window. "While I'm out of bed, I'd like to wash, if I may, Mrs. Matthews."

"Of course, Stanley. Me and Min'll leave you to it. There's a clean nightshirt in the bottom drawer—and clean unders, too."

"What has become of my army uniform, Mrs. Matthews?"

"Oh, I thought you knew. We burned them things, they was in such a sad state. And it just won't do to have you out and about looking like a Yankee."

"So nothing remains of what I came here with?"

"Well, we kept them shoes of yours 'cause they was so big. They're under your bed there. And your belt, too—didn't burn that, being good cowhide."

"Thank you, Mrs. Matthews."

"Levi, call me when he's done. I need to look to his other wounds."

"Yes, missus."

"And I thank you too, Levi," Stanley said, after the door had closed.

"Mastuh?"

"For the crutches. They'll suit me fine once I get used to them. No need to cut them, not yet anyway. An extra inch or two will help keep my left leg from touching the floor."

"Yes, mastuh."

"And for the help. It feels so good to be free of that bed."

"Yes, mastuh."

"Stanley. My name's Stanley."

Levi shook his head vehemently. "No, mastuh, ain't fitting. White folk is always 'mistuh' or 'mastuh' or 'missus.' The wee babes too. But 'Mastuh Stanley' be all right."

"Without your help, I wouldn't be standing here. I'd be buried in a shallow grave." Stanley turned to look directly at Levi. "I don't know what you think of me, Levi, whether you're still angry with me for what I did. You might even hate me, but right now, the only thing I can do is say, Levi Jackson, thank you for saving my life."

For a moment Levi stood motionless with his head down. He nodded slowly, almost imperceptibly. "Just doing what missus told me." Then Levi turned away when Stanley began to remove his nightshirt.

"Truth is, Mastuh Stanley, I don't hate you and I ain't sore, and I been praying every day for you."

"You have? What for?"

"I been asking the Lawd to show hisself to you."

"I don't know what you mean, Levi."

"Missus Davina, she say the Lawd brung you to Shiloh, and Scri'ture say Shiloh's another name for the Lawd. Maybe the Lawd's coming to you, Mastuh Stanley."

Stanley stood motionless at the dresser. How was God supposed to come to him and why would he want to? "I still don't get it, Levi."

"Just let the Lawd do it. Keep reading them Scri'tures to young Mastuh Willy and the Lawd'll show hisself."

Stanley finished washing and once again stood gazing out the window, dressed now in brightest white. A black man had been praying for *him*. His words were troubling, but it pleased Stanley that someone who had every right to hate him had showed such concern. Perhaps when he was rested he could make sense of what Levi had said

Levi stepped closer. "My Min done saved your buttons, Mastuh Stanley, and your buckle. Them buttons was so fine and bright, she just snipped them off before putting your jacket in the fire. I can fetch them for you, if you want, Mastuh Stanley."

"Thank you again, Levi, but there's no hurry." A pair of well-worn shoes, a leather belt with a useless buckle, and a handful of brass buttons, the grand sum of his earthly wealth. Nothing of any value to help him on his way to—to where?

"Maybe you had enough for today, Mastuh Stanley. Maybe you be getting back to bed and I be calling the missus."

Stanley lay back upon the bed, glad to rest his aching body. It was good that he had risen and managed to stay up for these several minutes. He had gained the window—and his own hands, not those of a stranger, had washed and dried his body. It had not been without cost—there was pain now, a great amount of pain, particularly from the still-healing wound in his left arm, which had borne much of his weight on the crutches. But it pleased him that he felt genuine tiredness, exhaustion from the physical labor of moving himself around, rather than the general weariness he'd been feeling for weeks now lying in this bed.

Mrs. Matthews came in a few minutes later and sent Levi away. "It's not surprising, not at all," she said when Stanley complained of the pain. She unwrapped the bandage on his arm. "See here? The bullet tore away a good bit of flesh, and it'll be some time before that arm gets tough and strong like the other." Then she wrapped the arm again so it wouldn't be rubbed raw by the crutch.

"Hmmmm. I'm at a loss," Mrs. Matthews said as she examined the wound from the musket ball in Stanley's back. "Dr. Comstock said a lot of thick, yellow pus would be a good thing, but there's been hardly any. Now I don't know what to think. The hole in your back is almost closed over, like the one in your chest. Do they hurt?"

Stanley chuckled. "A little when they're touched, Mrs. Matthews."

"And the ribs?"

"They didn't hurt the last few days, but they do now after working with the crutches."

"As they should, I'd say. Good, no need to bind your chest again. Now, lie back and rest. That's a lot for today. Try to get up every day and get your strength back and maybe soon you'll be able to try the stairs." Mrs. Matthews turned to go, but hesitated. "Pastor Blackwell is coming to visit on Sunday. He'll preach and then we'll have dinner. That's five days—might be something for you to try for, and we can set a place at the table for you, if you're able."

"How will your preacher take to you having dinner with a Yankee in your house?"

She walked slowly to the door. "I've got to do some thinking on that," she said, opening the door slowly. "But he's always preaching about saving souls. Maybe he'll think a Yankee's worth saving too." A moment later he heard her footsteps going down the stairs.

Maybe, just maybe, he would be able to get down the stairs to have Sunday dinner with the preacher. And then he would go outside. How warm the sun would feel—if it didn't rain, of course. That didn't seem like much to hope for, but then again, it had been a long time since he had hoped for anything at all.

His leg would heal. It wouldn't be as strong as the other, maybe not the same length either, but he would walk again. Perhaps he would always use a crutch, or a cane—maybe a fine hickory or walnut walking stick.

Stanley knew the real reason Mrs. Matthews was so eager to get him out of that bed and down the stairs: She wanted to get him out of her house, and he couldn't blame her. Her husband and son had been killed in battle, but she had been gracious to him. She had taken him into her house, tended his wounds, fed him, and nursed him back to health.

He had been in her house for three weeks. Perhaps another month and his leg would be healed, and he would be sent away from Matthews Hill. But what would become of him? Where could he go? What could he do? To whom could he turn?

CHAPTER 17

WHEN STANLEY AWOKE THAT FIRST SUNDAY OF MAY, THE house was already alive with activity in anticipation of the arrival of Pastor Blackwell. Stanley heard the commotion of a family at breakfast in the dining room just below, and he knew that soon Willy would climb the stairs to bring him his own plate of fried eggs, warm buttered bread, and tea made from herbs. But Stanley was determined that today would be the last day he would take a meal in this room.

Stanley struggled out of bed. He was now able to manage it on his own several times each day, and he had become quite accustomed to using Levi's sturdy crutches to go back and forth across the room to the window. With no little pride in his progress, Stanley was able to use the pitcher and basin to wash himself, and to use the chamber pot too. Stanley had just finished his washing and was standing at the dresser looking out at the sunbathed farmyard when Willy, dressed neatly in his go-to-meeting clothes and carrying a steaming plate of food, opened the door.

"You're up?"

Stanley grinned. "I hate staying in bed, Willy. Today, I'm going to try the stairs."

"You can't—you need help. I'll fetch Mama. She's on the veranda waiting for Pastor Blackwell."

"No, Willy. I have to do this myself."

Willy shrugged. "Won't do no good if you fall, you know."

"I know, Willy. I'll be all right."

"Anything you need, then?"

"Well, this nightshirt is a problem." Stanley tugged at the folds of flannel. "It's like a woman's skirt. I could sure do with a pair of trousers—I might have to cut them because of the wrappings. And a shirt maybe."

Stanley had finished eating when Willy returned a few minutes later. "These were Papa's," he said, handing the trousers to Stanley. "Found them and this shirt in Mama's dresser."

The faded brown duck trousers were well-worn but clean; the shirt was of white flannel like the nightshirt, but much better suited to day wear.

"And I borrowed this knife from Luke," Willy said with a wide, toothy grin. "He's downstairs in the parlor, so I just went in his room real quiet and took it."

Stanley shook his head. "You're a clever one, Willy."

The trousers were too large in the waist and too short in length for Stanley, but sufficiently generous in the legs that, after cutting a slit from the cuff to the knee in the left leg, Stanley was able to draw them on without difficulty. The sleeves of the shirt were too short, so Stanley rolled them up above the elbow.

"There," Stanley said, making a final adjustment to the suspenders. "That's great, Willy. Thanks." Armed with his crutches, he limped to the stairs. Stanley carefully lowered himself onto the floor at the very top of the stairway and handed the crutches to Willy. "See you downstairs."

Willy stepped awkwardly down the stairs, clunking one crutch or the other into the banister or wall with each step. "He's coming down," Willy called into the parlor, the small, plainly furnished room at the northeast corner of the house. "Mama told him to try, and he's trying."

Ruthie and Davy appeared instantly in the parlor's doorway.

A few moments later Anna appeared as well, more beautiful in her Sunday dress than Stanley could have imagined.

Finally, Luke strolled into view beside Anna. "Don't know what the fuss is about," he said.

Anna laughed. "Don't you want to see if he falls head over heels?"

"And maybe breaks his neck?" Luke's tight smile seemed to Stanley more hard and cruel than his words. "That I *would* like to see."

With all five of the Matthews children watching with upturned faces from the doorway to the parlor, Stanley began to slide carefully downward from one step to the next, using his hands and arms, along with his right leg, to support his weight, while he kept his left leg angled straight down the stairs. Stanley actually found the descent quite easy, and only slightly painful when his left leg bumped each step, but he grunted and groaned all the same, as if he was expending great physical effort, and this seemed to impress the smaller children very much, and Anna, he noted with a furtive glance, seemed unable to take her eyes off him.

Willy stood at the ready with the crutches. "You going into the parlor, Stanley?"

Stanley looked into the room to the right. There was a large dining table and several straight-back chairs toward the front of the unoccupied room.

"I think I'll sit in here, out of the way," Stanley said.

"And now you're down, how do you expect to get back up?" Luke's tone was mocking.

"Well, Luke," Stanley said, without turning to face him, "I suppose I'll just go about it the same way, only backward."

The clop and clatter of hooves and carriage wheels signaled Pastor Blackwell's arrival and sent the five children scurrying back to their seats in the parlor. Stanley had just settled himself in the dining room when Mrs. Matthews opened the entry door and showed the preacher inside.

The parlor and dining room lay on opposite sides of the small entryway at the bottom of the stairs. Pastor Blackwell spotted Stanley immediately. "Who do we have here, Mrs. Matthews?"

Fear showed on Mrs. Matthews' face. "Ohh...that's...that's Stanley, Stanley Mitchell. Wounded in the fight, he was, now seems to be on the mend."

Pastor Blackwell was a tall and spindly man with a narrow, pinched face that appeared a bit broader because of his thick, closely cropped black beard. He was dressed all in black, except for a bright white shirt, closed at the collar with a black, four-fingered necktie. He stuck out a long, bony hand toward Stanley. "Always pleased to meet a true son of the South."

"He ain't no son of the South," Luke called out from the parlor. "He's Yankee."

"Oh." Blackwell quickly withdrew his hand and stood unblinking over Stanley. "And how's that, Mrs. Matthews?"

"I found him when we were looking for Aaron. Stanley told us where to find him."

"You should have left him. Only trouble will come of it."

"But, Pastor Blackwell," Mrs. Matthews said, "how many times you told us to show mercy to widows and orphans. This boy *is* an orphan, and Scripture says, 'If thine enemy be hungry, give him bread,' so ain't we supposed to—"

"Enough!" the preacher said, turning quickly to face her. "You would lecture me?"

Blackwell stalked across the entryway into the parlor, where he greeted each of the children by name. Mrs. Matthews followed and sat in a spindle-back rocking chair in the front corner of the room. Pastor Blackwell stood, open Bible in hand, to Mrs. Matthews' right, in front of the fireplace, just within Stanley's view.

"As we all know, our little church at Shiloh is no more," the pastor began, his piercing blue eyes fixed on Stanley. "It was destroyed by the Yankees on the second day of the recent battle, and what little was left, they cut into little pieces and took as souvenirs of their great victory." Blackwell paused, still glaring at Stanley. "And word came to me just yesterday that the city of New Orleans has surrendered to Yankee naval forces."

Mrs. Matthews gasped loudly and shook her head in dismay.

"Pastor Blackwell!" Luke's tone was hard and critical. "Hearsay like that ain't for Yankee ears."

"I wish it was hearsay, Luke, but it isn't. It's a sad fact." The pastor turned his attention back to Mrs. Matthews and all of her children. "Your loss has been so great. You have given your husband and father and your son and brother to our righteous cause. They have not died in vain, and their sacrifice is well noted and is even now being rewarded in eternity. My prayers and my sympathies will always be with you.

"But I am here on this fine Lord's Day morning to tell you, as I have done and will continue to do from house to house, that the church of Christ is not to be found in any building. I take as my text the first two verses of the fifth chapter of Second Corinthians: 'For we know that if our earthly house of this tabernacle were dissolved, we have a building of God, an house not made with hands, eternal in the heavens. For in this we groan, earnestly desiring to be clothed upon with our house which is from heaven.'"

"Amen, pastuh." Stanley recognized Levi's soft, low voice. The entire Jackson family had gathered outside on the veranda to hear the preaching through the open parlor windows.

"We have always been a small gathering. How many times have we encouraged one another with the words of the Lord Jesus, 'For where two or three are gathered together in my name, there am I in the midst of them.' I count seven within this house and seven without on the veranda, so this morning we are gathered as a church of Christ."

Levi's muffled "Amen, pastuh" came again from outside. Stanley knew the pastor had omitted his own Yankee soul from the tally, but he listened to every word the preacher spoke, for

Blackwell's tone and manner, which had been harsh at the start, was now appealing, even friendly.

But when Blackwell's sermon drew to a close over half an hour later, try as he might, Stanley could recall only a few short phrases.

"Yes, Shiloh Church is no more," Pastor Blackwell said, "but the gathering of the saints together for worship and fellowship is still vital to the life of our small flock. Presiding Elder Harwood and I have determined that, beginning on Sunday, the first of June, Shiloh Church will once again meet for worship at eleven o'clock, Lord willing. With the Yankees moving on toward Corinth this past week, Mr. Sewell has agreed to loan the church a parcel of his land. The church will gather in a grove of trees beside the road to Crump's Landing where it crosses Snake Creek."

From her corner rocker Mrs. Matthews smiled and nodded in approval.

"Mr. Sewell's bottomland is rich and fertile," Blackwell continued, "with groves for a camp meeting and pastures for grazing your animals. It will be a mile or two farther than Shiloh, but much preferred over our battle-ravaged church grounds, at least for now.

"We will meet each Lord's Day throughout the summer months, and wait upon the Lord to provide a suitable location for the winter. A feast of love and fellowship will follow our time of worship, food for the soul and for the body, so bring something to share." Pastor Blackwell leaned a little to his left and peered into the dining room at Stanley. "And be sure to bring along that Yankee boy. Maybe he'll get some religion."

"Then I ain't going!" Luke said.

"Oh, yes you will, boy," Mrs. Matthews said.

"Now, now, young Luke," Blackwell said, "even Yankees need saving, and to get saved, they need to hear the preaching. Many a soul has been saved at a camp meeting."

Luke made no reply, and Stanley found himself wishing he could see the sullen look that undoubtedly clouded the boy's face.

"We must also consider the future of Shiloh Church," Blackwell said, again addressing Mrs. Matthews. "The last few weeks of traveling from house to house have taken me back to my circuit riding days, before Shiloh Church was built. We must decide if we should rebuild."

"Of course we should rebuild," she said, "but how, with our men gone away? For the first time I recall, our lives are completely dependent on our slaves. Levi and his boys do all the plowing and planting and reaping—and they'd be the only ones could help build that church, too, but I don't see how we can spare them."

"Just so," said Pastor Blackwell. "Even with those whose menfolk are still living, the ones at home are either too young or too old to do the heavy work. As I see it, we must wait until this war is done and the Yankees have all gone home before we can rebuild the church."

"But, Mama." It was Anna's voice. "Aaron was killed there. How could we ever...?"

For a few moments it seemed no one had anything to say.

Pastor Blackwell ended the silence. "Time will heal us. It always does. Until then, we'll have the meetings beside Snake Creek, and I'll preach from house to house, if I must, but it's best for all the saints to assemble together." Then he took a deep breath and said quietly, "Let us pray."

Pastor Blackwell prayed a long and eloquent prayer, the best Stanley had ever heard. The pastor prayed for the dispersed flock of Shiloh, for the camp meeting to come, and for the progress of the war and the departure of the Yankee invaders. He also prayed for "comfort amid their sorrows" for Mrs. Matthews and for each of the children by name. And then he prayed for "the young man in the other room to get the true gospel religion, and then get on to where he's going and leave this fine family in peace."

But for the slave family who remained on the veranda listening, the pastor prayed not a word. And Stanley thought this most peculiar.

———•——

The way Luke saw it, Sunday dinner was a sacred occasion, but countless wrongs were committed that day, all in the name of feeding the stranger in their midst. And the stranger wasn't Pastor Blackwell.

It began with Mama's insistence that the Yankee remain at the table for dinner. "He made all that bother to come down," she said. "I'm pleased he's getting better."

She put him in Papa's place. "He can't sit like the rest of us," she said. "Needs to put that bad leg out kinda sideways." Only Papa sat in that chair—ever—and his two eldest sons always sat beside him, Aaron to his right, Luke to his left. In all the months since he'd gone off to ride with Colonel Forrest, Papa's place had sat empty, and it was only after word came of his heroic death and the memorial down at the church that Mama stopped having Aunt Min set a place for him.

Mama's place was always at the opposite end of the table, but Pastor Blackwell sat there and Mama sat to his right. Next to her was Davy, then Ruthie next to the strange Yankee. All through that endless dinner hour Ruthie would now and again look down at that Yankee's bound-up leg splayed next to her chair, then beam a cute smile up at him. And at least twice, Luke saw the foolish girl reach down to run her hand back and forth over the rough surface of the bark wrapping. Then she'd giggle and the Yankee would make a stupid face at her.

Willy sat just to the right of the Yankee. He, too, seemed unaware of this offense to Papa's memory and prattled away with the Yankee like he was a lifelong friend. Willy wanted to know everything about that Yankee, where he came from, what he did, what he learned at school. This last subject seemed of great interest to Willy, and also to Anna. Luke watched her cock her head a little to the side when the Yankee spoke about the many things he had learned.

Even Pastor Blackwell raised his bushy eyebrows when the Yankee said he'd studied Latin, and when the two carried on a short conversation in that old-fashioned language, the pastor smiled—he actually *smiled* at the Yankee—and said, "As you might imagine, young man, it's been a long time since I met any-one in these parts who could speak Latin. You were well taught."

Not once during that dinner did Luke lift his head and look at the others directly; rather, from the corners of his eyes, he saw everything, and his ears burned at all the friendly prattle with that Yankee. When dinner was finally done, and Mama had dismissed the children, Luke raced across the yard to the barn, jumped on Duke, and galloped up the lane toward Owl Creek, still wearing his Sunday best.

CHAPTER 18

AFTER TAKING A LIGHT SUPPER OF HAM AND CHEESE AND bread with Mrs. Matthews and the children in the dining room, Stanley hobbled outside to the veranda to sit on the red-cedar bench. As he bathed in the warm glow of lamplight through the parlor window, gentle westerly breezes had cooled his face and driven away the last of that Sabbath Day's heat. Clouds had gathered; the sky had darkened, bringing on early nightfall. Rain showers had rolled in and passed on, but Stanley had remained, weary but not yet wishing to return to the confines of the upstairs bedroom.

Sometime later a rough hand touched Stanley gently on the arm, waking him with a start. "It's late, Stanley. Clock just struck half past eight. Mustn't get a chill, now."

Stanley reached for his crutches. "Of course, Mrs. Matthews."

"No, stay a while, if you want." Mrs. Matthews sat down next to Stanley. She was still wearing her Sunday dress, but now wore a white apron over it. "I put Ruthie and Li'l Davy down for the night, and Willy done turned in, too—too big a day for him, all tuckered out, I guess. Summer heat comes on right powerful in May, and we'll all be dripping sweat 'til October. But it's lovely now, for sure."

"Can I ask you a question, Mrs. Matthews?"

"Sure."

"Back in Ohio, we call this a porch. Why does everyone call it a veranda?"

Mrs. Matthews laughed softly. "I can tell you, it sure ain't 'cause we're uppity. About five years ago, maybe six now, Ben went over Memphis way and came back with our two horses, Duke and Earl. Well, Ben seen some of them rich folks' houses, and he took a fancy to their large porches—verandas, they called them. Well, he come back to the farm all full of this idea of him and Levi building a veranda onto the south and west sides of this house, and by gum, they did it the next winter."

Mrs. Matthews laughed again, but moments later her words were full of loss and sadness. "I miss my husband every day, Stanley. He was as good a man as any woman could want. He knew farming and he worked hard to build up this place. Twenty years ago, there was nothing here but trees, and Ben and Levi cleared the land and built our first house, just a cabin, really, and a cabin for Levi and Min, too, and they planted our first crops." Mrs. Matthews heaved a deep sigh. "Why am I telling you this? Aren't you only a stranger, Stanley?"

"I *am* interested, Mrs. Matthews, and I do care about your family."

"Well, we tried cotton for a while, but we only got about a hundred sixty acres here. You need lots more to grow cotton, and lots of negroes, too, if it's your main thing, so we went with hogs. Hogs is easier—they eats most anything, and now with the war, the army's got to have lots of pork. Well, we cleared more land and planted other crops, Indian corn and alfalfa and sweet potatoes and vegetables, some fruit trees, and sweet sorghum for molasses too. There was always lots for us and the Jacksons, and some to sell. Maybe ten years ago, we had a barn raising, and then in fifty-six, Ben built this house onto the old house—that's the kitchen and larder now. It's all 'cause of Ben this farm is what it is."

Mrs. Matthews paused to take another deep, heavy breath.

"And now he's gone. It's all on my shoulders now. But enough about me and my worries. How are you feeling, Stanley?"

"Tired for sure, Mrs. Matthews, and my back aches some —probably not used to sitting in chairs so much. I should go upstairs in a few minutes, but it's so pleasant out here. I've felt like a prisoner—"

"Oh, that ain't what I wanted. I'm sorry—"

"That's not what I meant, Mrs. Matthews. You've done nothing but good by me. You've been kinder to me than I deserve. No, it's everything I haven't been able to do that makes me feel like a prisoner." Stanley turned to look at her. "That's why I had to try those stairs this morning. I had to do something *more* today. I just had to see something besides that room."

"You gave me such a start." She punctuated her words with a sharp pat on Stanley's arm.

"I'm sorry for that, but you told me to try, so I did. Will Pastor Blackwell cause any trouble for you?"

"Oh, I should think not," Mrs. Matthews said, shaking her head. "He raised his voice and said his piece, but he was prob'ly right. Even if he don't speak of it, word'll spread anyway there's a Yankee here."

"The last thing I want is to cause you more trouble. I've caused enough already. What about the meeting at Snake Creek?"

"Oh, you'll be the talk, but never you mind. I got to think about that—you know, what to say about you and all." She swatted a mosquito away from her arm. "I will say this, young man, things is sure different since you came, and I ain't sure if it's more good or more bad."

"You just called me *young man*, Mrs. Matthews—not *boy*."

"Did I? I guess I did. I've heard you tramping back and forth upstairs, so I know you're trying real hard to get better. I guess I respect that."

"Maybe another three or four weeks and I'll be strong enough for…"

"For what?"

"I don't know."

"You ain't up to going anywhere, so what do I do—just turn you out and send you on your merry way?"

Stanley thought he heard genuine concern in Mrs. Matthews' voice.

"You wouldn't last a day," she added. "You talk too good. Everybody'd know you ain't from hereabouts. Our boys'll find you and hang you for a spy. You may be only sixteen, but you look older. They'll hang you sure. They won't care."

"Maybe I should return to the army. They would probably transfer me to the Invalid Corps because of my leg."

"What's that?"

"It's a special unit for wounded men who can't fight anymore. They work at hospitals or in army offices."

"How would you get there? And then you'd have to prove you're one of them, wouldn't you? Most of the ones you knew before are likely gone—or dead."

"I guess I need to think about that."

"We'll talk about this again," Mrs. Matthews said, turning sideways to look at Stanley. "Meantimes, you just finish your healing and keep being good to Willy."

Stanley smiled and nodded. "No need to tell me that, Mrs. Matthews. The first part is hard, but it's easy to like that boy."

"Yes, he's my blessed one." Her tone had become soft and sweet. "I think Willy's taken a shine to you. Won't let anybody take your meals up but him. Not that Luke would, or Anna, for that matter, but he don't want me or Min to do it neither. And he can't hardly wait every morning for his reading lesson. His eyes going bad's been hard for him, and I think he likes looking after you. Makes him feel important."

"He's always got a bright smile when he brings up my breakfast. I know he can't see me smiling back, but I *tell* him I am. Makes me smile now just thinking about it."

Mrs. Matthews patted Stanley's arm again. "I think you're taking to my boy."

Stanley listened to the soft patter of raindrops among the broad leaves of the large oak that overspread the farmhouse. Mrs. Matthews was right. He was taking to Willy, and to the other occupants of that house, including Luke, if he was honest with himself. But a few days ago she had said she wanted him gone, and she was right about that too. He had no place here, and he would not overstay his welcome. But he was sure going to miss Willy when that day did come.

"I've never had a brother." Stanley was surprised that he'd spoken those words aloud.

"Now, Stanley," Mrs. Matthews said. "Be careful about that. Willy ain't your brother and I'm afraid how he's taking to you, and how it'll be when you leave, whenever that is."

A boundary had been clearly staked out. *Read for Willy and be good to him, but it's only for now. It will soon end.* After several minutes, Stanley began to reach for his crutches, then stopped. "Am I still your enemy, Mrs. Matthews?"

She laughed again, though only a little, and quietly. "No, not no more. Truth is, I don't think much on you being a Yankee. More like you're just a boy with no mama or papa who needs our help."

Not an enemy, but not a friend either. Still, the conversation had been friendly, even when it was serious, and there was one thing that had been on his mind for several days. "Mrs. Matthews, there's something I need to tell you."

"About Willy?"

"No, about me, I guess—and you, Mrs. Matthews."

"Well, go ahead and speak your mind. That's what we do in this house."

"It was that first night," Stanley said, once again looking only at the floorboards between his feet. "The night you brought

117

me here. I was awake when you came in, but I pretended I was asleep."

Stanley felt Mrs. Matthews stiffen beside him. "So you saw me?"

"Yes. I saw you taking Aaron's clothes out of the dresser."

"I didn't know—that was a private time, just me and my boy."

"Yes, Mrs. Matthews."

"You could've said something."

"I almost did, but I didn't want to intrude."

"You did anyway."

"And I'm sorry. But you taught me something very important that night."

"And what might that be?"

"I saw how much you loved Aaron, and I've never known anything like that in my life."

"Was it so bad, living with your aunt and uncle? Sounds like they're well put."

The slight edge to the woman's words didn't surprise Stanley. "They are. Uncle Charles invested heavily in the railway, and when it was finally built, he made his money back many times over. He also owns a large foundry in Ironton, right on the river, that makes iron and steel parts for steamboats, like boilers, engines, paddlewheels, and such. My aunt and uncle live in a huge house with lots of windows. It's painted bright white with glossy black trim, and there's a wrought-iron fence, made right at his own foundry, all around the place. And a carriage gate. And they have five servants—a cook, a maid, a stable boy, a gardener, and a butler."

"A butler? What's that?"

"The head servant. He manages the house, and he's the boss of the other servants. So yes, my aunt and uncle are rich, but you know what, Mrs. Matthews? I never saw my aunt put a dollar in the offering plate at church without complaining about how they were always looking for more money."

Mrs. Matthews shook her head slowly. "'God loveth a cheerful giver.'"

"And at dinner today," Stanley said, "I thought of their house and how whenever they had guests to dinner, I was always sent off to eat in the kitchen and then up the back stairs to bed. But you set a place for me and invited me to sit at *your* table with *your* family, a Yankee and a stranger, and that—"

"And Luke sulked over it all through dinner."

"And when I asked you if I could read for Willy, you laid your hand on my shoulder."

"I did?"

"Yes—just like I saw you do with Willy before. And you did again when you woke me just now. I don't remember my mother, and my aunt never touched me that way, not once."

"Oh, you poor boy," Mrs. Matthews said.

"Lots of money in that house, the best of everything, you could say, but never a hug and never a kind word. No love."

"And no God, from what I gather. Well, Stanley, by now I should think you know things ain't like that in this house down here in Tennessee. For one thing, we got no white paint, and for another, we got no back stairs. But we do have God in *this* house."

Stanley reached for his crutches a second time.

"Need help?"

"I think I'll just need someone to carry my crutches up, Mrs. Matthews."

"I can do that. I want to see just how you're thinking to do them stairs. Let me fetch a candle."

Stanley sat on the third step from the bottom and, using his strong arms and one good leg, he lifted himself to the next step, just as he had told Luke that morning he would, and five minutes later he stood at the door to his room.

"That'll get a little easier every day," Mrs. Matthews said, handing Stanley his crutches.

"I'd like to come down for breakfast, if that's all right, Mrs. Matthews."

"I thought you would. I already told Min to set a place for you tomorrow." She paused for a moment. "So, Stanley, how'd that leg of yours come to be broke?"

Stanley chuckled. "It's not something I'll be proud to tell my children—a mule kicked me."

Mrs. Matthews laughed a little too. "A mule?"

"A mule. When I got shot in the arm, I started for the rear to find a hospital. I walked backward so I wouldn't get shot in the back—and then I got shot in the chest. I was knocked over backward, and I lost nearly all sense of where I was or what was happening."

Mrs. Matthews looked down and shook her head in dismay. "Oh, my…"

"I got up and stumbled down the hill toward the creek, where men were trying to hitch teams of mules under heavy fire. The mules were real skittish, and I must have gotten too close to one, because he kicked me in the side of my leg, and that was that. While I was lying on the ground, another ball hit my belt buckle, and it knocked me nearly senseless again. That's where your son found me."

When Mrs. Matthews looked up, Stanley saw tears in the corners of her eyes. "You've been through a lot, Stanley, and you're still just a…a young man. I'll say good night now, but there's one more thing." She put her right hand into the pocket of her apron, then extended her closed hand toward Stanley. "I've been meaning to give you this."

Mrs. Matthews opened her fingers. In the palm of her hand lay a shiny, though somewhat misshapen, musket ball.

"You saved it!" Mrs. Matthews could not have done anything better for him. Stanley felt his own eyes grow warm and misty. "Thank you, Mrs. Matthews. I'll treasure it always." He examined the ball in the candlelight. "It will always remind me of you, Mrs. Matthews, no matter where I am."

"Stanley? What I said about you healing up and getting on your way? And what Pastor Blackwell said today? I've been thinking I oughtn't be in such a rush to see you gone. There's Willy, of course. And besides, if you get strong enough, maybe you'll be some help with the crops, maybe the livestock, whatever Levi can put you to. Lord knows we need all the help we can get."

"Of course, Mrs. Matthews. I'd like to repay your kindness however I can."

"I'll need to think about this. I can't pay you, but there'll be room and board, same as you got now. And another thing I've seen since you been reading to Willy. That boy's been chattering on and on that you read real good and you know a lot of things, and now Anna's taken to reading again herself, and she ain't done that in months. Don't know what to make of that yet. Don't know if it's got anything to do with what Willy's been saying, but I'm thinking it's good for her."

"Perhaps I should tell you one more thing, Mrs. Matthews."

She looked uneasy. "Another secret?"

Stanley smiled and shook his head. "No, Mrs. Matthews, no more secrets. I've never had a home, at least not somewhere I ever thought of as my home. But being in your house these four weeks, even being shut away upstairs here, I'm beginning to think that—"

"Hush," Mrs. Matthews said, touching the tip of her finger to Stanley's lips. She turned quickly away and took one slow step down the stairs, then a second, halting and unsure, it appeared to Stanley. She looked back over her shoulder, and Stanley knew the warmth he felt growing within him was good and true.

"We'll see, Stanley Mitchell. We'll see."

CHAPTER 19

BREAKFAST SOON BECAME STANLEY'S FAVORITE MEAL OF the day. Usually awake with the first crow of the rooster, he would lie abed until the dawn brought enough light for him to see his way about the room. Then he would rise as quietly as he could, so as not to disturb Willy. It was during his daily washing that he usually heard the first clank of a skillet or the clink of a china teacup that told of Min's arrival in the kitchen below.

Using one arm for support and the other to hold the crutches, within a few days Stanley found that he could bump and slide himself almost noiselessly down the stairs. His skillful use of the crutches allowed him to move across the dining room, careful not to give himself away by bumping into the table, or one of the chairs, or the large pinewood hutch against the wall. Having arrived undetected beside the kitchen door, he would pause for a moment to gather himself, poke his head around the corner, and say, in his deepest voice, "Good morning, Min."

To Stanley's great amusement, the black woman always jumped in surprise at the sudden interruption, and what splendid exclamations she uttered: "Law-be, see what I done? Done drop the spoon in the pot. Ain't no manners at all, you nawthuns." Indeed, the first day or two he did this, Min seemed genuinely annoyed at his antics. "Now, mastuh, you shoo," she would say. "Got no call being here. Let me be with my cooking now." But within a week Stanley was convinced that, despite her vehement protestations, Min was looking forward to the nonsensical morning ritual as much or more than he was.

"Good morning, Min," Stanley said one morning three weeks after the first time he'd risen from his bed to try out his crutches, and he saw Min jiggle with laughter. "Got something for my friends, Min?"

"Got eggs today, Mastuh Stanley."

"Eggs?"

"They works hard, and it *good* for them," Min said as she handed Stanley four boiled and shelled eggs wrapped in a small patch of cloth. Stanley stuffed the eggs into the pocket of his trousers.

In the past three weeks, Stanley had not only conquered the twelve stairs, thereby gaining access to the entire house and veranda, but he was also striving to expand his world farther every day, rain or shine. The three steps leading from the veranda down to the yard between the house and the barn had been particularly challenging, but Stanley was determined not to sit down and slide ignominiously into the dirt. Rather, he used the crutches and relied upon his powerful shoulders and arms, and the support of his now exercised and strengthened right leg, to descend the steps one by one. He'd been taking those steps now for several days, adding the farmyard with its dozens of squawking chickens to his domain.

For the past several mornings the weather had been fair and warm, and rather than wait inside for the seven o'clock breakfast hour, it had become Stanley's practice to cross the nearly bare ground of the yard to the barn, with several clucking chickens chasing after him, hoping this large human creature would strew cracked corn for them.

From the window of Stanley's room, the barn had seemed a mysterious but interesting place. All he could see of the interior was what little was exposed to the light of day by the yawning doorway; all else was shrouded in darkness. But as he approached at ground level in the dim light of misty dawn, he could look through the interior of the barn to an equally wide doorway opposite the one he was entering.

In the first two stalls to the left of the entryway, a pair of large draft horses nickered softly at Stanley's arrival and poked their heads eagerly over the gates of their stalls. A simple, wooden sign with the name "Duke" carved in it was nailed near the top of the gate of the first stall. The second bore a similar sign with the name "Earl."

"It took a few days," Stanley said softly, "but you like me now, don't you? I'll bet it's just because I always bring food." He reached out and stroked the side of Duke's face. "No apple or carrot this morning, big fellow," he said, taking the cloth-wrapped eggs from his pocket. "No sweets either, just an egg. Min says it's good for you, but I've never heard—"

Duke snatched the egg with his lips from Stanley's open palm, chewed it a couple of times, and swallowed it. "I guess she was right." Stanley stroked Duke's face for another minute or two, and then went to Earl's stall, where the second egg was likewise consumed.

"Now I've got to say good morning to the girls." Stanley gave each horse a final pat on the nose and crossed to the stalls of the mule team, Lily and Penny, on the opposite side of the barn. As he had with Duke and Earl, Stanley fed each mule a hard egg and petted them affectionately.

Levi entered through the barn's rear entrance carrying two buckets of water, which he set on the floor next to Stanley. "Look like you knows mules, Mastuh Stanley."

"Horses mostly, and only a little," said Stanley. "My uncle had a stable boy, so I didn't have much to do with his horses, but I did some riding at school. I feel like I owe these two something."

"Lil and Pen, mastuh?"

"The way I see it, they helped save my life, so I guess I'm just saying thank you."

Levi smiled. He picked up one of the buckets, opened the door to Lil's stall, and emptied it into the watering trough against the far wall. "Yessuh, Mastuh Stanley. I been thanking them two critters for years. They ain't strong as Duke and Earl, but these two work all the long day, and be good the next day, too."

Levi closed Lil's stall and hoisted the second bucket. "They pull lots of stuff, and not just the plow and the wagon, mastuh. Them critters pulls us, too. Cain't do much without them."

Levi finished with Pen and shut the door to her stall. "You being nice to Lil and Pen, and Duke and Earl, too—it's kinda like that Gold Rule. You got to be good to them so they good to you."

"Will you teach me how to drive them?"

Levi's grin was quick and wide. "Oh, sure, Mastuh Stanley, easiest thing in the world. You already done the hard part."

"What's that?"

"They likes you."

———

No bell was rung. No call went up. Breakfast was taken exactly at seven o'clock. Each sleepy child knew the rule of the house—meals were served at the appointed hour and none other. Stanley was always first to the table. As he waited for Mrs. Matthews and the children to gather, he thought of what new wonders the day might bring, what new things he might do.

As the hour neared, the children appeared, drawn both by their gnawing stomachs and the sweet aromas of Min's cooking and baking. Willy came in first, barefoot as he always was except when it was cold or rainy or Sunday, and he was soon followed by Ruthie and Davy.

Mrs. Matthews entered from the kitchen. "Our hens is good layers, better than two dozen this morning." She greeted Stanley with a warm "good morning," then went around the table kissing each of her children on the forehead.

Anna came in a few minutes later, dressed like her mother in a pair of tan duck trousers and a plaid flannel shirt. Stanley greeted her cheerfully, to which she responded to the room in general and to no one in particular, "Gamorning."

Just as the pendulum clock began to strike, Luke appeared as he always did, still clad in his nightshirt, and when Stanley said "good morning," Luke didn't so much as nod in Stanley's direction. Mrs. Matthews slowly shook her head as she bowed to bless the table.

The fare was always simple. Fried eggs this morning—poached or scrambled some other mornings—with bread and butter, and a heap of grits, or "greeyits," as Stanley soon learned to call them, although it took him a little longer to develop a liking for them. When breakfast was done and Min had cleared away the dishes, Mrs. Matthews read a psalm and prayed for God's blessing on the day.

When Stanley opened his eyes, Levi was standing in the doorway to the kitchen. "Missus Davina, you say I's to tell you when we be getting the critters to new pasture? Well, a storm be coming up, and it be coming up quick-like. Won't be no spring shower neither, and we need to get it done in a hurry, missus. I hitched the wagon for you, too, missus."

Mrs. Matthews jumped to her feet. "Then this morning we drive cattle and sheep. You all know what needs doing. Ten minutes and I want everybody out to the southwest pasture. That means you, too, Luke."

Luke's cold, hard eyes stared at Stanley across the table. "What about him? He eats our food but don't lift nary a finger."

"Look to yourself, Luke. Ten minutes, no more."

Luke threw a mean look at his mother and ran upstairs.

"Anna, I'll need you out there, too," Mrs. Matthews said, apparently unaffected by her son's temper. "Willy and Ruthie will look after Li'l Davy. I've got something special for Stanley today." The other children scattered and Mrs. Matthews disappeared into the kitchen.

She returned moments later with a large knife and a big smile. "Don't worry, Stanley, won't hurt at all." She knelt on the floor and turned up the loose left leg of his trousers. With one quick flick of the knife, she severed the leather strap that bound the wrapping around Stanley's leg. Then she carefully removed the bark and straw wrapping. Stanley rubbed the flesh of his thigh, now free and exposed, and so very pale.

"Can't have you going about one leg in and one leg out neither. I've laid out another pair of Ben's britches in my room and I'll get Min to stitch these up again. Levi made a cane for you, too. Go on in there and put them britches on and see how that cane works for you."

Stanley went into Mrs. Matthews' bedroom and closed the door. He stripped off his old trousers, with the left leg split to above the knee, and pulled on the new ones, identical to the old, but less worn. The coarse material felt rough against the skin of his unbandaged leg. He adjusted the braces and picked up the cane.

Levi had made the walking stick from heavy, strong wood. It wasn't straight and thin like many Stanley had seen, as if they were made more for show than for service. From the handle, crowned with the skillfully carved image of a horse's head, the shaft tapered gradually, not with a smooth and polished line, but rough-hewn, as if a large blade had peeled the wood away in long, slightly concave strokes.

Stanley ran his fingers down the length of the stick. It was smooth and just a little greasy, as if Levi had rubbed the cane to a fine, dark sheen with oil or wax. It was a unique work of craftsmanship and artistry. Levi must have labored many hours making it, and the fact that it was a gift from a man he was coming to admire more each day only added to Stanley's appreciation. The walking stick instantly became Stanley's most prized possession, next to the musket ball Mrs. Matthews had given him.

Stanley wrapped the fingers of his left hand around the horse-head handle and leaned heavily upon the cane. It was as strong as it looked. He opened the door. His first steps were halting and cautious, but he hobbled back into the dining room, already thinking of what new places he might go with his new cane. "This is wonderful, Mrs. Matthews—my own walking stick. I've never seen anything like it."

"Levi said that's hickory, just like you wanted, and that's Duke's head he carved in the handle."

"I thought so. Thank you, Mrs. Matthews, and I'll thank Levi, too. It will take some work, and I'll need to be careful, because I can feel how weak my left leg is. Can I help today?"

"No, Stanley. Let's get over to the barn and take the wagon down the pasture."

Stanley laid the cane aside, took up the crutches, and followed Mrs. Matthews across the farmyard to the barn. She climbed into the driver's seat and took the reins while Stanley lifted himself into the back. As Mrs. Matthews steered the wagon along the narrow lane, a fresh breeze stirred the leaves of the trees; many were turned upside down, exposing their light undersides. Dark clouds rolled in from the west.

"We got four pastures," Mrs. Matthews called back over her shoulder, "and every week or so we drive the animals from one to the other, for new grass, you know. Shoulda been done two days ago, but we was getting the tater field ready, and yesterday was the Sabbath, so we got to do it today, and when it comes up a storm, we got to be quick about it."

"What happens to the livestock when it storms, Mrs. Matthews?"

"Oh, there's a few trees in all the pastures."

Mrs. Matthews drew the wagon up next to the fence line. Levi's sons had already removed the rails from the fence that separated the acreage of the northwest pasture from the south-west pasture. Of the almost fifty sheep Stanley counted, most headed for the taller, greener grass as soon as the way was open. However, the fifteen head of beef cattle seemed to have no desire to follow the sheep.

Luke and Anna rode the horses, Duke and Earl, back and forth across the pasture, driving the wayward steers ever closer together and toward the opening in the fence. Stanley had never seen anything like it, the way brother and sister guided their mounts with such ease and skill, like the steps of the minuet and waltz he had learned at school, but without any music that he could hear. But most of the time, Stanley gazed at the slender, graceful form of the lovely Anna, so tall and confident in the sad-dle, her long, honey-brown hair billowing behind her as she rode. Anna, who still seemed to have nothing but loathing for Stanley.

For Stanley, it was all over much too soon. Levi's boys were replacing the rails in the fence just as the first heavy drops of rain began to fall. Mrs. Matthews clucked softly to Lily and Penny and turned the wagon back toward the barn.

CHAPTER 20

THE FOLLOWING DAY WAS SUNNY AND WARM, SO STANLEY practiced hard with the cane. It was painful and exhausting work to build up his left leg so that it could hold more of his weight. Each step was a fight to keep his left foot from turning outward, for above all, he wished to walk normally again. He supposed he would always need a cane, but he would not accept forever walking in such an ungainly manner that he would be seen as "the cripple." So Stanley went back and forth across the farmyard and then, dripping with sweat, hobbled around the back of the house to the stone-walled well for a long, cool drink of water. Refreshed, he completed the circuit of the house and sometimes ventured across the yard to the barn.

Willy sidled up to Stanley at the well while he was dousing his sweating head with a bucket of cool water. "Stanley, my eyes are badder than they was. Heard you going round the house, though. My eyes are getting real dim now. Mama says I can't leave the yard unless I'm with somebody."

"I'm sorry about that, Willy."

"Your leg getting better?"

"A little every day, I think, but sometimes it feels like the muscles are tied in knots."

"I'm sorry about that, Stanley."

Stanley drew another bucket of water and poured it over his head and shoulders.

"Stanley," Willy said, "I been thinking maybe you can take me."

"To the graveyard?"

"Yeah. I ain't been to Aaron's place for a couple weeks, and I can't go on my own now."

"Sure, I'll go with you."

"You will?" Willy's smile was warm and bright; his vacant eyes searched for Stanley's face.

Stanley leaned so close that his shadow fell across Willy. "But that's about two hundred yards, and I can't make it that far yet. Maybe Saturday, or maybe next week. But the lane can't be muddy, and if I can't make it all the way, we'll turn around and try again another day. Deal?"

Willy nearly jumped with joy. "Deal." And the two shook hands on it.

"Almost, Willy, you almost have it. Listen once more. 'In him was life; and the life was the light of men. And the light shineth in darkness; and the—" Stanley felt something warm and furry brush against his leg. It was a cat he had seen several times sleeping lazily on the veranda. "Look at this little fellow."

"King George III? He's Anna's cat. Don't like other people much. Seen him turn on Luke, and once on Anna, too."

"But he seems to like me."

"Can't make him like you or not. Maybe just likes your voice."

King George III walked back and forth on the floor between and around Stanley's feet. Stanley leaned forward and offered his hand. The cat rubbed both sides of his face against it and purred loudly. Then Stanley stroked the top of the cat's head and ran his fingertips down the animal's spine. The cat arched his back with delight.

131

"Come on up here," Stanley said, gathering the cat up in his arms. King George III made no protest, and Stanley petted the cat's head, neck, back, and sides. "You look just like a little striped tiger, you do, except you're gray. A little brown and orange, too."

"Can't believe he's letting you do this. King George III is mighty partic'lar about people."

"Why's he called King George?"

"*The Third*, always King George *the Third*. It's 'cause we got other cats. You seen them—they're *working* cats. They eat mice and chipmunks, even squirrels sometimes, and keep varmints out of the corn crib and the barn and the house."

"Yeah, I've seen those other cats, but they never come close like he does."

"Well, King George III ain't like them other cats. Never seen him hunt, hardly ever seen him get up off this veranda, less it's raining. Never does anything, that cat, and that's fine with the other cats. They bring him varmints—not dead, 'cause cats don't eat another's killing—and he finishes them off real quick-like, and then eats them. It's like he's the king or something, like his kingdom's this farm, and we're his loyal folk, doing all the working just for him, like old King George III from England, so that's what Anna called him. How come you like cats?"

"Aunt Bess had two cats. I liked them just fine, but Uncle Charles hated them."

"Kinda like Luke. Only time I seen King George III move fast is when Luke comes near him."

"Hey, what's this?" Stanley said. "It looks like His Royal Highness has fleas. One just jumped onto my hand."

"Needs a bath. I'll tell Anna and she'll pester Luke until he does it. Another reason he hates Luke."

"Do you know how to do it?"

"Give that cat a bath? Sure, but I can't, you know, my eyes—"

"I'll do it," Stanley said, "if you tell me how."

Willy pondered this while Stanley continued to pet King George III. "All right," the boy said, "but if he turns on you, I told you so. We do it out back by the well. Need lots of water. But Anna will get mad if she finds out."

"Where is she?"

"Parlor, prob'ly reading. She's always reading now."

"Good." Stanley put King George III gently down on the floor. The cat walked unhurriedly down the length of the veranda and laid down heavily in the sunshine. "Now, let's get back to the lesson."

A half hour later, Willy was able to remember the first eighteen verses of John's Gospel, not just once to Stanley's satisfaction, but a second and third time for good measure. Then they went around to the back of the house and filled a large barrel tub with several buckets of water drawn from the well.

"Can we get some hot water from the kitchen?" Stanley said.

"Think so. Aunt Min always leaves a kettle on the stove. What for?"

"Don't you think King George III will prefer a warm bath to a cold one? When I was in the army, the only bathtub we had was a freezing cold creek. I hated it, and so did most of the men, so we usually just went dirty and stank."

Willy wrinkled his nose and went toward the door to the kitchen. "I'll get a blanket for drying him, too."

A few minutes later all was ready—tub half filled with tepid water, a large bar of lye soap, a jug of cider vinegar, and an old blanket that had obviously seen this duty on multiple occasions, given its many sewn patches.

Stanley started for the front of the house.

"Careful when you get him," Willy said.

"Will he bite me?" Stanley called over his shoulder.

"Likely not, but he'll set on you with them claws when he sees that tub."

The battle raged for better than fifteen minutes. From the

moment King George III perceived the intent of Stanley's gently cradling arms, it became the cat's sole purpose to hack those arms to ribbons of bleeding flesh. Through the first thorough soaking, to a lathering all over with the lye soap, to a thorough rinsing away of the lather, then on to a liberal dousing with the vinegar followed by another rinse, then yet another lathering and rinse, Stanley learned all of King George III's tricks and used his powerful hands and arms to force the cat into uneasy submission.

When the bathing was finally ended, Stanley wrapped the struggling cat snugly in the blanket and held the writhing bundle against his chest with his right arm. Then he picked up his cane with his left and hobbled toward the front of the house.

Anna's shrill voice stopped him dead. "Just what do you think you're doing with *my* cat?" She stood at the top of the steps, one hand clutching a book to her chest, the other splayed defiantly on her hip. The flickers of green in her eyes had been fanned to full blaze.

"Uh...he had fleas."

"So you gave him a bath? See he got you a couple of times. Serves you right."

Stanley looked at the long, red scratches on his hands and forearms. "Yeah, but he wasn't too bad."

"Looks to me like you got off easy." Anna watched Stanley hobble up the steps onto the veranda.

"What are you reading?" Stanley asked.

Now it was Anna's turn to stammer. "Um...uh...*The Deerslayer* by—"

"James Fenimore Cooper. Good book. Do you fancy yourself more like the Wild Rose Judith or the Drooping Lily Hetty?"

Stanley was pleased to see Anna flush at this comparison to the two Hutter sisters—Judith, the quick-witted, sharp-tongued, and steel-tempered beauty, versus the slower-witted, but more spiritually minded and thoughtful Hetty.

Stanley felt Anna's heated gaze upon his back as he moved

down the veranda. "If you must know," she said, "I fancy myself the best of both."

Stanley turned to face Anna.

Their eyes met and held.

Stanley smiled his warmest smile. "Perhaps you are at that," he said. And as he turned to walk toward the end of the veranda, Stanley smiled a second smile within himself at how the color in the girl's face had risen all the more.

"What're you doing *now* with my cat?" Anna called after him.

"Oh, King George III and I are just going to sit over here in the sun and dry off."

Much to Stanley's own amazement, King George III allowed Stanley to rub him all over with the blanket again and again, both to dry his matted fur and to warm him. Indeed, most curious of all was that after a few minutes of Stanley's soothing ministrations, the cat emitted a low throaty rattle that increased in volume until even Anna, who had held her ground several feet away, could not ignore it.

"Turncoat," she hissed, as she turned and stalked off into the house.

CHAPTER 21

L ATE SATURDAY MORNING, AFTER WILLY'S LESSONS WERE through, Stanley announced, "I think my leg is ready. Let's try the lane up the hill to the graveyard."

A few minutes later, Stanley and Willy set off through the farmyard, past the barn, and out through the gate in the fence to the fields beyond, now green with alfalfa. Stanley noticed a narrow lane, just a pair of well-worn wagon wheel tracks that led off to the left behind the barn and disappeared into the trees. "Where does that lane go?" he asked.

"To the Jacksons' cabin," Willy said. "Ain't no call to go there, unless Mama says go."

Stanley toiled up the gradually sloping lane, leaning heavily on the hickory walking stick. The pain was bearable, a deep, aching soreness from all the work Stanley had done in the past several days to build up his weakened muscles. Step by step he tried to bend his left knee, and allow his left leg to take more and more of his weight, but about halfway to the graveyard, Stanley needed to stop for rest.

"'Even the youths shall faint and be weary,'" Willy called, "'and the young men shall utterly fall, but they that wait upon the LORD shall renew their strength; they shall mount up with wings as eagles; they shall run, and not be weary; and they shall walk, and not faint.'"

"What's that?"

"More Isaiah," Willy said with a smile. "Stanley?"

"Yes."

"You know how I told you it wasn't too hard—my eyes and all? That weren't true. It's hard, sometimes real hard, like you and your leg, but I seen you working at it—ha! can't hardly see you at all—and I figure we're kinda the same that way. We both got something bad, you know what I mean, Stanley?"

"I think so. We both have something wrong that we wish wasn't wrong, but there's nothing we can do about it except make the best of it."

"Yeah. Wish I could talk like you, Stanley."

Stanley turned to face Willy. "How you talk isn't important. That just comes from schooling, and anybody can do that. My uncle could speak very well, and everyone seemed interested in everything he said, but I knew him, and his words were nothing but words. Do you understand what I mean?"

Willy nodded slowly, thoughtfully.

"What's much better is the meaning of your words," Stanley said, "and nobody can learn that in school. That comes from your heart. And that's how *you* talk, Willy. And you know what else?"

"What?"

"That's something I'm learning from you."

Willy looked bewildered. "Really?"

"Really. Back in Ohio, I just said and did what was expected of me, and nobody cared what I thought or felt. Since coming here I've started to look inside myself, and I've learned that you and your mama, and Levi and Min, too, really do care what I'm thinking and feeling."

Willy's eyes, now moist and glistening, never left Stanley's face.

"And I'll tell you something else, Willy."

"What's that?"

"I think I'm going to make it. Let's go."

Ten minutes later, Stanley and Willy stood atop the crest of the hill under the expansive branches of the oak that shaded the graveyard. The graveyard was quite small, perhaps twenty feet square, and bordered with a low white-washed picket fence. Stanley pushed open the gate and stood aside to let Willy enter first.

Three things within the fence drew Stanley's attention. Two wooden crosses, painted white with black lettering, stood close to the western side of the enclosure, near the left rear corner. The grass before the leftmost cross was full and green, while the earth before the other was packed firm in a slight hillock, nearly devoid of vegetation. The third thing Stanley noticed was a large rock, opposite the two crosses in the far right corner.

"What's this rock, Willy?"

"That's the setting rock."

"The setting rock?"

"Yeah, that's what Mama calls it. Sometimes she comes up here and sets a spell."

"Was it always here?"

"Oh no, Levi done that. He dug it up somewhere down by the creek and had Duke drag it all the way up the barn. Coulda just drug it here, but Levi said the grass woulda got all tore up. That's when you was sick."

"How did Levi get it here from the barn?"

"Long time ago, before I remember, Papa and Levi built a hoist backside the barn, so Levi just lifted that big old rock up and drove the buckboard under it, then he drove it up here, maybe a month ago now. Levi says that's Papa's rock, seeing as Papa ain't buried here, but we can remember him just the same."

"Levi is rather clever."

"Cleverest I know. Seems ain't much Levi don't know." Willy searched the ground before him with his nearly sightless eyes. He took several halting steps forward and to the left, then reached out to touch one of the white crosses. "This Aaron?"

"Yes."

"I'll pray now." Willy knelt before the grave and was silent for a few moments. Stanley thought he should kneel as well. Using the cane for support, he tried hard, so very hard, to bend both knees and lower himself gently to the ground, but the left knee would not, could not bend completely. Stanley almost wept at the effort of it, then decided it would be best simply to sit upon the setting rock.

It was the simple prayer of a child, such as anyone might pray, and his words were those of a child talking to his papa. And yet it seemed to Stanley there was something more happening here. Willy spoke with simple, sincere words of his deepest desires to his "heavenly Father," upon whom he seemed to depend completely.

Willy prayed for himself, that he would be able to remember more and more of the Bible, and that he would obey his mother and be helpful to her. "And give me a good mind about my bad eyes so I ain't blaming you for it."

Willy went on to pray for his mother, for each of his brothers and sisters in turn, and then he prayed for Levi Jackson and his family as well. Lastly, the boy prayed for his new friend Stanley, and while this made Stanley smile, he also shifted uncomfortably upon the rock.

"In Jesus' name I pray, amen." Willy stood and looked around. "Stanley?"

"I'm right here," Stanley said. He rose stiffly and limped over next to Willy.

"This is the highest spot on Matthews Hill, and I used to come up here sometimes just to see what I could see. Can't see anything now. Tell me what *you* see, Stanley."

"Sure, Willy. Let's start over here." Stanley guided the boy to the fence along the south side of the graveyard. "We're facing south now. Feel the sun on your face?"

"I feel it—south. We're looking toward the house and the barn, right?"

"That we are, just below. Beyond that I can see the lane that leads down to the trees—"

"That goes to the road to Chambers Store."

"There are pastures on either side of the lane, with cows and sheep in them."

"Prob'ly some beef on the hoof, and the milk cows, too. Sheep are for wool, and once in a while, we eat one."

"I see smoke in the distance."

"A fire?"

"Don't think so. It's very faint and spread out, so it can't be a house or barn fire. Could be a brush fire, but isn't Corinth down south there?"

Willy nodded. "Think so."

"That could be smoke from the army, like campfires, or maybe they're fighting again."

Stanley learned much from Willy during their short visit to the graveyard. He learned that hogs ruled the woods that surrounded the Jackson place, and that the Tippetts, whose farm lay in a shallow glen just to the northwest, went to the Baptist church in Purdy, the county seat, and they had no slaves, so the Matthews didn't have much to do with them. Owl Creek was a favorite place to picnic during warm weather, and Aaron had built a raft and tried to float all four miles of Owl Creek to the Tennessee River, but the raft broke up on some rocks about halfway down. And it would be Tater Day soon, because Levi and his boys were hard at work in the tater field tending the young sweet potato shoots.

"Willy, I know the river is over there to the east, but I can't see it, just the trees along the bank, and I know Shiloh is down there, but I can't tell exactly where."

"Sometimes, I'd see smoke from the riverboats. See any now, Stanley?"

"No, just woods mostly, and a few cleared places, hayfields maybe. Can I ask you something, Willy?"

"We're friends, ain't we?"

"In your prayer you said you hoped both Luke and I would see the light of Jesus. What did you mean by that?"

"The light of Jesus?" Willy laughed a little, quietly. "That's easy. We was just learning it the day you washed King George III. 'In him was life, and the life was the light of men.'"

"That sounded strange when I read it to you. Still does."

"Mama says if you don't know Jesus, it's like you're dead, or asleep, and then he gives you the light and you wake up."

"What if I never get that light, Willy?"

"Stanley! You got to! Or you'll be damned to hell forever."

"Hell—like hellfire and brimstone? My aunt used to threaten me with that."

"All I know is it ain't no place I want to be forever. Could be real dark, too, 'cause when this king asked some folks to dinner, most folks took a bath, but this one man didn't, and he got throwed out in the outer darkness and there was all kinda weeping and gnashing of teeth—that's one of my favorite bits—weeping and gnashing of teeth."

Stanley was dumbfounded. The troubling images of hot, flashing teeth and the flood of tears had continued to plague his dreams during the dark hours. How could this young boy have known?

"Don't know what hell is, really. Don't want to know, either. But there won't be any good there, and you'd be without God forever. You got to believe in the light of Jesus, Stanley."

"How do I get that light, Willy?"

"That's easy," Willy said. "'Ask, and it shall be given you; seek, and ye shall find; knock, and it shall be opened unto you.'"

"Now you're talking in riddles, Willy."

Willy laughed his high, shrill laugh. "That ain't no riddle,

Stanley. That's gospel. All you got to do is ask and Jesus will give you his light."

A movement from down the lane beyond the farmyard caught Stanley's attention. "Someone's coming."

"What do you mean?"

"Someone's coming up the lane—a wagon—looks like a man driving a black wagon."

"With four black horses?"

"Yes."

"Then we gotta stay here awhile, Stanley. Maybe just set in the shade under the oak tree 'til he leaves."

"Why's that?"

"That's Mr. LaVache, and he's a bad man, the kind that oughta be burned in hellfire. Best he not see you."

CHAPTER 22

*D*AVINA WISHED HIM GONE THE MOMENT SHE CAUGHT A glimpse of his black wagon coming up the lane, alternately bathed in brilliant sunlight and, moments later, nearly hidden in deep shadows cast by trees that lined the lane. His team was the envy of Memphis, Ben had said once, four beautiful and spirited black Arabian stallions. Davina eyed them admiringly as he drove the wagon into the yard close to the house, then swung it around and drew it to a halt next to the barn. He turned in his seat and rattled the heavy chain that bound two blacks to the side of the open wagon. One was a young boy, the other an even younger girl, both his prisoners and his valuable cargo.

Arms crossed, Davina stood at the top of the veranda steps feeling both amusement and revulsion. He had apparently fallen upon hard times since last she saw him. The black-painted wagon had faded to dark gray, and the brilliant gold lettering that announced to all his name and profession had half peeled, leaving faint traces where the gold had been.

The man looked faded as well. His broad-brimmed black slouch hat was stained white with sweat all around the band, and his formerly dark wavy hair had gone mostly gray, as had his closely trimmed moustache and goatee. Gone was the frock coat and perfectly matched trousers—made by the finest tailor in Memphis, he had claimed. Gone also was the floral brocade waistcoat he'd been so proud of, and the bright white shirt with frills at the collar and cuffs. Now he wore a tan three-button shirt and brown trousers—of wool, it appeared to Davina, the ordinary garb of ordinary folk.

He climbed down from the wagon with a certain degree of caution. Davina had never seen him climb down; he had always jumped to the ground. She also saw that his usually spotless, shiny black boots were dull with dust and spotted with mud.

He was still a handsome man, she had to admit that. His face was finely chiseled, although more obviously wrinkled now, its only blemish a two-inch-long diagonal scar from below his right eye to near the corner of his mouth, a scar hardly visible when the skin of his face was darkened by the sun, as it was now.

In fact, the only thing about him that remained as Davina remembered it was the pair of revolving pistols with polished handles that he wore at either hip, slung from a thick, black leather belt in black calfskin holsters, adorned all over with round and diamond-shaped silver studs that gleamed in the sun.

He strode briskly across the yard and stopped at the bottom of the steps. Then he removed his hat and bowed low. "Good day to you, ma'am. Jean-Baptiste LaVache at your service."

The manners were still perfect, too. But Davina knew better. LaVache's voice was smooth, its tone both rich and soothing, and more often than not, it reminded her of something sweet and syrupy, like sorghum molasses. And yet, it was at the same time rotten to the point of making her stomach churn, like the time she had discovered the decaying body of one of the barn cats under the veranda.

"There's no call for your services here, Mr. LaVache," Davina said, not mimicking the man's lyrical, drawn out "Lah-Vaaah-shuh," but rather sticking to a curt and crisp "LaVatch," as if it soiled her to speak the name. "And I trust you'll recall that your last visit ended when my husband drew down on you with his scattergun. Told you to never pass this way again, he did."

"So he did, ma'am. Please forgive the intrusion, Mrs. Matthews, but I wished only to pay my respects to you, and offer my sincerest sympathies at your recent misfortunes."

"The deaths of my husband and son are no mere misfortunes, Mr. LaVache."

"No, ma'am, most assuredly not. I beg you will pardon me if you think me disrespectful, ma'am, but I assure you, no disrespect is intended and my sympathies are indeed sincere. Mr. Matthews was a good man, as was your son, I'm sure."

"Then your sympathies are received and you should get on your way." Davina nodded her head in the direction of his rig. "Pretty young, ain't they?"

For a brief moment Davina detected a hint of anger in LaVache's gaze.

"The Yankees are making it hard for folks around here, and selling at any age helps pay their creditors." LaVache stepped forward and rested his booted foot on the lower step. "Ma'am, if I may—"

Davina's glare stopped LaVache in his tracks.

After a moment's consideration, he withdrew to his former position. "Ma'am, if I might express my concerns for your well-being. It must be a great burden working this farm now. Certainly, there must be countless difficulties after losing Mr. Matthews."

"And that's not your concern."

LaVache smiled warmly up at Davina. "Yes, ma'am, but perhaps I might be allowed to ease your burden a little."

"How? By selling me one of those negroes you have there?"

"Oh, no, ma'am." LaVache sounded truly indignant. "Mrs. Matthews, I couldn't help but notice on my way up the lane what a fine brood of blacks you have working the fields—mending your fences, I think they were—and one or two of those particularly fine young boys out there would certainly be worth an equally fine price indeed."

"You want to get one of the Jackson boys?"

"Both, if you'll allow it, Mrs. Matthews. That would yield a substantial amount of capital that would be of great benefit to your farm."

"Oh, I know your dealings, Mr. LaVache. You'll try to get both for the cost of one, half what those good boys are worth. And then haul them off to sell to some big slave pen in Memphis or some plantation down the river for a huge profit."

"I believe I offer a valuable service, ma'am." LaVache half-turned and pointed at the black wagon by the barn. "Your neighbors, the Trimbles and the Hodges, have already improved their situation through such an arrangement."

"There'll be no like arrangement here, Mr. LaVache. I'll not be taking children away from their mama and papa."

"Your warm-hearted generosity does you credit, but if you'll allow me, Mrs. Matthews, their kind holds to no like domestic sentiment, and will run off given the chance. I know of four blacks in Hardin County, and one right here in McNairy, I might add, that have run off to the Yankees. Drovers they'll be, or servants to Yankee officers, but those blacks will still be traitors through and through, and not one of them gave a rearward thought to their women and children as they were running away. No, Mrs. Matthews, their kind aren't attached to their own kin as we are. I've even seen mothers give up their babies without shedding a single tear."

"I'm sure you have, and I'm just as sure those mothers had no more tears in them to shed. Now, on your way, Mr. LaVache."

"Then perhaps one of the small females. You could still reap a handsome profit and you would have one less mouth to feed."

"No, LaVache. Be gone, or I'll get my gun."

"All right, ma'am, I'm going. Would you be so kind as to send for one of your blacks to water my horses and my two negroes?"

"I'll fetch a pail of water myself for your two negroes. But for you and your horses? Do it yourself. The well's around back."

"Never you mind, ma'am." Again LaVache doffed his hat and bowed. "Good day to you, Mrs. Matthews." LaVache walked a few paces toward his wagon, then turned again to face Davina. "I nearly forgot, Mrs. Matthews, I was told you've been sheltering a Yankee."

Davina felt her knees about to give way. So, this was the true purpose of the slave trader's calling on her.

"If it's true," LaVache said, "I strongly suggest you turn him over to me. It just isn't proper for a good southern woman like you to be seen giving aid and comfort to the enemy. Is he still here in your house, ma'am?"

Davina fought to steady her voice. "No, Mr. LaVache, he is not. Left a while ago with nary a 'thank you, ma'am,' or even a good-bye. Went off down the lane, south toward Corinth, maybe."

Davina held LaVache's gaze as he searched her face with his coal-dark eyes. And it was true—mostly anyway. Stanley wasn't in the house, and they hadn't spoken to each other since breakfast, but she had seen Stanley hobbling *up* the lane with Willy toward the cemetery rather than down the lane toward the road to Chambers Store.

"Well then, he's likely trying for the Federal lines," LaVache said, apparently satisfied. "It's probably not wise for me to pursue in that direction with my blacks. My business here is concluded, Mrs. Matthews. Again, please accept my condolences, and if you do come upon difficult times, ma'am, which I believe you shortly shall, please be so kind as to send word to your good friend Jean-Baptiste LaVache."

With a final touch to the brim of his hat, LaVache climbed aboard his faded, peeling wagon and, with a sharp crack of his whip, disappeared down the lane in a cloud of dust.

Davina walked slowly to the end of the veranda and looked up the lane toward the cemetery. Willy and Stanley had started to walk back toward the farmyard. The tall Yankee's steps were measured and careful, his left hand gripping the cane, his right upon Willy's shoulder to guide the way. Davina knew that her last words to LaVache had been neither measured nor careful. She had spoken without hesitation and without thought to what effect her words might have. The lie had come so naturally to protect one whom she had, in that moment anyway, thought of as her own. This perception both surprised and troubled Davina.

But as Willy and the Yankee boy drew nearer, she knew that her deception had been a good and righteous act. Her words would have been no different had Stanley Mitchell been born a Matthews.

CHAPTER 23

———

IF LEVI JACKSON HAD LEARNED ONE THING DURING HIS twenty-one years on Matthews Hill, it was that there were certain times each year when it mattered little whether one was white or black. Tater Day was one of those times. The work would be hard and dirty and tedious, but he couldn't help looking forward to that day in late May when the sweet potato shoots were ready to be planted, because on that day the toil would require the combined efforts of every soul at the farm, without exception.

About the first of the month, Levi and his sons, Jeremiah and Micah, had tilled two four-foot-wide beds along the entire length of the field and seeded each bed with ten bushels of sweet potatoes from last year's harvest. Over the next three to four weeks, those seed potatoes had sprouted in the dark, rich earth, warmed by the strong May sun. Levi had checked the growth of the new potato shoots daily until the experience of years told him planting time had come.

The field lay on the gentle northern slope of Matthews Hill, just beyond the graveyard and across the lane that bisected the farm and led down to Owl Creek. At something less than an acre and a half, the field would not produce a huge crop of sweet potatoes. Even so, about twenty thousand shoots had to be harvested from the seedbeds and immediately planted in the freshly tilled soil.

Ben Matthews and Levi had learned much from other farmers in the area, and year by year, the two had worked hard to improve their methods to get as much as possible done in the twelve hours or so of daylight each day. Each crop had its own special times for plowing, planting, thinning, weeding, and harvesting. Schedules had to be planned and followed if there was to be enough food for both man and beast for the coming year, and if any profit was to be made through selling what was unneeded.

Levi scanned the sky. There could not be a better day for Tater Day. It promised to be warm and humid—usually was this time of year—but the full heat of the sun would be broken occasionally by billowing clouds with gray undersides that spoke of rain showers to come, maybe that afternoon or evening, surely by tomorrow.

Of the seventeen inhabitants of Matthews Hill, only Li'l Davy and Levi's two youngest boys, and Min, who was charged with keeping the gang fed, would escape the rigors of Tater Day. Everyone else, including Stanley Mitchell, gathered by the buckboard at the edge of the tater field.

Davina Matthews stood shoulder to shoulder with Levi. "You're the field boss, Levi. Tell us what to do." It was an agreement Mistuh Ben had told him about before he went off to the war, but it nonetheless pleased Levi to hear Missus Davina speak of it.

"First, I ain't calling no rest 'til lunch," Levi said. "You need water? You get it quick, and back to work. It's Amos's job to keep driving down the well to fill them buckets so we got water all day long. Keep filling them buckets, the clean ones there, 'cause it'll be warm today, even with them clouds coming up."

The twelve-year-old boy smiled sheepishly and went to stroke the muzzles of the mule team, Lily and Penny.

"Now," Levi said, "Miss Anna and Mastuh Willy done cut them shoots last year and done 'em good. Cut 'em clean, now, just an inch above the dirt, but Mastuh Willy, 'cause of your eyes, you got to feel 'em now, so careful about them fingers. Miss Anna, you and Mastuh Willy oughta work close, maybe on op'site sides, so you can keep an eye on him." Anna and Willy went to the back of the wagon. Each took two wooden buckets and a pair of sharp shears and Anna guided Willy toward the beds of tater shoots.

"The rest of us is planters. There be three teams a-planting. Missus Davina and Mastuh Luke, you be one. You take them ten rows at the top, and Miss Ruthie, you be their runner. You run on up and get a bucket of shoots and take it to your mama." As the three workers headed off to begin work, Levi couldn't help but notice how weary Luke already looked. "Jer and Micah, you be another team. Abby, you be their runner—and no dawdling, girl. You take them next ten rows." Levi watched his three children to see they were headed in the right direction.

Other than Levi, only two persons remained standing at the rear of the wagon, his eight-year-old daughter, Naomi, and Stanley Mitchell. "Naomi, you be our runner." The girl nodded, picked up a bucket from the wagon, and ran across the field toward the shoot beds, pigtails flying.

"Now, Mastuh Stanley," Levi said, "I got to tell you one thing about the water. They's two buckets, one for the whites and one for the blacks. See?" Levi pointed to the bucket painted with a white *W*. "Two cups, too. Same water, different buckets."

Stanley nodded.

Levi picked up a pole about four feet in length from the back of the wagon. An iron point about six inches long was fastened to the end of the pole.

"That looks like a spear," Stanley said.

"That it do," Levi said with a laugh. "I call this my hole-pole, 'cause it makes holes right quick. Easy work, but doing it all day be the hard bit. Just stick it in the dirt and shake a little, like this." Levi plunged the pole into the earth until the iron point was buried in the dark soil. Then he shook the pole side to side before taking it out. "See? Shake it to open it up some, break the dirt some. Like I say, easy work. Now, you do it, Mastuh Stanley."

Stanley did as he was shown, and the resulting hole in the earth looked every bit as suitable as Levi's. "Every foot, then, make them holes, Mastuh Stanley. You'll see when you gets used to it, you faster than me planting. Go on down the row, then come back up the next."

As Levi had predicted, Stanley learned the repetitive plunge and shake motion very quickly. He laid aside his cane and used the pole for support as he worked his way, foot by foot, down to the end of the long row.

He paused to wipe the sweat from his brow with his shirt-sleeve. Levi had assigned his teams wisely. At the top of the field, the smaller hands of Anna and Willy snipped away rapidly on opposite sides of the seed beds. Luke stood leaning on his hole-pole about three quarters of the way down the first row, staying just ahead of his mother, who was on her knees planting the shoots one after the other. Stanley knew that no one but Mrs. Matthews could keep Luke in check for the entire day. Ten rows away, Micah and Jeremiah seemed to have a smooth routine going. Micah dug the last hole in their first row while Jeremiah was about even with Mrs. Matthews in planting the shoots. Micah looked up and flashed Stanley a toothy grin. Stanley smiled in return and began to work up the next row toward Levi.

"You think you can get down so's you can plant some?" Levi asked when Stanley came abreast of him.

Stanley tried to lower himself to his knees next to Levi, but could not. "It'll take another week or two for this left knee to work right, but maybe I can sit down and plant the shoots."

"Only takes a few seconds to plant each one and then you got to move, Mastuh Stanley. No, try to sit and do that, and before long you'll be done for the day. Digging them holes is what you good for today, so you keep digging, and if I get too behind, I'll get Jer or Micah and set him a-planting."

From the start, Stanley established a routine. He started at the top of a row next to the lane and hole-poled all the way down to the end. Then he worked his way up the next long row, arriving at the lane about three quarters of an hour after he had begun. Only after Stanley had taken two cups of water to Levi from the unmarked bucket did he allow himself the respite of a cool drink of water and the added refreshment of removing his hat and pouring another cupful over his head and down the back of his neck. Then he went back to work.

"Give us a song, Levi," Mrs. Matthews called out.

"Must we, Mama?" Luke said.

Stanley chuckled under his breath. Luke had been quiet until then.

"Hush, Luke, and mind your holes. Set them straight. Go ahead, Levi."

"Yes, missus."

> *O shout, O shout, O shout away, and don't you mind,*
> *And glory, glory, glory in my soul!*
> *And when 'twas night I thought 'twas day,*
> *I thought I'd pray my soul away,*
> *And glory, glory, glory in my soul!*

It was a good song to work by. Levi sang the first "O shout" softly, the second louder, and the third louder still, and he did the same with "glory, glory, glory." Stanley started to plunge the holes in tempo with the song, and even began humming the tune.

> *O shout, O shout, O shout away, and don't you mind,*
> *And glory, glory, glory in my soul!*
> *O Satan told me not to pray,*
> *He want my soul at judgment day,*
> *And glory, glory, glory in my soul!*

The past few days Stanley had often thought about Willy's prayer at the cemetery. He had even tried to pray himself a few times, as Willy had said to, but Stanley had always ended his "prayers" in confusion, wondering why God would ever listen to his feeble ramblings. Surely, he must have more important things to do. Was it Satan telling him not to pray, as the song said?

> *O shout, O shout, O shout away, and don't you mind,*
> *And glory, glory, glory in my soul!*
> *And everywhere I went to pray,*
> *There was something in my way,*
> *And glory, glory, glory in my soul!*

"Willy, let's switch sides," Anna said. For the last hour she and Willy had snipped shoots smoothly together and the planters never had to stop their work for lack of shoots to plant.

"What for?"

"Because all I see is you and the shoot bed and the fence behind you, and I want to see the whole field, see what's going on, you know."

"All right, can't see much anyway."

What Anna particularly wanted to see was Stanley. Luke had said the Yankee had neither the strength nor the stomach for hard work, and although Anna suspected differently, she would see for herself what sort of field hand this uninvited visitor would make.

It was immediately obvious to Anna that Luke was wrong. From beneath the brim of her straw hat, she peered across the field at Stanley while she continued to snip, snip, snip the shoots just as Willy was doing, more by touch than by sight. Stanley worked away, head down, poking those holes in the ground, and when he had gotten well ahead of Levi, he made his way over to the wagon to fetch a cup of water for Levi from the bucket without the white *W*. And several times, Anna saw the Yankee glance over in her direction, but whether he was looking at her or checking on Willy, she couldn't tell.

————•————

It was inevitable that sooner or later that day, Stanley would cross paths with Luke. And about midmorning, as Stanley was hobbling back toward the wagon after taking Levi his second cup of cool water, Luke took his hole-pole in hand and walked quickly toward the wagon, arriving at the water bucket just moments before Stanley.

Luke ignored Stanley, who stood but a few feet away panting and sweating. Luke grabbed the drinking cup with the white *W* painted on it and dipped it into the water bucket with the *W.* Then he turned his back to Stanley and drank slowly, a small sip at a time, while he looked out over the field of knee-high alfalfa across the lane. When he'd finally drained the cup, he dipped it into the bucket a second time and resumed his leisurely drinking.

Stanley had waited long enough. There were still thousands of holes to make and thousands of shoots to get into the ground. He grabbed the second tin cup, filled it from the unmarked bucket, and gulped the water down.

Luke spun around. "What do you think you're doing?" he said, loud enough to be heard across the field. "That cup's for them negroes." Luke shook a pointing finger at the boy Amos, who stood beside the wagon silent and wide-eyed. "See this *W*? That means whites only. You can't be that stupid a Yank, can you, drinking from the blacks' cup? And see the *W* on that there bucket? Same thing—whites only. Other one's for the blacks."

Stanley dipped the cup into the bucket again, but before drinking, he straightened himself to his full height and looked down at Luke. "I think of it this way," Stanley said in a voice no one else could hear. "I don't think I have any cooties that will hurt them."

Stanley quickly drank the second cup of water and set the

empty cup down next to the bucket with a loud clank. A multitude of hateful emotions played across Luke's face. His hand tightened on the spear-like tool at his side.

Stanley turned and limped away. He resumed his work and had another half row done before Luke stopped his fuming and returned to work beside his mother.

Levi struck up another song, one which his children obviously knew:

> *O come my brethren and sisters too,*
> *We're gwine to join the heavenly crew;*
> *O hallelu, O hallelu, O hallelujah to the Lord.*

"Do me first, Pappy," Naomi called from the seedbed, where she was picking up another bucket of shoots from Anna.

> *Oh, there's Lil Naomi, she makes me mad,*
> *For you see I know she's going on bad;*
> *She told me a lie this afternoon,*
> *And the devil will get her very soon.*

The girl squealed with delight as she raced across the field toward her father, and when Levi started the chorus again, everyone joined in the singing, everyone except Stanley, that is, who didn't know the song, and Luke, who was just being himself.

> *O come my brethren and sisters too,*
> *We're gwine to join the heavenly crew;*
> *O hallelu, O hallelu, O hallelujah to the Lord.*

For verse after verse, as the planting continued, Levi inserted either the name of one of his own children or one of the Matthews children. He even sang a verse for Luke, although the boy never looked up from his hole making to acknowledge it. "Last verse, now, for Mistuh Stanley." And all the children merrily chimed in:

Oh, there's Mistuh Stanley, I know him well,
He's got to work to keep from hell;
He's got to pray by night and day,
If he wants to go by the narrow way.

To the delight of nearly everyone, Stanley removed his hat and bowed. The tune was strange and the words awkward, and rarely had he even tried to sing, but when the final chorus was begun, Stanley leaned upon the hole-pole, hat in hand, and sang along with joy in his heart, all the while looking across the rows at Anna, who had raised her head from her work and was returning his gaze.

In the heat of midday, Levi called a short break and everyone dove into a tray of ham sandwiches that Min had Amos drive out to the field. Then it was back to work again.

Through it all, Stanley plunged hole after hole, and when there were no more holes to dig, he stood and watched as Levi planted several shoots. Then he took a bucket of shoots, limped over to the last row, and sat in the dirt. He stuck a shoot into the first hole, mounded up the loose soil around it, and tamped it firm with his hands. Then he scooted on the seat of his pants to the next hole, and then the next and the next, until there were no more sweet potato shoots to plant.

CHAPTER 24

ANNA SAT QUIETLY ON THE STRIP OF TRAMPLED GRASS between the sweet potato field and the lane. She had been on her knees all day. The legs of her trousers were almost black from the moist earth. But her back hurt most of all from bending and reaching over the tater shoot bed. She inhaled deeply, heavily, not a gasp from exhaustion, but rather a breath that filled her with refreshment, that drove away some of the weariness and eased the stabbing aches in her joints and limbs.

Across the tater field Stanley got slowly to his feet. He stretched, brushed what dirt he could from his trousers, and began to hobble up the row. Every step seemed painful to him, and Anna saw him wince several times, but he had endured the day. *A wretched and crippled moron blue-belly, that's what you are now, and that's all you'll ever be.* It was odd that those words she had spoken to him came so readily to mind, but as she watched him limp across that field for the final time that day, she was troubled. Perhaps she had thought less of that Yankee boy than she ought.

All of the children were weary and filthy, either sitting or lying down on the grass. Anna and the other Matthews children sat next to each other—Luke on the right, then Ruthie, Anna, and Willy, while the Jackson children sat some yards distant to the left. But Mama and Levi and the buckboard wagon were nowhere to be seen.

Stanley sat down on the grass next to Willy and tousled the boy's hair. "What's going on, Willy? Where's the wagon? I was hoping for a ride down to the house."

Willy laughed his high, shrill laugh. "You'll see," he said, "just sit and wait. You'll see."

With a loud huff Luke lay back on the grass and threw an arm over his face.

"How are your hands, Willy? Those shears must have been rough on them."

"Yeah, but I've had worse," Willy said. "The gloves helped, but I still got a couple of blisters. See?" Willy held his hands close to Stanley's face.

"I can't see anything for all the dirt, Willy."

"Anna's are lots worse. Show him, Anna."

"Oh, Willy, they're all right," Anna said, but she held her hands out toward Stanley anyway. Her usually soft, delicate hands were swollen and reddened. The swellings of several blisters could be clearly seen and the inside of both thumbs had been rubbed raw.

Stanley frowned.

"Just think how they'd be without the gloves," she said.

"Can anything be done?" Stanley asked.

"Mama's down the house for witch hazel. That'll help. Might help with your leg, too—I mean, it must be hurting."

Stanley had just opened his mouth to reply when the clatter of the wagon coming over the crest of the hill caused all of the children to jump to their feet.

Over the years it had become the custom, whenever a long, hard day of planting or harvesting was done, to picnic down by Owl Creek. For much of the day Min, while minding the smaller children, had been cooking, baking, steaming, and roasting. As much a part of the routine of the day as the planting itself was this greatly anticipated evening meal.

"'Ho, every one that thirsteth,'" Levi called out, "'come ye to

the waters, and he that hath no money; come ye, buy, and eat.'"
And with a huge laugh he drew the wagon to a halt beside the
sweet potato field.

Stanley nudged Willy. "More Isaiah?"

"Yep," Willy said with a big, toothy smile. "Levi always says
that when it's picnic time down by the creek."

"But the sun's going to set soon, maybe an hour. Won't it get
dark?"

"Don't matter," Anna said, and then realized that she had
just repeated the first two words she had ever said to the Yankee
boy. *Miss Don't Matter*, he'd called her, but now Willy and Stanley
seemed like old friends. Almost—should she even think it?—like
brothers. She'd also seen genuine concern in his eyes when he'd
looked at her hands, and she thought she should respond in kind.
"Stanley, you go hop in the wagon next to Aunt Min and catch a
ride down the creek."

———————

The smaller children had run ahead and were already frolicking
in the waters of the creek by the time Levi steered the team along
the creek bank. Several blankets had been spread on the ground,
and Min's wondrous preparations were upon laid—a large platter
with several slabs of smoked and slow-roasted pork ribs, another
platter with a pair of roasted chickens seasoned with herbs, one
bowl filled with eggs boiled hard, another with sweet peas, a third
heaped with some sort of greens flavored with bits of onion and
fatback, plenty of corn bread, and three sweet potato pies for
dessert. No fancy dishes or silverware had been brought from the
house, only a stack of large wooden bowls, another of wooden
cups for water, and a few serving ladles—eating would be done
with one's own fingers.

Grimy hands and faces were washed in the stream. Dripping,
shivering children were called to the "table." The white folk sat in
one group, the black folk in another. Stanley thought he should

sit as well, but hesitated. He dearly wished to sit cross-legged on the ground, even if it meant sitting shoulder to shoulder with Luke, but he simply could not. His strength was gone, his leg would take no more strain that day. Stanley turned and retreated to sit on the back of the wagon.

Mrs. Matthews quieted everyone. "Let's all bow our heads while I say the blessing."

After a hearty "Amen," the feasting began in earnest. Mrs. Matthews turned to Anna. "Take Stanley some food. He worked hard today."

Anna took one of the large bowls in hand and looked over at Stanley. "What do you want?"

"A little of everything, I guess."

"Even the greens? I heard Yankees don't eat greens."

A chorus of giggles erupted, but Stanley heard no spite in Anna's words or tone. He laughed a little himself. "Yes, the greens, too."

Stanley noticed that Luke watched his sister's every move as she went to each of the serving bowls and platters. Finally, she rose and brought the filled wooden bowl and a cup of water to Stanley.

"It smells wonderful," Stanley said, smiling what he thought was his best smile. His eyes met Anna's. "Thank you."

Anna nodded. "You're welcome." Then she returned to her place.

Words were few, no running conversations as were common at dinnertimes, just the occasional comment that the food was all "lip-smacking" or "finger-licking" or "bone-gnawing" good. When the last of the day's light faded, Levi came to the wagon and lit several pitch torches, which he stabbed into the ground here and there about the picnic ground.

Stanley ate until he could eat no more. He set his empty bowl down and drained the last bit of water from his cup. Mrs. Matthews came and stood beside him, smiling. "You worked hard today, Stanley. Couldn't have asked more of you, young man. Now go and cool off in the creek—do you good, and you'll sleep good tonight for sure."

"Thank you, Mrs. Matthews, I think I will. Is there a spot deep enough to swim in?"

"Not here. Down where it joins Snake Creek, though. Didn't know you could swim."

"My friends and I went swimming nearly every day in the summer back in Ohio."

For Stanley, there was nothing odd about bathing in a creek; he had done it dozens of times in the army. He studied the bank of the creek in the dim torchlight, planning each careful step down into the flow. The water was pleasantly cool, not icy cold, as the stream would have been back in February and March. Stanley waded several yards downstream to remove himself from the rest of the picnickers. He found a quiet spot about two feet deep and lowered himself gently to the creek bottom so that only his head was above the water. He smiled, recalling Anna's words from their first meeting. *No creek muck here.* Her tone had certainly softened since then. She seemed to be more—friendly? Caring? No, he couldn't use those words, not yet. Pleasant? Yes, that was it. Anna was being more pleasant.

Stanley washed his sweaty hat and, several times, poured a hatful of water over his head to wash the grit from his hair. Then he stood and made his way carefully back to the bank of the creek and up out of the water.

The picnic was at an end, and Levi and Min had already loaded everything into the wagon. Stanley gave Min his arm to help her up onto the back of the wagon, then he climbed up to sit beside her. Levi spoke his soft "Giddap," and Lily and Penny pulled the wagon back onto the lane. The children, in little bands of two or three, set out on their trek back over Matthews Hill —but Anna, Stanley saw, walked alone. Luke was nowhere to be seen.

Stanley wanted to jump down to walk with her, but he knew he couldn't risk dropping from the moving wagon. To break his leg again would mean losing it entirely, and besides, he knew a leg that couldn't bend enough to sit on the ground would never endure the quarter-mile walk back to the house. Not yet—soon maybe, but not yet.

The warm glow of the set sun on a bank of low clouds to the west was the last remnant of the day's light. "Do you think it will rain tonight, Levi?" Stanley called out.

"Might it could, Mastuh Stanley. Thought it would this morning, but the air don't feel it no more. Be mighty fine if it do, or we back at it hard in the morning." Levi laughed with just a hint of private glee. "Might be you driving these girls tomorrow, Mastuh Stanley. How about that?"

"Whatever you need, Levi." But Stanley wasn't entirely sure what he was volunteering for.

He elbowed Min's arm gently. "Back in Ohio, my uncle's cook lady, Aunt May, was superb, but that meal we just ate was about the best I've ever had."

"Oh, Mastuh Stanley," Min said, jiggling with quiet laughter, "that's 'cause you was famished, and famished food's always more good."

"Maybe, but I think it's because you know your way around food, and I think you always put in something special, something that nobody sees."

"I been hearing you a smart one, Mastuh Stanley." And by the bright tone of her voice, Stanley knew without looking at her face that Min was beaming.

CHAPTER 25

*L*EVI HAD KNOWN FOR AS LONG AS HE COULD REMEMBER that farming always depended upon the grace of Almighty God for all that was needed to bring crops to harvest—sunshine and warmth, rich soil and good seed from the year before, freedom from harmful blights and insects, and enough rain at the proper times throughout the season to bring tender green shoots to fruitful maturity. As in years past, there had been enough rain, but the tender shoots planted in the tater field needed immediate watering. The clouds that had darkened and lowered during the evening of Tater Day passed over Matthews Hill during the night without yielding even a brief shower.

The sun rose warm with the dawn, and the day promised to be hot and dry. Levi was at the rear doorway of the barn at first light. A large cistern stood next to the doorway under the eave of the roof to catch rain water for the livestock.

Levi knelt and lifted a large wooden mallet over his head. *Cain't never have too much water. Wish I could save it, but no time for that.*

"What are you doing, Levi?" It was Stanley, with his usual morning treat for the horses and mules.

Levi lowered the mallet. "Got to water all them taters today, or they done, Mastuh Stanley. Gave what I could to the animals, but now I got to empty this and put it in the wagon." Two blows with the mallet knocked out the large bung at the base of the cistern. Levi watched the water stream down the path and disappear into the trees. "Shame, losing that water," he said, shaking his head, "but cain't heave it full."

"I'll help you."

"Oh no, too heavy for you and me. Like to break our backs. No, when the water gone, we roll it over and get it up on the wagon with the hoist there." He pointed out the pulleys and ropes hanging between the rafters. "Then we get Jer and Micah and some buckets and go down the creek for water and back to the taters—all day long, almost. Like I said, Mastuh Stanley, we be back at it in the morning."

"You said something about me driving the team today?"

"I seen you done it right fine last week, and it ain't hard. And heaving them buckets? Well, Mastuh Stanley, that be frightful hard on you, and you got to carry two, and you got the cane."

"Then I'll be your teamster for the day. Do you think if I give Lily and Penny double treats, they'll be extra nice to me?"

Levi hooted with laughter until tears flowed. "You try, Mastuh Stanley, you just try, but I'm a-thinking those two girls cain't be bought so cheap."

———

It was another toilsome, back-breaking day. Stanley drove the wagon back and forth from the tater field to the creek fifty times by his count, and there was no hurrying the team along if Lily and Penny were to last the day. When Stanley swung the wagon around and pulled up close to the bank of the creek, Jeremiah and Micah already had their four buckets full of creek water and handed them up to Stanley, who dumped them quickly into the cistern. The boys moved with speed and grace, exhibiting both strength and agility, and on each trip the cistern was filled within five minutes—fifty buckets per load, about one hundred gallons in all. As Stanley returned to the driver's seat, his soft "giddap" was punctuated by the sounds of the boys splashing and laughing in the coolness of the creek, a reward for their labors, which they would enjoy throughout the day.

"Haw, Lil. Haw, Pen," Stanley called out, just as Levi had taught him to do, and the team turned toward the left. Stanley stopped the wagon exactly where Levi wanted it, close beside the tater field. Levi worked the field alone. He also had four wooden buckets that Stanley filled from the cistern and handed down to Levi. "Sun so hot, them shoots start falling down, and I got to cool them down right quick," he explained to Stanley. "While you gone, I run and put them fires out."

Levi emptied the rest of the water in the cistern, and sent it along to the tender sweet potato shoots, by hoisting one end of a long open-ended trough, another of the slave's wooden inventions—not unlike the brace he had made for Stanley's leg, just longer and wider. Levi rested the trough on the tail end of the wagon just below the bung in the cistern. He then angled the trough toward the furrow between the first two rows. The tater rows had been laid out according to the gentle slope of the land, so that the far ends of the rows were slightly lower than the ends nearest the lane. With one or two blows of Levi's mallet, the water gushed out of the hole at the bottom of the cistern and down the trough with enough force that the water flowed down the entire length of the furrow. Within two short minutes of his drawing up next to the field, Stanley would call out, "Gee, Lil. Gee, Pen," and turn the wagon around toward the creek again.

Each of the fifty tater rows was watered in this manner, and when it was done, over five thousand gallons had been hauled from the creek to the field. With the sun already set, the four saviors of the tater shoots, now bone-weary and famished, rode the wagon down toward the barn.

Stanley and Levi unhitched the wagon and began the evening ritual of caring for the hardworking mules. "What will we do tomorrow?" Stanley asked.

"Well, now, Mastuh Stanley," Levi said, scratching the wiry stubble of his beard, "if it don't rain, maybe we back at it tomorrow. First few days, maybe a week, them shoots will die right quick if they don't get wet. But it do feel like rain, and I got other stuff needs doing. Oh, I near forgot. Min, she say she need more firewood soon. Have to set Jer on that."

"I had regular firewood detail in the army, rain or shine. I think I can do that, and I'd like to know if my leg can stand up to it."

CHAPTER 26

THE NEXT DAY, THURSDAY, MAY 29, WAS JUST THE SORT OF day Anna hated. It rained. And it wasn't the wind-driven downpours of thunderstorms that passed quickly on, but rather a steady, soaking rain that lasted well into the afternoon. And so Anna had to stay inside to give Ruthie her lessons in history and arithmetic while Davy sat nearby, drawing on a scrap of paper.

"Seven times eight is fifty-eight," Ruthie recited. "Seven times nine—"

"Stop, Ruthie, that ain't right." Anna knew that her voice sounded too harsh, but her aggravation grew stronger with every wrong answer, and Davy's giggling didn't help one bit. "That's three times you said it wrong. Seven times eight is fifty-six, not fifty-eight. It ain't that hard. Start again."

A heavy thud from behind the house went almost unnoticed by Anna, but her two charges immediately looked up from their lessons. The sound was repeated once, twice.

"Levi's chopping wood," Ruthie said.

"Uh-uh, Ruthie. Jer does it most times. I bet it's Jer," Davy said, and before Anna could stop him, the boy jumped from his seat and dashed out through the kitchen to see who was right.

Within seconds, the boy ran back into the dining room. "Ha! You was wrong, Ruthie, ain't Levi."

"It's Jer?"

"Ain't him neither, and it ain't Luke 'cause he never does it."

Anna felt a smile form on her lips. Her mood was instantly a little brighter, but she didn't know why. "Back to work, both of you!"

The seemingly endless lesson of sevens continued. Davy, who was supposed to be working on several simple addition problems Anna had given him, finally scribbled a couple of times on the paper in front of him, then folded his arms over the paper and laid his head down. Ruthie failed again, this time at seven times six.

Anna took a deep breath and let it out slowly. "Ain't no use. Like flogging a dead mule, both of you. I'm done. Tomorrow it better be perfect."

Anna stood and walked into the parlor, where a tall, narrow stack of shelves next to the fireplace held the family library. She had returned *The Deerslayer* to its place a few days ago, and she was eager to begin the sequel, *The Last of the Mohicans*. She grabbed the book and returned to the dining room. The house was too damp and close; the air outside would be better. She took up one of the wooden chairs and went through the front door onto the veranda. Her steps were soft as she walked slowly around the corner of the house, then down the long side of the house that faced the barn. She set the chair down near the door to the kitchen, where she was just able to see who was wielding the axe that rainy day.

It was Stanley, just as she had thought. The Yankee grunted as he swung the axe, splitting the log cleanly in two. Willy picked up the two pieces and stacked them in the shelter behind the larder.

Anna opened the book. She skimmed the introduction and started in on the first chapter. It was a feature peculiar to the colonial wars of North America, that the toils and dangers of the wilderness were to be encountered before the adverse hosts could meet.

Stanley grunted again, different and louder this time. The log split just as before, but Stanley didn't straighten up immediately. He remained bent almost double. He breathed in and out several times, heavily. Then he lifted another piece of wood onto the chopping stump and hefted the axe over his head.

Sitting with her legs tucked under her, sheltered from the rain, with the slight stirring of the air cool upon her face, Anna began the first long paragraph again, realizing that she was indeed witnessing the toils, if not the dangers, of the wilderness.

Several axe blows later, Stanley again bent double and groaned. Anna looked up from her reading. Leaving the axe buried in the stump, Stanley used both hands to massage his left leg above the knee.

"You okay, Stanley?" she heard Willy ask.

"It's the muscle, Willy. Feels like it's trying to tie itself in knots again." Then Stanley gulped down a cupful of water and went back to work.

Anna couldn't recall any of what she had read. She went back to the beginning. This time a word caught her eye. *Hardy.* Yes, the Yankee was all of that. He was soaking wet from the rain and his own sweat, and the axe handle must be wet and slippery, but he would probably toil away until he had split a month's worth of wood.

Then another word. *Rugged.* Anna looked up at Stanley, still unaware of her presence. He was all of that, too. She had seen that the day he first managed the stairs, and on Tater Day, too. But now the Yankee, with his dark, neck-length hair matted and dripping, seemed the very image of ruggedness. How hard and strong his arms looked when they tensed just before he swung the axe—how wonderfully that left arm had healed and strengthened. How broad his shoulders were—thick, rounded bulges of muscled flesh showed above his shirt at the base of his neck— with every blow of the axe the flannel fabric was stretched taut across his back, almost to the point of being torn in two.

Stanley raised the axe again. He wavered for just a moment, then swung with a powerful grunt. No sooner had the axe struck home than Stanley let go of the axe handle and grabbed his left leg. A sharp cry split the damp, heavy air. Anna jumped up. She ran a few steps toward the end of the veranda nearest the Yankee, then stopped herself. Stanley dropped onto his right knee and kneaded his left with his hands.

Willy stood next to Stanley and patted the kneeling Yankee's shoulder. "You got to drink more water, Stanley, and some milk, too, and you got to eat something. Then you should rest."

Stanley's groans quieted. Anna returned to her chair, and as she picked up her book again she thought she heard Stanley weeping softly. That Yankee boy—no, Stanley was no longer that wounded and deformed enemy. He was hardy and rugged, hard-working and eager to prove himself. She marveled at how Stanley fought against the pain and awkwardness, and she couldn't help wondering, as she picked up the chair to return it to the dining room, what Stanley might have been capable of with two good legs under him.

A sudden uneasiness fell upon Anna. In the short time she had been on the veranda, she had said his name over and over within herself. Never again would she call him *that Yankee boy*.

CHAPTER 27

*F*ROM THE MOMENT HE TURNED HIS TEAM DOWN ADAMS Street, Jean-Baptiste LaVache knew something was wrong. Most Saturdays the streets of Memphis were empty by midafternoon, particularly when the weather was stifling, as it was that last day of May. The bell tower of Calvary Episcopal Church stood tall against the sky just seven blocks away—usually an easy drive, even with a fully loaded wagon, but today the street was nearly choked with buggies and wagons. Several times LaVache had to steer around a rig someone had abandoned in the street. City folk huddled in small groups along both sides of the street chattering, but he wasn't of a mind to stop and inquire. LaVache finally drew the rig to a halt across from the church at a large two-story building that occupied half the block. A sign across the top of the building proclaimed "Forrest & Maples, Slave Dealers."

Josiah Maples, clean shaven with gray hair and a thin face, spotted LaVache as soon as he pulled up. He came out of the office, ledger and pencil in hand, as LaVache was climbing down from the wagon. "Jean-Baptiste, welcome home," Maples said, shaking LaVache's hand vigorously. "What did you bring me today? Looks like a full load."

LaVache nodded. "The southern route worked out well. Some of the folks are leaving on account of the Yankees. I picked up those young ones in Hardin County. The boy is fifteen and the girl is twelve. Then I got this family, five of them, in Hardeman. I know you and the colonel like to keep them together, but that's no account to me. That last one I got just inside the county line, the McMurray place. He's thirty or thirty-one—Old McMurray couldn't say for sure. I have papers for all of them."

LaVache waited until Maples had finished scribbling notes in the ledger. "Why is everyone in the streets, Josiah? What's going on?"

"Let's go inside and talk while I do the figuring."

Inside, Maples sat at his paper-strewn desk. "Rumors are flying that Corinth has fallen to the Yankees. Don't believe it myself, but some folk say they've heard it from other folk from down that way. The *Appeal* hasn't printed a word about it, they say because their agent hasn't been able to get messages through the enemy's lines. I'll wait to see it in print before I believe it." Maples waved a bony hand toward a small table beside the office door. "There's today's issue. See for yourself. Not a word about Corinth."

Maples shuffled a few papers and set to work. LaVache scanned the paper. There was a lot of war news from Virginia, and Vicksburg seemed to be holding strong. The only war news of local interest was a brief notice that the Federal river fleet had started to bombard Fort Pillow, the last bastion of defense above Memphis. However, it was the considered opinion of the editor that the citizens of Memphis were safe because Fort Pillow would never fall.

The *Daily Appeal* made no pretense at being anything other than a pro-Confederate newspaper, and while LaVache's sentiments were akin to theirs, it would be madness to believe every printed word. According to the editor, the Union was on the verge of collapse and the Confederacy would win the war by year's end. But LaVache couldn't help thinking that the city folk were right to be worried, because the Yankees were as relentless as they were numerous.

Maples slipped his pencil behind his ear. "How does twenty-five hundred for the lot sound?"

"Federal greenbacks?"

Maples shook his head. "You know better."

"Then it sounds like not enough." LaVache had paid twenty-eight, and he needed something for his trouble and expenses. "How's four thousand?"

"Too much. You know the market's not what it was even three months ago."

LaVache nodded.

"Some folks think the Federals will swoop in here and free all their slaves, so they're leery of investing now. I'd have been looking at fifty-seven hundred, maybe six thousand at auction. Now I would be lucky to get forty-five."

"Well, I paid three for them, and I've got feed and food and lodging and livery to pay."

"I understand, Jean-Baptiste. What would you say to thirty-three?"

"I would say 'good day' and take my catch around the corner to Fremont's."

Fifteen minutes later, LaVache left the office smiling, with a bank draft in hand for thirty-six hundred dollars Confederate, and the eight blacks had been secured within the slave pen.

LaVache climbed aboard his empty wagon and took up the reins. The rumors from Corinth were troubling, and would likely be proven true within a few days. If Corinth was gone, there would be no railroad to the east, and with the Federal fleet bombarding Fort Pillow, upriver was cut off as well. And if Memphis was taken, as he was certain it would be—he had seen with his own eyes how ill prepared the military authorities were to defend the city—there would be no downriver either—no river at all, in fact, to support his trade. He would have to move inland. And immediately, before the panic set in.

LaVache steered his empty wagon into the street and turned

left on Second Street. He had made his plans weeks ago. He had even gone so far as to speak to his agent, Mr. Lide, should the eventuality arise—he just hadn't thought it would arise so quickly.

A few blocks south he came to the office of the *Memphis Daily Appeal*. A clerk helped him with the wording of two advertisements that would be placed in Sunday's edition, as well as the two days following:

Passmore, Lide & Marshall
R. E. Agents and Auctioneers

For Sale

MAGNIFICENT HOUSE
On Pontotoc and Shelby Streets

House, Contents, Lot, Stable,
Four Negro Servants

This house contains seven well-furnished rooms. Lot fronts 80 by 200 feet. Lovely view of the river. Sale includes all furnishings and household servants. Here is a chance for an investment. We will sell to the highest bidder, for Confederate money, at the premises, on Tuesday, June 4th, at 10 o'clock A.M.

AUCTION SALE
Four Beautiful Horses

Fine, six and seven-year-old black stallions, pure-bred Arabians, with papers, foaled at Transylvania Plantation, East Carroll Parish, Louisiana. A one-time offer of such a matched team.

There will be a Public Auction, at Market Square, to the highest bidder, for Confederate money, on Wednesday, June 4th, at 10 o'clock A.M.

With a heavy sigh, Jean-Baptiste paid the clerk six dollars and left the office.

It was his usual Saturday evening ritual, whenever he was in town, to dine at the Bon Ton, and then ride downtown to the Magnolia Saloon. But that night he would take his supper at his home on Shelby Street that overlooked the Memphis waterfront.

He had expected this day ever since the Federal victory at Shiloh, and it had been confirmed the first of May, when he read the awful news of the fall of New Orleans in the *Appeal*. For Jean-Baptiste LaVache, the glorious days of the slave trader were ended.

CHAPTER 28

S UNDAY MORNING, STANLEY ROSE SOMEWHAT EARLIER THAN normal. He took extra care watering and feeding the horses, Duke and Earl, and the mules, Lily and Penny, for he knew that all four would be pressed into hard service that day.

"I'd like you to drive the carriage tomorrow," Mrs. Matthews had said quietly the evening before, as they sat on the veranda.

Stanley sat in stunned silence for a few moments. He had seen Levi dusting and polishing the carriage for more than an hour Saturday afternoon, and while he hadn't thought deeply about it, he did think that if he was expected to go to meeting, his status as a Yankee would require him to ride in the back of the buckboard with the Jackson children.

"Me, Mrs. Matthews?" Stanley had asked. "Shouldn't Luke have that privilege?"

"You're right, it's a privilege," Mrs. Matthews had said, "and it's mine to say who gets it. You've worked real hard, Stanley, and Luke's done mostly nothing."

A few minutes before the appointed hour of eight o'clock, Mrs. Matthews and Anna came out of the house. Stanley first gave his arm to the mother as she climbed up to the front seat of the carriage, then turned to offer the same service to Anna. She was wearing a dress, the first time he had seen her so attired since the day of Pastor Blackwell's visit, and it graced the girl's slender form in such a way that Stanley knew he would need to take great care throughout the day to keep from staring at her. It was a simple calico dress, ivory in color and patterned with small blue and yellow flowers, with a full skirt that fell to within an inch or two of the ground. Narrow strips of white lace encircled both her neck and her wrists, and she wore a large, floppy bonnet of the same fabric, also trimmed with lace.

With a polite "Thank you," Anna took Stanley's offered hand and climbed into the rear seat.

Stanley limped forward and stroked Duke's huge face with his hand. He was doing the same to Earl when Luke came crashing out of the house, slamming the door behind him. Luke ran to the carriage and leaped into the driver's seat beside his mother.

"Luke, I've asked Stanley to drive us this morning," Mrs. Matthews said matter-of-factly.

"No, Mama, ain't his place," Luke said, taking up the reins.

Stanley moved out of the way as quickly as he dared in case Luke put the whip to Duke and Earl. "It's all right, Mrs. Matthews. I'll sit in the back with Anna."

In fact, Stanley would have gladly yielded the privilege of driving in order to sit in the rear seat next to Luke's beautiful sister, but Stanley stood beside the carriage looking up at Luke and his mother, waiting patiently for the situation to resolve itself. The play of conflicting emotions that contorted Luke's face seemed almost comical to Stanley, for he knew Luke was wrestling with a most disagreeable choice. To remain where he was and drive the family to church meant that Stanley would sit out of his sight in the seat directly behind, close beside his sister.

Stanley put his foot on the step to the rear seat.

Luke turned and glared down at him. "Nope. *This* ain't your place. But," he added, nodding his head at the open seat next to Anna, "*that* ain't your place neither. You drive, Yank."

"Stay close by me," Mrs. Matthews said when they arrived. "I won't lie, but them folks don't need to know all of it. They'll know you're a Yankee, but don't talk much—no use them knowing you're a powerful smart Yankee. No harm in them thinking you're simple."

Stanley was only too happy to comply as they left the carriage in an area of open grazing land and walked toward the trees.

The site that had been selected as the temporary meeting place for the people of Shiloh Church was under the shady canopy of a grove of trees, about a third of an acre in size, within a sharp bend of Snake Creek near where the creek flows into the Tennessee River. Workmen had cut down a number of small trees and saplings, cleared away the underbrush, and graded the ground almost level. Carpenters had built ten long, low, split-log benches and placed five on each side of a central aisle.

A dais made of pine boards, perhaps six feet wide by twelve feet long, had been built in the center of the grove. Over the dais a roof had been erected, higher in the front and lower at the rear to shed rainwater. A simple wooden pulpit stood in the center of the dais near the front. The dais was open on all sides except the rear, where a pine-board wall eight feet high and extending twenty feet to either side of the dais had been raised.

"Just like they done for camp meeting," Mrs. Matthews told Stanley, when they had seated themselves. To Stanley's ear, her voice seemed strained, nervous even. "Only lots smaller, 'cause at camp meeting we have a few thousand people, and lots of tents all around. Good for now, but not if it rains."

The faithful arrived a few at a time or, occasionally, in large families. They sometimes shouted, sometimes whispered greetings to one another and then took their seats upon the timber benches. One gray-haired woman spotted Mrs. Matthews and, letting out a squeal of delight, rushed to her. The two embraced warmly.

"Why, Winnie Johnson," Mrs. Matthews said, "how long has it been?"

"About eight months shy of a full year—so good to see you, and so sorry about Ben, and Aaron, too—must have been terrible. Did you hear the horrible news?"

"What news, Win?"

"Why, the Yankees done took Corinth. Our boys just left it to them. The railroads too. Just horrible."

"That is sad news, Win."

"And who's this fine-looking boy? A friend of Aaron's back from the war?"

Stanley took firm hold of his cane and struggled to his feet. He took the woman's fleshy hand in his and shook it gently.

"Good to meet you, Mrs. Johnson. I'm Stanley Mitchell."

"My, he's a tall one. Been hurt in the war, Stanley? Whereabouts?"

"Uh, yes, ma'am—uh, right here, at Shiloh."

Winnie looked at Mrs. Matthews. "He don't sound like he's a Tennessee boy."

"No, Winnie, he's from Ohio." It amused Stanley how calmly Mrs. Matthews spoke those few words.

"Ohi...Ohhhh?" Winnie Johnson suddenly seemed short of words. She lowered her voice to a whisper. "He's a Yankee?"

"Yes, Winnie," Mrs. Matthews said with a bright smile, and when she went on, her voice was light and cheerful. "Just before he died, Aaron told me to take care of this boy, so I took him in. All done in he was, almost dead. I couldn't just leave him die, Christian charity and all, you know. I had to. You'd prob'ly done the same. And he's a good boy, don't never sass or cuss, and he's taken to working hard. My new field hand, that's what he is. I done good by him, and now he's doing good by me. Fact is, don't know how I'd be getting on without him. Providence, that's what it is."

Winnie Johnson walked slowly away shaking her head, and it wasn't but a minute or two before looks of wondering contempt were being hurled in Stanley's direction. Sixty or seventy people had now gathered in that small open-air church, and soon every one of them knew that a Yankee was in their midst.

And every one of them was white. Levi and Min, along with their children and all the other slaves, never entered the sanctuary but gathered in the area behind the dais—and behind the pine-board fence. Stanley now knew why it had been erected.

Pastor Blackwell appeared and, Bible in hand, strode up the center aisle. As he ascended the two steps to the low dais, all the people stood, unbidden. Pastor Blackwell greeted the congregation and raised his voice in a brief prayer of invocation. Then he said, "This hymn has long been a favorite of this flock, so you should all know the words." There were no hymnbooks such as Stanley had seen in Aunt Bess's church, and he didn't know the words, but he liked the lively tune, and soon found himself humming along as the people sang loudly and joyfully.

> Blow ye the trumpet, blow!
> The gladly solemn sound
> Let all the nations know,
> To earth's remotest bound:
> The year of jubilee is come;
> Return ye ransomed sinners, home;
> Return ye ransomed sinners, home.

Pastor Blackwell had a pleasant singing voice, a strong, vibrant baritone well suited to leading the congregation, and in tune, as far as Stanley could tell. Beside Stanley, Mrs. Matthews sang heartily, as did Willy, and Stanley thought he heard Anna's soft voice once or twice. The small voices of Ruthie and Davy were inaudible amid the throng, and at the opposite end of the low bench, Luke appeared to not sing at all.

Meanwhile, from behind the wall of pine boards rose a chorus of joyous, lively voices, somewhat strange to Stanley's ear, yet appealing—louder and fuller than those of his own race in front of the wall.

Ye slaves of sin and hell,
Your liberty receive;
And safe in Jesus dwell,
And blest in Jesus live:
The year of jubilee is come;
Return ye ransomed sinners, home;
Return ye ransomed sinners, home.

After the singing, the people remained standing while Pastor Blackwell read from the fourth chapter of Ephesians. He ended with these words: "There is one body, and one Spirit, even as ye are called in one hope of your calling; One Lord, one faith, one baptism, One God and Father of all, who is above all, and through all, and in you all."

Ephesians. Willy had been learning some verses in Ephesians by heart, and Stanley was rather surprised how quickly one of them came to mind: *For by grace are ye saved through faith; and that not of yourselves: it is the gift of God: not of works, lest any man should boast.*

Pastor Blackwell was a forceful and convincing preacher. While his words entreated, his fiery eyes scanned the congregation, resting here or there on this soul or that, and whenever his gaze wandered in Stanley's direction, Stanley sat a little straighter and focused his senses to hear every word and catch every nuance. The preacher sometimes held his Bible high with one hand and gestured emphatically with the other. At other times he set the Bible on the pulpit and waved one or both of his hands over the entire assembly. Once or twice he drew his hands close to his breast and spoke softly, shoulders hunched, to make a particularly fine point. Stanley watched and listened, struggling to clear his mind and comprehend. Once, Pastor Blackwell pointed a long, bony finger directly at Stanley, or so he thought, and Stanley searched his heart, trying to understand which of the pastor's words were meant for him.

182

Although the expansive gestures of the preacher added force to his words for those who saw him, Stanley couldn't help thinking that they were lost upon the multitude of dark-skinned folk out of sight behind the wall. Looking the preacher in the eye, Stanley could assess the passion with which the man spoke, a passion lacking in some of the teachers he had had at school. He had learned the most from those whose passion for their subjects was obvious in the way they taught.

Stanley heard much to challenge him during that hour. But looking at the wall that stood between the pastor and the darker half of the congregation, he wondered: Why was the unity he had heard Pastor Blackwell orate upon so skillfully apparently limited? And were those limits found anywhere in the book the pastor so reverently held in his hands?

During the dinner that followed, Stanley did as he was bidden and remained beside Mrs. Matthews throughout. Her straight talk and his simple answers seemed sufficient for most of the curious. "'A soft answer turneth away wrath,'" she whispered to him several times.

However, as the time to depart for home drew near, Luke sauntered up with three of his friends at his heels. Apparently, they wished to see a real Yankee up close but were afraid to do so one or even two at a time, for they had all seen how large this particular example was.

"I heared the big ones is soft in the head," one of the boys said. "Got to be simple coming amidst us all."

"And he don't seem in no hurry to leave, neither," said another. "Yep. Got to be soft in the head."

Luke stood as tall as he could and stared at his mother. "Nah, that Yankee ain't soft in the head. Fact is, he's right smart, and I can prove it."

"Luke, leave him be," Mrs. Matthews said, "right this minute. Now go on."

Luke didn't move. "Oh, yeah, he's real smart. He even talks the Latin, you know, like that Julius Caesar."

"Aw, go on."

"No way."

"Can't nobody simple talk the Latin."

"Go ahead, Yank," Luke said, smiling at the chorus of disbelief from his friends. "Go ahead and show us some of your fancy northern learning."

Mrs. Matthews laid a hand on Stanley's arm, perhaps thinking he might do something brash, but Stanley gave her a quick wink and took hold of his cane. He got slowly to his feet and looked down at the four boys.

"Latin, huh? Let me think." He drew the moment out for what seemed a long, heavy minute or two, appearing to ponder the question very deeply. "Yes, I think I have one. *E pluribus unum*. I think that's correct."

"Ha!" Luke said. "You could say anything at all and can't nobody know it's Latin or not."

"Yeah," said the nearest of Luke's friends, "but I heared it before. It's on the old money, or something, I think. What's it mean, Yank?"

"Out of many, one," Stanley said. "It's the motto of the United States of America."

"Aw, we ain't them no more," the second follower said. "Ain't our motto 'cause we's Confederates."

"But it sounds a little like Pastor Blackwell's sermon, doesn't it? He said God can make us all one in Jesus."

Stanley resumed his seat, noticing that a slight smile curled the corners of Mrs. Matthews' mouth. But when Luke stalked away, silent and sullen, her smile faded.

CHAPTER 29

⎯⎯•⎯⎯

*T*HE NARROW LANE THAT LED TO THE JACKSONS' CABIN WAS hardly distinguishable in the diffused, shadowy gray remains of another dying day. The uneven, stony path challenged every step, compelling Stanley to take added care not to fall. He probed the ground ahead with the cane in his left hand while he clutched Willy's Bible in his right. Despite his caution, Stanley stumbled several times, every jolt causing him to wince in pain. Now and again he heard the snorts and grunts of hogs to the right or left of the lane, and he hoped none would charge out of the woods at him, which he'd been told they sometimes did without warning. Run away he could not, not even to dodge behind a nearby tree for cover. He would be completely at the mercy of the beasts.

Stanley knew his fear was foolish. A split-rail fence bordered the lane on both sides to control the roaming swine. Yet a dark memory that, weeks ago, he had packed away in the farthest corner of his mind suddenly came back with a vengeance. No, tonight's darkness wasn't as deep, and there were no flashing teeth, but his fear and dread seemed as thick and real as when he had lain helpless and hopeless upon that bed. *But I'm not helpless anymore, and I'm not hopeless either. Levi's family needs me to read the Bible for them.*

A faint light shining through the trees, perhaps fifty yards ahead, signaled that he was nearing the cabin. It was a beacon to lead him, step by cautious step, toward the security that awaited within the slaves' cabin. As he drew nearer, the light took the shape of a small window thrown open to draw the evening air.

"Hello. Levi?" Stanley called out as he approached the door of the cabin.

"Hush, now. All you hush." Levi's own hushed voice came from inside. Then the door was opened wide.

"Evening, Mastuh Stanley." Levi stood in the doorway, framed by the warm glow from within. "Come on in and set a spell."

The cabin was of rough split-timber construction, like the Matthews' house, but much smaller, about twenty feet side to side and fifteen feet front to back, with only a single room. Min stood before the fireplace in the rear corner, stirring in a large, black pot something that filled the interior of the cabin with an exotic but enticing aroma—a fragrance that almost, though not entirely, displaced the pervasive odor of human perspiration.

The seven Jackson children sat quietly on a pair of low wooden benches on either side of a large wooden table in the center of the cabin, no doubt ordered to their places in anticipation of Stanley's arrival. Every face followed Stanley as he entered, and every young eye grew big with wonder when he shifted the Bible to his left hand and extended his right hand toward Levi. "Good evening, Mr. Jackson."

Anxiety played across the slave's face. He stared at Stanley's outstretched hand, then looked up into Stanley's eyes.

"It's all right," Stanley said. "I've shaken the hand of more than one free black man back in Ohio."

Slowly, and seemingly with great effort, Levi extended his hand to meet Stanley's. "But we ain't in Ohio, Mastuh Stanley, and we ain't free."

"True enough, but isn't a man allowed to greet a friend in his own home?"

"Friend, Mastuh Stanley? Ain't no friends between white and black."

"But *I* think of you as a friend, Levi. And not just because you saved my life. You also made this wonderful cane for me. It must have taken a great deal of time and care for you to make it—the sort of thing one friend does for another."

Holding Stanley's gaze, Levi seemed to ponder what he had just heard and then slowly nodded his head.

"And now we're working in the fields, side by side sometimes. And Min over there, she used to think I was a son of the devil, but I think she knows differently now."

"Lawd I do, Mastuh Stanley. You cain't be no devil and be wanting to read Scri'ture to my babies."

"Then as far as I'm concerned we're friends. And if anything ever comes of it, I'm just a stupid Yankee who doesn't know any better."

The children at the table all laughed, as did Min, and finally, Levi smiled and shook Stanley's hand again, this time vigorously. "Come set at the table with the young'uns. All you move a piece and let Mastuh Stanley set with you."

Levi went to the head of the table. "You set by me here, Mastuh Stanley." A place had been cleared on the bench to Levi's left. "This be the tribe of Levi," Levi said when both he and Stanley were seated.

"I know Jeremiah and Micah already," Stanley said, nodding at the two boys in turn. "How old are you?"

Jeremiah looked at his father.

Levi nodded his head once in return. "It good when friends talk."

"Seventeen, Mastuh Stanley," said Jeremiah. "Micah's fifteen."

Stanley wished he could be just *Stanley* to this family, especially the children, but he knew it could be no different. "And the names of your other children?" he asked Levi.

"Boys is all prophets of Scri'ture. By you be Amos and he be eleven—"

The boy beside Stanley shook his head vigorously. "No, Pappy."

"Oh, I plumb forgot," Levi said with a sideways wink at Stanley. "Amos twelve now, just last week we had cake. This here by me be Ob'diah. You is how old, Obie?"

"Six, Pappy."

"And the little one be Zech'riah—he only three. And my two girls be Ab'gail and Naomi. They thirteen and eight."

"Naomi, you fetch them bowls here," Min said, stirring the pot. "You done et, Mastuh Stanley?"

"Yes, ma'am, I ate supper up at the house."

The younger children all giggled, and Stanley saw Jer mouth the word *ma'am* at Micah.

"Then you got to et again. Cain't have no comp'ny that don't et."

Min swung the pot away from the fire and ladled an ample portion into each bowl, which Naomi then carried to the table. "That firstun's Mastuh Stanley's, girl."

While Stanley waited for everyone at the table to be served, he stirred through the stew set before him. There were several chunks of sweet potato, and the same kinds of greens and leeks he had seen in other stews, but he didn't think the meat was beef or chicken or pork.

With a steaming bowl at every place, and seven hungry children sitting with wooden spoons in hand, Levi waited quietly for Min to draw up her stool and sit at the opposite end of the table.

"Bow your heads, now," Levi said. "Fathuh in heaven, we's thanking thee for this good-smelling stew this night and we's praying thy blessing on it. And we's thanking thee for the life of this here critter, and bettering Mammy's pot that-a-way. And we thanking thee that brung this Yankee from away up nawth, so's he sitting at our table and reading your Scri'tures to this house. For Jesus' sake, amen."

Stanley picked up his spoon, but Levi laid his hand gently on Stanley's arm.

"Well, Mammy? Is it good?" Levi asked.

All of the children remained poised just like Stanley, with their spoons at the ready.

"It's good," Min said, after sampling a small spoonful.

"How good is it, Mammy?" a chorus of young voices asked.

"It's bowl-licking good."

The children went to work on the stew immediately, and Min laughed the way Stanley had seen her laugh in the kitchen up at the house.

"When Mammy say 'bowl-licking good,'" Levi explained, "we know it be so good, we be licking our bowls. You eat now, Mastuh Stanley."

The stew was different from anything Stanley had ever tasted, but it was most tasty and satisfying. He had eaten fully half of it before he paused, remembering that he had already eaten supper, and that his hosts had not, and that he really ought not to have indulged again so greedily. "Levi," he said, "what kind of critter is in this stew?"

The children erupted in laughter. "Hush now," Levi said, trying his best to suppress his own broad smile. "Well now, Mastuh Stanley, that varmint be possum, and possum stew be filling our bellies tonight. Jer'miah there be a right fine trapper, and there be a fat possum in that boy's trap this morning, thank the Lawd. Sometimes he get the squirrel, but they ain't fat like possum. It take three, maybe four squirrel to fix the stew, and it kinda good, but ain't never bowl-licking good like possum stew."

Stanley looked at Min. "It is very good."

"Thanks be, Mastuh Stanley," she said, her smile big and bright, "thanks be. I throwed in the fatback and the sorghum molasses for sweet'ning—yep, molasses do the trick."

When Stanley saw each of the children lick their bowls clean, he did the same—bowl-licking good indeed.

"Now, young'uns, hush," Levi said. "Mastuh Stanley be reading the Scri'tures now."

"What should I read, Levi? I've been reading St. John's Gospel with Willy."

"That good, but I been thinking on something from Isaiah the prophet."

Stanley chuckled to himself. "Folks around here seem to like Isaiah. The first words I heard Willy remembering were from Isaiah."

"A lot of good gospel in Isaiah," Levi said, his tone firm and serious. "You read chapter fifty-five—ain't long, but it got good gospel."

Stanley opened the Bible and found the place. "I think I've heard this before, Levi. It's what you said on Tater Day before the picnic."

"You right, Mastuh Stanley. Now, listen up, you young'uns."

"'Ho, every one that thirsteth,'" Stanley began. He steadied his voice and pronounced each word distinctly. "'Come ye to the waters, and he that hath no money...'" Only a few minutes of reading, thirteen verses in all, but from the oldest to the youngest, each of the slaves in that humble cabin listened to every word. And Stanley understood the significance of Levi's choice. Truly they were a people without money, and yet they treasured those words of Isaiah the prophet most dearly.

Stanley finished the reading and laid the Bible on the table.

"I thinks on them words out in them fields," Levi said. "I go out in joy and peace, Mastuh Stanley, and I been teaching my young'uns to do the same. The plowing and planting and watering and all, that be just like the word of the Lawd, and it all be grace. You know what I'm saying, Mastuh Stanley?"

Stanley stared blankly at Levi. "Not really."

"It like this, Mastuh Stanley. I go on out in that field and I plant them seeds, but them seeds cain't grow unlessen they got the dirt, and the Lawd made that, and they got to have rain, and that be from the Lawd, too, and they got to have sun, and that be the Lawd's too. All I does is plant and weed. For us ones here, the seed be the word, just like you read, and the weeding be the punishing when we done bad. Yep, the word of the Lawd, it been planted in me and my Min and my young'uns, and maybe you, too, Mistuh Stanley. Yep, good gospel there."

Levi prayed then for Min and each of his children by name and for himself. Then, much to Stanley's surprise, Levi prayed for the members of the Matthews household as well, including Luke. "Now, Lawd," Levi prayed, "we ain't asking you to shake the heavens and the earth, like you said you going to, just shake this one boy, Lawd." Lastly, Levi again thanked God for Mastuh Stanley's visit to read the Scriptures for them.

As soon as Levi pronounced the amen all of the children jumped up to attend to various tasks. The two girls, Abigail and Naomi, cleared the bowls and spoons from the table and then took a bucket outside to get water from the well behind the cabin. The older boys—Jeremiah, Micah, and Amos—took charge of their little brothers, Obadiah and Zechariah, and prepared to bed them down for the night.

Between the pair of windows in the end of the cabin to Stanley's right, the boys lowered three narrow beds that had been folded up and out of the way during the day. The wooden frame of each bed was secured to the hewn-log wall with a pair of strong iron hinges. The opposite corners of each bed frame were suspended from the bed above with thick rope, and the top bed was likewise suspended from the roof rafters. The result was a neat stack of three bunks that occupied the barest amount of space possible. Two pairs of identical beds were folded down along the front and rear walls of the cabin.

Levi, Min, and Stanley remained seated at the table. "That's amazing," Stanley said. "I've never seen beds like that."

"Yep, Mastuh Stanley," Levi said, "with Mammy putting out

them babies right reg'lar, I had to think how we's all fitting in this cabin."

"Willy said you're the cleverest man he knows, and I see why."

Levi grinned with pleasure.

"I should be going," Stanley said, taking hold of his cane and rising from the table. "Min, your stew was very good. Thank you."

"Aw, Mastuh Stanley, wasn't nothing. You a mighty curious one, though."

"How's that?"

"Well—how come you good to us blacks here? Ain't like any whites I know."

"Now, Minerva, that ain't no—"

"No, Levi, it's all right," Stanley said, sitting down again. "The cook in my uncle's house was a tiny black woman named May—less than five feet tall, I think she was. I ate more meals in Aunt May's kitchen than in the dining room, and Aunt May always talked to me, sometimes about what I was learning at school, sometimes about her family, and sometimes just talk. She's the only person who cared about me, and she's the only one I said good-bye to when I left for the army." Stanley looked at Min, and then at Levi, still seated on their wooden stools at opposite ends of the table. "I always thought the black folks back in Ohio were just ordinary folks, a little different for sure. But I'm learning that Rebels are even more different."

Levi and Min exchanged a curious look and smiled. Then Levi gave Min a little sideways nod, whereupon she stood and went to the back corner of her kitchen. She was back in an instant with a small cloth pouch in her hand. "Dat for you, Mastuh Stanley," she said, placing the pouch before him.

Levi's smile was even bigger than Min's. "Go ahead, Mastuh Stanley, undo it."

Inside were the brass buttons from Stanley's uniform and his damaged belt buckle. All had been polished to a luster Stanley hadn't been able to achieve for dress parade even on his best day.

"Thank you, Levi. Thank you, Min."

"No," said Levi, "that's us saying thanks for coming here, Mastuh Stanley, and we ain't got nothing to give you but what's yours."

"But it means a lot to me." Stanley stood and again offered his hand to Levi, who accepted it gladly. "I should be going so your little ones can sleep. Shall I return tomorrow evening?"

"That be real fine, Mastuh Stanley," Levi said, "if it be fine with the missus."

"It is, Levi. Mrs. Matthews asked me to come here for the reading after we returned from meeting yesterday. But Min, if you feed me that good every night, I'll get fat and even slower than I am now."

The cabin rang with laughter.

"Now, Levi," Stanley said, wiping away a happy tear, "I was wondering if you would light a torch and walk with me back to the barn. I would rather not pass that way in the dark again."

CHAPTER 30

*L*AVACHE CHECKED HIS POCKET WATCH. SHORTLY AFTER two o'clock. He drank the last swirl of tea from his cup and poured what remained in the pot on the small fire he had built beside the road. Then he tossed his rucksack under the seat of the wagon and climbed aboard.

"Only five or six more miles to Somerville, girls," he called to the pair of chestnut mares he had purchased. He'd been living like a foot soldier for three days since leaving Memphis. Showers had soaked him several times. Saturday night he'd slept under the wagon to prevent a complete soaking, and Sunday had been hot and muggy from start to finish. A good meal and a soft bed at the Fayette and he would be right as rain.

His days of thundering along the byways of western Tennessee, covering fifty or sixty miles in a single day, were past. He grieved the loss of his four coal-black Arabian stallions. It would be a week tomorrow since he'd sold them, and the four thousand dollars he had garnered from the sale was little solace. Perhaps this was what one experienced upon the death of a loved one, he thought, even though he had never held anyone so close.

Their names had been chosen by their breeder, Mr. Richards —Aziz, the strongest of the four; Ghalib, almost tireless, even on the hottest summer day; Tayyib, the even-tempered one; and Karim, the noblest steed he had ever seen and his favorite whenever he rode through the city streets. Fine animals like that were hard to come by, and few in Memphis could afford to buy even one of them, let alone all four, but a man no one seemed to know had outbid the few familiar citizens. An agent for the Federals, no doubt, and soon LaVache's four beautiful steeds would be burdened by four fat Yankee generals.

The chestnuts had cost him only an eighth of what he had gotten for the stallions. The pair were strong and healthy, but they were only two and they lacked the endurance of the Arabians. He would have to rest them more often, and when they were on the road, the pace would be slow—too slow. He would have to be content with fifteen miles a day, twenty at most, and he would have a lot of time—too much time for his liking—to think about the way things had been before the vexing Yankees.

A real estate speculator, hearing of LaVache's desire to sell his house quickly, had offered less than half its worth. The pangs he'd felt in parting with the house were mild when compared to his stallions, because he had spent most of his days during the last five years driving his magnificent team along the many roads of southwestern Tennessee, whereas he couldn't remember the last time he had spent more than a week in the large brick house.

It wasn't so much the house that he would miss, but rather its beautiful view of the river and the short walk or ride to the Cotton Exchange, the slave markets, and the familiar Businessmen's Club. The camaraderie of the Club was a thing of the past, as were his many acquaintances among the fairer sex, but LaVache had never allowed those relationships to become entanglements, and of that he was glad.

The fall of the city had been swift, but LaVache had been prepared. Late in the afternoon on Wednesday, June 4, word spread through the streets that Fort Pillow had surrendered and that Federal gunboats were steaming unmolested down the Mississippi River toward Memphis.

When the Federal fleet appeared before the city just after

dawn on Friday the 6th, a small flotilla of ramshackle Confederate gunboats and rams steamed out to meet them. While reports of Confederate and Federal guns rang through the streets of the city, LaVache walked calmly to the bank. His funds on deposit with the Bank of Tennessee in Memphis had grown to over twenty-two thousand dollars Confederate after liquidating his property. He arrived just as the manager, Mr. Hawkins, with many a worried glance over his shoulder toward the river, approached and unlocked the door.

"All of it?" Hawkins asked, upon hearing LaVache's request.

"All of it."

Hawkins stiffened. "Will a bank note suffice?"

"Yes. Make the note payable to your office in Somerville. And none of those shinplasters," LaVache added. "Only genuine Confederate currency." Paper currency issued by the bank or railroad might well be worthless outside of Tennessee.

LaVache returned to the house on Shelby Street. He packed what remained of his personal belongings in a large satchel and then sat on the veranda to watch the progress of the battle. The issue was never in doubt. A short time later, when the cannonading had lessened to a burst now and again, he summoned his stable boy, who hitched the chestnuts and drove the wagon around to the front of the house.

LaVache climbed aboard and tugged the brim of his hat down low over his eyes. Then he drove away to the east with hardly a rearward glance. Memphis was gone to the Yankees.

Somerville had always seemed pleasant; it had been a regular stopping place on LaVache's trading route. There was a comfortable hotel, the Fayette, where people knew him—the kind of place he could stay for a week or two without anyone thinking it strange. It was exactly the sort of place to stay while he planned what to do next, but it was much too quiet to consider as a permanent residence and, even worse, it was in territory under Yankee control.

LaVache reached the town just before the bank closed for the day. The spectacled bank manager smiled happily when LaVache presented the note from the bank in Memphis and asked him to deposit it, but the smile faded a few moments later when LaVache told the banker he would be withdrawing the entire sum in cash within two weeks.

Across the street, LaVache took a room at the Hotel Fayette. Then he drove his rig a few hundred feet down the street to the livery, where Chet Adams was an old and trusted friend. LaVache paid for fourteen days livery for his team and added an extra forty dollars to have Chet build a small, hidden compartment in the floor of his wagon, underneath the seat, and make some other changes to the black slave wagon.

"It's got to open from below," he told the curious liveryman, "and it's got to have a lock and be large enough to hide the chains, and maybe the pistols, too."

"Where you going, Jean?"

"You heard about Memphis?"

Chet nodded.

"I have to move south, so I won't be passing this way again."

Chet nodded again, looking saddened.

LaVache felt the same—the way of life he had loved was coming to an end. "Everything I own now is in this wagon, Chet, so I need to keep it safe until I get where I'm going. It's the Yankees driving me out. They're freeing lots of slaves and putting some of them to work driving their wagons or building their forts. Would you buy a slave now?"

Chet shook his head.

"There you have it," LaVache said. "Yankees have killed my business, so I've got to head south and find a place that's *free of them.*"

CHAPTER 31

LEVI JACKSON WAS AMAZED AT HOW EASILY HE AND THE Yankee boy had got along since he first came to their cabin a week before. Levi had taken to welcoming Mastuh Stanley with a warm handshake, and as the evenings passed, the slow torch-lit stroll back up the lane toward the barn became a time for chatting about the next day's work, or for more serious and personal talk.

Whenever Levi assigned Mastuh Stanley any chore, the boy would work at it until it was done. "No need to ask my permission, if he's willing," Missus Davina had said the first time Levi had asked her for Stanley's help. "Just tell Stanley yourself what you need doing."

Mastuh Stanley was more than willing. He was smart and steady, and he used his growing strength and vigor whether working on behalf of the white folk or the black; it made no difference. And how that boy managed to do the things he did with that bad leg still amazed Levi. But above all, Levi could look the young man in the eye and know that he spoke straight. Mastuh Stanley was a truth-teller.

"Say, Levi?" Mastuh Stanley said as they started their evening stroll up the lane, "I've been thinking about something Willy said the day I took him up to the graveyard, the day that slave trader was here."

Levi snorted loudly. Then he spat a thick wad into the dirt. "What words I got for that varmint ain't fitting, Mastuh Stanley."

"Why does he upset you?"

"Always looking to steal one of my young'uns."

"But you're all needed here, and the way I see it, you're like family to Mrs. Matthews. She would never sell any of your children, no more than she would her own."

"But they ain't my own."

"What? Of course they are. And Min? They're your family."

"But me and Min ain't wed right."

"Of course you're married."

"No, we ain't. Never had words said by a preacher."

Stanley looked puzzled. "I don't understand."

"Well, Mastuh Stanley, ain't something I likes to speak of, but you been good to me and my family."

"And you've been good to me, Levi."

Levi nodded slowly and heaved a great sigh. "Back twenty year or more, over Carolina way, Mistuh Ben's papa, he bought me and Min in Charleston. We never seen the other 'til then, and we was gave to Mistuh Ben and Missus Davina when they got wed, and then they come out here. Come down the river over yonder all the way from Georgia, and down about Al'bama way, Mistuh Ben say, 'We a Christian family and cain't have nothing lewd going on, so Levi and Min done got to be wed.'

"So they tie the boat to a tree, and they cuts a branch, just a skinny one with some leaves, and Mistuh Ben say, 'We knows your kind likes jumping over the broom, but we ain't got no broom, so this here branch'll do.' So me and Min jumped, didn't hold hands or nothing, and weren't no kissing then neither."

Levi kicked a stone and sent it skipping up the lane. It hadn't been a happy occasion for either of them, each knowing nothing about the other, and they had said only a few words to each other before that day. Still, Levi saw the hand of God in it, and in the brief moment of silence, he blessed the Lord for giving him Min and the children, just as he had done countless times before.

"Then Mistuh Ben say we married," Levi said. "And he say 'What you be calling yourself?' And I say, 'What you mean, Mistuh Ben?' And he say, 'Your family got to have a name,' so I say 'Jackson.'"

"You chose your own name?"

"Yep, Mastuh Stanley. I knowed we was going to Tennessee, and the only man I knowed of in Tennessee was Pres'dent Jackson, and Mistuh Ben liked it lots that I named us for Ol' Hick'ry."

"But Levi, you and Min love each other now."

"Oh, yessuh, Mastuh Stanley! And it weren't long in coming neither, cause Jer'miah be born almost eighteen years ago. But Min still ain't my wife, not by law, and Jer'miah ain't my son by law, ain't none of my young'uns mine by law."

"But how can that be, Levi?"

How could that be? It was the kind of thing that was never talked about with white folk, and hardly whispered among the blacks. But with Mastuh Stanley it was different. When it came to whites and blacks, he didn't seem to care about how it was supposed to be. They had called each other *friend*. Could that really be?

"Me and Min and my young'uns is owned by Missus Davina," Levi said. "We all her prop'ty, just like a horse or mule, and she can sell her prop'ty anytime she want. That be why that slave-man upsets me so much, Mastuh Stanley."

"But she'll never do that. She knows this is your home and they're your family."

"Seems like. That slave-man gone for now, but this land be hers and the cabin my own hands builded be hers, and all us living in it be hers, and maybe she be needing money, maybe she up and sell me or Min or a young'un or two."

"But I'm a stranger, and look what she's done for me. She's

not in any hurry to turn me out, not anymore, so I don't think she'll ever sell you or any one of your family."

Levi touched Mastuh Stanley lightly on the arm, causing Stanley to stop and face him. "I don't like thinking about it, but if Missus Davina die, then Mastuh Luke prob'ly own us, and he ain't like the missus."

"That *would* be terrible," Mastuh Stanley said. "I'd be worried, too. But Mrs. Matthews is in good health."

Levi kicked another stone up the lane and started walking, his head down. They were getting close to the barn now. He had prayed for Luke for years, but it seemed the more he prayed, the harder that boy's heart got.

"I'm sorry I upset you," Mastuh Stanley said, "but I'm glad you told me. It's like you're living under a dark cloud, but there's such happiness in your house."

Levi laughed a little. "Well, Mastuh Stanley, I been bought by Jesus. Missus Davina can sell me if she wants, but cain't nobody touch my soul no more, and cain't nobody touch my Min or my young'uns that way neither."

"And that makes you happy, Levi?"

"That be grace from the Lawd, Mastuh Stanley. But one more thing I got to say, and that—well, if Mistuh Ben's papa don't buy me and Min, then I don't know Min at all, and maybe I don't know the Lawd neither. The Lawd done made it go that way, and I been thanking him every day for that."

The dark, hulking shape of the barn was now visible against the night sky. They walked the last score of paces in silence.

Mastuh Stanley leaned against the corner of the barn. "Levi, I don't know God. Or even where he is."

"But I think the Lawd know you, Mastuh Stanley, and all about you, too."

"So how do I find God?"

"God's the one does the finding. And," Levi added with a

wry chuckle, "I think he been looking in on you right here on this dark path tonight."

"I'd like to pray like you and Willy and Mrs. Matthews, but what do I say?"

"Mastuh Stanley, the words ain't important, just the words only the Lawd hears, your heart-words."

"That's strange. I said almost the same thing to Willy on our way up to the graveyard."

"Then I think you know, Mastuh Stanley. Now just do what you know. Lot of times I think, 'Lawd, be merciful to me, a sinner,' and I know he hearing this poor slave down here. Maybe a fine thing for a Yankee to do, too."

CHAPTER 32

*A*NNA HAD BEEN SITTING ON THE PORCH EVER SINCE SHE saw Stanley Mitchell disappear out of sight behind the barn in the direction of Levi Jackson's cabin. Ruthie and Li'l Davy were already tucked in for the night, and the only disruption to the tranquility of the evening came from Luke and Willy, who sat upon the thin carpet in the parlor playing game after game of checkers. Every so often Willy, who now could not tell red from black and was sometimes convinced that his older brother was taking unfair advantage, raised his voice in protest. An argument inevitably ensued until Mama called from the dining room, where she spent most evenings knitting, "If you boys can't play in peace, you'll not play at all." But as Anna noted whenever she chose to turn and look in through the open window, Mama's warning merely caused the brothers to carry on their argument with coarse whisperings until one or the other tired of it.

From as far back as her memory took her, Anna had always loved Luke. Born just thirteen months apart, they were the closest in age of all the Matthews children. Anna had been the protective older sister, eager to pass on the wisdom of age, such as to look for mud wasps that liked to crawl up between the floorboards from the ground below, or which plants would cause an itchy rash if they brushed against them, or how to steal food from the kitchen when Aunt Min wasn't looking.

It had been a couple of years ago—perhaps after that thing with Micah, although Anna couldn't say for sure—that Luke had stopped seeing her as his big sister. He'd started to grow taller—she had only an inch or two on him now—and as he grew, the precious, cheerful boy faded away and a quick-spoken, easily riled youth took his place. Anna thought he probably considered her his little sister now, and more often of late, one word came to mind whenever she thought of him—bigheaded. *Please, Lord, I miss the old Luke. Let him grow out of it soon.*

Twilight gave way to nightfall and Anna continued to sit quietly. The moon, not quite half-full, slowly rose from its hiding place in the east, and Anna's thoughts turned toward retiring for the night. Then she saw a tall shadowy form emerge from behind the barn, limp awkwardly across the farmyard, and disappear toward the rear of the house. Anna remained a few minutes more. Then she stood and walked quietly along the veranda.

For the last several days, she had observed Stanley's evening routine. Before turning in for the night, he would go to the well behind the house, where he would remove his shirt and hat, draw two or three buckets of cool water, and wash away the sweat and grime of the day.

Anna paused at the end of the veranda near the larder. She remained hidden within moon-shadow, waiting for Stanley to finish, but tonight he had paused partway through his usual evening washing. His shirt hung from the side of the well and the water was drawn, but Stanley stood motionless, leaning over the well. At first Anna thought he might fall in, and she almost called out. His large hands grasped the stone wall of the well and his head hung low between his shoulders. A faint murmur reached Anna's ears, a voice, low and soft, almost a continuous groaning that seemed to come from somewhere deep within him. She longed to hear but could not, all except the last, for when Stanley's muted words were done, he stood straight, lifted his gaze toward the starry night, and said, "Amen."

When had she last prayed like that? Had she ever? Anna stood motionless and watched as Stanley first took a drink from the bucket of clean water and then began to wash himself. Then he emptied the dirty water and drew more fresh water. He took his shirt from where he'd hung it, plunged it into the bucket, and began to wash it vigorously.

Anna stepped off the veranda. "Good evening, Stanley." The trembling of her own voice disturbed her.

Stanley froze. "Oh—Anna—I didn't hear you. Hello."

Anna stood facing Stanley, her hands clasped demurely in front of her. "You're back from the Jacksons', I see."

"Yes," Stanley said, turning to look at her. "I enjoy visiting them, but those hogs rooting about in the woods scare me. Levi still walks me back to the barn every evening."

Anna giggled a little. "Scared of them hogs? A big, strong boy like you?"

"Think about it—I can't run away, and if one of those brutes charged at me, I'd be completely at its mercy, and I don't think mercy is something a hog is known for."

"You're right. I'm sorry," Anna said, trying hard to make her words sound genuine.

Stanley resumed washing his shirt, working the lye soap into a lather that glimmered faintly in the moonlight.

"Stanley, I'd like to say something to you. I've been thinking about it for some days, and I'd best not delay another."

"Do your worst. I can take it."

Anna thought she detected a playful tone in Stanley's words. "Ain't like that." She laughed a high, nervous little laugh. "Ain't like that at all, Stanley. I just want to say I'm sorry."

Stanley stopped his washing. "Sorry for what, Anna?"

"I been so mean to you. Mama's told us everything you told her, and I know you ain't had a good life, and I seen you working out in the fields with Levi, like Papa and Aaron done when they was here, and now you're helping however you can, and Mama's feeling better about things, and looking better, too. She's not so much worried as she was."

"I'm glad to be of some use."

"But I think it's more than just you helping out. It's kinda like you being here is helping Mama not be so sad about Papa and Aaron. I don't know why, but it just seems that way."

Stanley returned to washing his shirt. "I don't know what to say to that, Anna, but thanks for telling me."

Anna walked up beside the well and stood next to Stanley. "I'm just wondering what you're aiming at here?"

Stanley emptied the wash bucket, lowered it into the well and drew it up filled. "What am I aiming at? You mean, what am I doing here at the farm? I've been asking myself that same question lately." Stanley threw his shirt into the clean water and began to rinse the lather from it. "I can't say. What I mean is that today was a good day, a hard day for sure, but it feels good to do the work. I feel like I'm doing something worthwhile. And from what you just told me, I guess I am."

Stanley straightened and used his powerful hands and arms to wring the shirt as dry as he could. "I've noticed a change in your mother as well, and I think it's a good thing to be able to repay her for helping me when I needed it."

Stanley threw the damp shirt casually over his shoulder and turned to face Anna. She heard his breath catch in his throat, and much to her surprise, it delighted her to think she might have caused it.

"And tomorrow?" Stanley said, standing tall and looking down at her. "I expect I'll work much as I did today, but I haven't made any great plans for the future, if that's what you're asking, and I don't know where I'll go when your mother does ask me to leave."

"I seen you that day you and Willy walked up the cemetery," Anna said, "and I seen you and him all the while until LaVache left. You got a kindness for that boy, and it sure would be a sorry day for him if you went off, and it started me thinking that you ain't such a bad sort and I oughta think better of you." Anna's eyes left Stanley's and wandered down over the still wet skin of his bare chest to the dark scar that appeared nearly black in the moonlight. Her gaze lingered a few moments. She tried to imagine the shock and pain the ball had caused when it first struck, and then, suddenly aware that she was staring, Anna lowered her eyes farther until they came to rest upon her own hands, which she still held clasped in front of her. "You...you like Willy, don't you?"

"I sure do. He's quick. He learns fast, and he's always so joyful. I'm learning a lot from him."

"You're learning from Willy? Like what?"

"He said it this way: we both have a physical problem, and even though the problems are different, in a way we're alike. I can't think how hard it is for Willy with his blindness. It must be much worse than dealing with a bad leg. Up at the cemetery he prayed to God for a good attitude about his blindness."

"That's our sweet Willy," Anna said.

"And when I see how he depends on God, well, I think I need to learn that. And another thing. No one has ever needed me before, and Willy needs me. I enjoy reading for him and doing other things for him, like taking him places he can't go by himself, and up to Aaron's grave—oh, I'm sorry."

It took a moment for Anna to grasp why Stanley had stopped so abruptly. "It's okay, Stanley. Really. I know you didn't kill Aaron. Forget what I said before."

He hesitated, watching her eyes closely. "All right." After a pause, he went on again, more slowly. "That makes me think one more thing about Willy. Please don't take this wrong—I've never had a brother, or a sister for that matter, and I know you've all just lost your big brother, and I know I can't *ever* think to replace him in *any* way, but Willy has become like a brother to me. Do you know what I mean?"

And Anna did know, deep inside, and she felt warmed by Stanley's words. She looked up at him and nodded. "I think so."

"Does this mean you like me now?"

"No, I ain't saying that," Anna said, thankful the flush in her face was hidden in the soft moonlight. "But I heard all them folks at meeting again yesterday, saying how the Yankees have taken Memphis, and how they hate the Yankees so, and I knowed when you was driving us home that I didn't hate you no more."

Stanley opened his mouth to reply, but Anna went right on. "I didn't much like myself and what I was letting myself think about you—hating you like Luke does—ain't proper, and ain't Christian. The Bible says we have to put away all bitterness and anger and evil words, and I seen how Luke's been about you, and I don't want that for me."

Stanley smiled. "So you're saying you don't want to squish me between your toes?"

"Do you remember every word I said that day?"

"Every word." His smile grew wider.

"Oh, I'm so ashamed." Anna covered her face with her hands and shook her head, then looked up again. "They was angry words I shouldn'a said. I'm hoping you forget about that, too. I'm just saying I don't hate you no more, and now you're tolerable—just tolerable—to me. And I'm sorry for the way I been to you."

"I accept your apology, Anna, and now we're done with this. Right?"

Anna stared up at him. In the reflected moonlight that danced beautifully in his eyes, she saw only warmth and gentleness and sincerity. In that moment she knew, in spite of herself, that the young man standing before her was more than just tolerable.

"Right," she said.

"Did you finish reading *The Deerslayer*?"

Anna hesitated, wondering what that book could possibly have to do with what they were talking about. "Yes," she replied, "days ago."

"And were you happy with the ending?"

"Not a bit. It was just so…so sad. I cried and cried."

"Why's that?"

"Because Judith finally learned it's what's inside a man that counts—that's what made Natty Bumppo so good and strong. And for a fact she loved him, and I think he loved her back. So *she* begs *him* to marry her, but he can't because his gift is living in the forest with them Indians rather than with the white folks." Anna leaned closer and cupped her hand to her mouth as if about to reveal a great secret. "I say he shoulda taken the girl and lived in a nice little house someplace with a fireplace and had some babies."

"So," Stanley said, after his laughter subsided, "what are you reading now?"

"I'm about halfway into *The Last of the Mohicans*."

"Another great book, and the ending is—"

"Don't tell me!" Anna said, stamping her feet.

"I have an idea, though. When you come to the last five chapters, why don't we read them together?"

"Together?" Luke would be infuriated. In fact—Anna turned quickly back toward the house, scanning the veranda and windows. "I think I should say good night now." She started toward the house.

"Anna?"

The simple, pleading way he said her name felt so good to Anna. She stopped, but didn't turn around.

"Are you worried about Luke, that he'll be angry if he sees us talking and reading?"

Anna turned back toward Stanley. "He will. I know he will, and he'll say something mean, and maybe yell and carry on." Anna paused for a long moment, gazing up at Stanley, searching her heart for a small portion of Judith Hutter's strength. "But I'm his big sister, and I don't have to do as he says. He's getting taller and he's for sure stronger than me, but the way he's been lately, he just seems—small. Know what I mean?"

"I think I do."

"And as I said," Anna said, "I can't let his hatred have power over me. I ain't like that." Then, with a demure wave of her hand, she added, "Good night, Stanley. I'll think on me and you reading sometime."

CHAPTER 33

ANNA ENTERED THE BARN SHORTLY AFTER TWO O'CLOCK Wednesday afternoon, her stride quick and purposeful. Duke was gone, but the saddle still hung from its wooden peg inside the empty stall. Luke liked to ride bareback.

Anna knew where to find him. "Come on, Earl, let's ride down to the creek."

Anna took her time saddling Earl, and when she finally did mount and set out along the wagon lane toward Owl Creek, she allowed the large horse to walk at a slow, easy pace. It was a typical June day, hot, the air heavy and oppressive, with broken lowering clouds that told of thunderstorms later that afternoon or evening.

At the graveyard Anna dismounted and stood holding the reins. Aaron's grave and her father's memorial stone both stood as silent reminders of the twin tragedies that had brought with them anguish the likes of which she had never imagined. *The valley of the shadow of death*—she knew what that meant now. She also knew she had not conquered it—only the good Lord could do that. She had only endured. Still, the heaviness she had felt at first was gone, and she even found herself daring to imagine herself somewhat content, at peace. Almost, but not quite.

There was another trial yet to come.

She sat on the setting rock and closed her eyes. She prayed

for the strength to do what was needed, for the right words to say, that she wouldn't get angry but instead have a peaceable spirit so that she might speak true, loving words.

She stood and walked toward the gate in the low fence. "Thank you, Lord, for everything that's happened," she said aloud. "It's been real hard, and it still is, not having Papa and Aaron, but I really do mean that, because I think you brung Stanley here for something good. I was so bad to him. Please forgive my wicked thoughts and words. And please be with me now."

Anna climbed astride Earl and guided him back onto the lane. She paused under the shade of the arching oak. Yes, there was Duke grazing near the picnic spot by the creek. "Let's go, Earl."

Having a strong horse at full gallop beneath her always stirred Anna body and soul. It never failed to lift her spirits. After the short dash down the lane, Anna reined Earl to a halt by the stream and jumped down. "Hi, Luke."

"Hi." Luke was sitting on the bank of the creek, his legs dangling toward the slowly flowing water. His fishing pole was stuck into the ground, its line trailing limply in the stream's flow, while he occupied himself honing the gleaming blade of his large hunting knife on a smooth stone he had taken from the creek.

"Catch anything?"

"Nope. Nothing's biting today, but it's still better than being down the house—like it's become that Yankee's house."

"Oh, Luke, it ain't. It's still our house as much as ever."

"But he's always around, always with Willy, always making like he's a nice boy, always working so hard, pleasing Mama and all."

"Actually," Anna said, sitting down next to her brother and putting her arm around his shoulders, "that's what I want to talk to you about."

"The Yankee?"

"Yes—Stanley. Luke, I can't hate him anymore like you. I've made peace with him."

212

Luke turned his head slowly and looked at Anna. His eyes looked darker, colder, more bitter than ever. "You what?" Luke said.

"Luke, we've been taught not to hate anybody. I can't be Christian and hate Stanley. It ain't right and it gnaws away at my insides like something's in there trying to get out. So I done made up my mind to be decent to him."

"Decent? He don't deserve decent after what he done."

"Maybe, maybe not, but Mama's forgiven him and I can be decent anyway."

Luke flung the stone into the creek. He jumped up and jammed the knife into the sheath at his side.

Anna stood to face him.

"I know what he's about," Luke said. He began to pace back and forth along the creek bank. "He ain't got no family, so he's taking this one. Scheming his way onto this farm, then worming his way in, winning you people one by one, first Willy, then Mama—and the blacks just *love* him." Luke stopped just inches from his sister's face. *"And now you, Anna?"*

"'You people'? That's what we are to you?" Anna turned away from Luke's hot, heavy panting. "Stanley ain't like that, he ain't scheming and tricking us. All I seen is how good he is to Willy—*our brother*, Luke—and sure, he's obeying Mama and he's working hard every day, something you oughta be doing, too."

"A scheme, that's all it is." The disdain in Luke's voice was thick and heavy. "He'll get you all thinking how wonderful he is, and how this farm can't go on without him, and in the end, he'll throw you in the hog pen. That's what Yankees do."

"Stanley ain't that way. He's just a boy like you, Luke, but he ain't got no papa *or* mama. And he ain't a soldier neither, 'cause he can't fight. Sure, we all wish them Yankees would leave us alone and go back north, but Stanley's one Yankee we'll be thanking the Lord for when winter sets in."

"I can't believe you said that. That Yankee will be long gone by then, if I have anything to do with it."

Anna whirled to face Luke again. "Then I'll pray to God you don't, because Stanley Mitchell's a decent boy, and he speaks true, more than you, I might say."

"What makes you say that?"

Anna moved close so they were again face to face. "I've talked to him." And even as she spoke, Anna heard the note of pride in her words.

"You what?"

"Yes, Luke, terrible as you think it, I talked to Stanley Monday night."

Luke's eyes burned. His nostrils flared. His hands tightened into fists at his side.

"And besides that," Anna said, unable to keep the sneer on her face from coloring her words, "I come to tell you, me and Stanley, we'll be reading books sometimes—*together*."

"You can't," Luke screamed. "I forbid it!"

"You *forbid* it? Just who do you think you are?"

"The master of Matthews Farm, that's who. Papa and Aaron are dead, so now I'm the man of the house and you'll do as I say."

"Oh no, I won't! You're still my little brother."

The sudden blow to the side of her face stunned Anna. She reeled backward and fell to her knees. Her eyes closed. *He will not see me faint.* She willed her eyes open again.

Luke had hit her with the back of his hand—that much she had seen—and hard, with all of his force. She lifted her right hand to her cheek. It was already tender; a large welt would soon swell beneath her eye.

Anna closed her eyes again. *He will not see my tears.* Didn't he know she loved him? She had always protected him, and this is how he repaid her? And with the back of his hand? She clenched her fists tightly in front of her and fought the fury building inside her. When she had galloped over the hill just minutes before, she had never imagined that her brother might actually strike her. But the searing pain bore witness to what her beloved brother had just done. *No, he will not see my tears.*

Anna stood, faced her brother, and calmed herself. Rage and violence were all she saw in him now, and yet ever so slowly, she turned her head to the left. "Here's my other cheek, Luke, just like it says in the Bible. Would you like to hit me again?" She closed her eyes in anticipation of the second blow, but after several long seconds, nothing had happened. Anna turned her back on her brother and walked toward Earl. "Sin is lying at your door, Luke," she called back over her shoulder, "just like the Lord said to Cain."

Luke's voice came hard at her back. "But that Yankee ain't my brother, and I ain't his keeper."

Anna put her foot in the stirrup and mounted Earl. "But maybe he could be, if you'd let him." She reined Earl around and started him at a slow walk up the lane. Now she allowed the tears to flow; she dabbed at them with the cuff of her flannel shirtsleeve. A few moments later, Anna cast a look over her shoulder, and there was Luke, once again sitting on the creek bank sharpening his knife.

CHAPTER 34

DUKE AND EARL WERE RESTLESS IN THEIR STALLS, MORE SO than Lily and Penny. Thunder had rumbled for about two hours. Heavy bands of rain had swept over Matthews Hill, and the occasional brilliant flash and deafening crash of a nearby lightning strike made the two draft horses jump and snort.

"Look here, big fellow, Min's sent cornbread covered with molasses—your favorite. It's just a thunderstorm. Settle down, Duke." Stanley stroked the side of Duke's head gently. "There, big fellow, there. I'll be right back. I've got to go over here and see my girls."

"Your girls?"

Stanley spun around. Anna took off her large straw hat and shook the raindrops from it. He had seen the reddish-purple welt on her right cheek at supper the night before, but no one else had mentioned it, and he thought it best not to inquire. "Young lady, that's the second time you've crept up on me."

"It was easy, what with the storm, and how you're so busy talking to the animals. And I wasn't creeping!"

"You're right. So what brings you out here so early on such a dreary day?"

"I need to talk to you," Anna said, following Stanley across to the stalls of the mules. "You know, without certain eyes and ears around."

"About what?"

Anna watched Lily and Penny consume their treats. "Oh, this and that."

Stanley grabbed a pair of buckets from the wall. "They need water. There should be plenty in the cistern now."

"Let me help, and I can say what I got to say."

Stanley and Anna walked toward the rear doorway of the barn. As he had predicted, it was over half full of rainwater that had run off the roof of the barn. They filled both buckets and walked back inside.

"You ever ride a horse?" Anna asked.

"As a matter of fact, I have."

"You have? I thought you was a northern city boy."

"Ironton is a town, not really a city. My uncle never let me ride his horses. But Mr. Fremont, the headmaster at school, had this rule." Stanley hooked a thumb in his suspenders, threw out his chest, and stood tall, looking down his nose at Anna. "'A fine gentleman must also be an able horseman.'"

Anna's merry laughter filled the barn. "You? A fine gentleman?"

"Yet to be proven, miss. Mr. Fremont taught lessons in what he called the 'equestrian arts.' But I only had a few months of riding before my uncle took me out of school and put me to work in his factory."

Stanley emptied his bucket into Duke's water trough, and Anna dumped hers into Earl's.

"When I enlisted," Stanley said, as they walked back toward the cistern, "the regiment was called the Fifty-third Mounted Rifles, so I thought I was signing up for the cavalry. Obviously, it didn't turn out that way."

"Maybe God had another way for you."

"Maybe. Why did you ask if I could ride? I haven't even thought about trying to mount a horse with my leg the way it is."

"I been thinking about us reading, and I only got three more chapters before those last five like you said. I know the perfect place, but we got to ride a ways on Duke and Earl. The wagon's too slow, and it'll take too long getting there and back."

"Where is this place?"

"Down next the river, near Shiloh. There's a bunch of old Indian mounds on the bank, and I think that's the best place to read them last five chapters."

"That sounds wonderful, Anna. They need more hay, and I've been climbing that ladder every day. Always step up with the right leg, then bring up the left. But I just can't climb that last bit to the floor of the loft."

"Oh, I'll go up and throw it down."

Stanley watched with equal parts admiration and jealousy as Anna clambered quickly and gracefully up the vertical ladder. After several pitches with the fork, a pile of hay lay at the base of the ladder.

"What about Luke?" Stanley asked after Anna had climbed back down.

"I done went and talked to him."

"Did he do that?" Stanley reached forward and touched Anna's right cheek, just below the swelling. She didn't move away.

She nodded. "I was hoping you wouldn't notice."

"How could I not? I saw it at dinner last night, but I didn't want to ask." His voice was tender—but as he continued, it trembled with anger. "That boy needs to be taught a lesson he'll never forget."

"Please, don't be mad at Luke."

"I don't think that's possible." In fact, Stanley thought the best way to deal with Luke was to pin him to the wall of the barn with the hay fork.

"I didn't want to wait," Anna said, "so I went and told him me and you'd be talking by and by, and maybe reading books even. He got madder than a hornet's nest stuck with a stick, but all I can say is, amen, Lord, let it be. I hope that'll be the end of it."

Stanley took a deep breath and calmed himself. "Then for your sake, Anna, I will let it be."

Stanley and Anna walked slowly to the doorway of the barn. He looked up at the low, dark clouds. It was still raining, but the thunder and lightning was passing on, and the rain would soon end, and then, perhaps, the sun would shine brightly.

"Anna, I don't want to cause trouble between you and your brother."

"It ain't you that's making the trouble. Thought it was you before, but not now. Luke knows what's right and wrong. Been taught it all his life. Fact is, Luke's had a hot streak for a year or two. I think it started when him and Micah had a fight." Anna pointed toward the rear doorway. "Right there behind the barn. Luke started it, and he got the worst of it, so Papa didn't do nothing to Micah. Didn't say a word to Levi about it neither. Mama thought he'd grow out of it, but he ain't, just got worse since Papa and Aaron died."

Stanley wished he could draw her close, touch her cheek again, comfort her.

"He done his worst to me, Stanley, and if he leaves us be now, I say it's a small price."

"Did you speak to your mother about going to the Indian mounds?"

"Yes."

"And what does your mother think about you riding off with a Yankee to read?"

"She ain't pleased, but she ain't angry, either. And not because of you, Stanley, at least not much, because I think she likes you, in spite of you being a Yankee. She says she's more worried about us meeting up with bad men, and she thinks you won't be much good in a fight, so she says take Willy along, 'cause ain't nobody going to harm a blind boy."

Stanley laughed, pleased that Mrs. Matthews had given her blessing. "That's a very good idea. Willy will enjoy it, and of course, he will vouch that nothing unseemly occurred between this Yankee and his sister."

Anna didn't flinch. She held Stanley's gaze even as the color rose in her cheeks. "There's something else, Stanley, something I didn't tell Mama about."

"What's that?"

"I want you to show me where Aaron was found. I need to know the exact place."

Stanley studied her quietly for a moment. "You want to go to the battlefield, and you want me to..."

Anna's eyes suddenly were shiny, moist. She lowered her head and spoke softly. "Stanley." Her voice was barely audible above the patter of rain. "I *know* it's a hard thing I'm asking, and after how I treated you before—"

"Anna, look at me." Stanley's firm voice caused Anna to comply at once. "We agreed we were done with all that, and that old Anna is a fading memory. I hesitated only because I wish there was someone else who might take you there. But I also realize that, besides myself, only your mother and Levi know the place."

"So you won't do it?"

The shadowy terrors of that early April Sabbath surged through Stanley's mind as he looked down at the beautiful girl. He opened his mouth to decline, and to explain why he could not view that dreadful scene again. But welling tears in hopeful, pleading eyes stopped his words just as surely as if she had pressed her delicate fingers to his lips.

"Yes, Anna, I will show you everything. That mark on your cheek shows what you already did for me." Stanley's own eyes began to moisten a little. "It will be my solemn duty and honor to escort you, if you will help me up on one of these big fellows." He gestured at Duke and Earl. "Deal?"

Anna dried her tears. "Willy said you like to shake on things." She took his huge hand in her own. "Deal."

"So," Stanley said, not letting go of her hand, "when do you propose to make this visit to the Indian mounds?"

"This Saturday," Anna said. Her smile was radiant, despite the gloomy weather, and suddenly her face had come alive. She was smiling at him, with him, because of him, and it was all that Stanley had dreamed it might be. Before him stood the true Anna, the girl whose lovely eyes now spoke only warmth and softness and joy to Stanley's heart.

But in only a moment that vision of loveliness turned and splashed her way across the muddy yard to the house.

CHAPTER 35

I T WAS EXACTLY AS STANLEY REMEMBERED IT—THE BROAD, gently sloping hayfield bordered by woodland, the winding creek about thirty yards to the left of the lane, the shattered, splintered trees—except it was all so very green compared to two months before. The budding trees of April were now full and leafy. The grasses of the trampled, muddy hayfield, which lay to the right of the lane, had grown over the ravages of foot and hoof, of ball and shell, and but a week or two hence would likely be cut down by the sharp blade of the farmer's scythe.

Stanley drew Duke to a halt nearly halfway across the hayfield. Willy, who had ridden bareback on Earl behind Anna, took his sister's offered hand and slid off the mount's haunches. Then he went to hold Duke's bridle while Stanley slowly and carefully swung his left leg over and down to the ground. His leg throbbed from the long ride; he massaged it with both hands.

"How does it feel?" Anna asked. The broad brim of her hat had shielded her from the sun, but Stanley saw that her face appeared red and mottled; her eyes were already moist.

"None the worse," Stanley said, reaching up to release his cane from a leather strap on Duke's saddle. "Your brother was over here," he said, taking Anna by the arm to guide her toward the creek.

"No, Stanley." Anna pulled her arm free. "Tell us what happened to you first."

"Yes, tell us, Stanley," Willy said. "Tell me so I can see it."

"But I'd like to forget that terrible day." Stanley searched Anna's face. Her eyes pleaded her case, deep and rich in the full light of day, the green hues much more than mere hints.

"That day brung you to us." Anna's voice was low and steady. "If I'm to know you, I got to know how and why. So tell me. Show me. All of it."

"All right, Anna." Stanley bent close to the girl's ear. "For you."

Stanley turned reluctantly from the girl's innocent beauty toward his field of terror. "The grass was much shorter then. It was a clear, beautiful morning; the sun had just risen. The Fifty-third Ohio was camped in this field."

Stanley led Anna and Willy across the lane toward a low rise in the center of the large hayfield. He leaned on his cane and spoke in low, even tones, with Anna to his right and Willy to his left. "As near as I can tell, Company E camped about here. They said we wouldn't be attacked, but we were ordered to form a line of battle anyway. General Sherman and his staff came riding up that morning while my friend, Gilbert Goode, was boiling coffee. The general told our colonel that he still didn't think there was going to be a fight, but then the enemy came yelling out of those woods to the right and fired off a volley. The general's aide fell off his horse, dead, and General Sherman rode away as fast as he could."

"There's something down there by the trees," Anna said.

"What's it look like?" Willy asked.

"It looks like a mound of dirt," Stanley said. They walked toward the line of trees to get a better look. "Stop," he said. "No closer."

"It's a grave, isn't it?" Willy said.

"Looks like it," Anna said. "How'd you know?"

"I can smell it, but not much."

"It's about fifty feet wide, Willy," Stanley said, "and there's a small, wooden sign with the letters 'CSA.' There must be dozens of Confederates buried there."

"All together?"

"Yes, Willy, with no markers and no names—all unknown."

"So if Mama didn't find Aaron..."

"Yes, he would have—either here or some other place."

"Good thing Mama brung him home to bury him."

Anna looked at Stanley, her eyes again brimming. "Show me where you were."

Stanley turned to his left and walked back toward the center of the field. After a few minutes looking here and there, and walking back and forth, with a sharp nod of his head he finally settled on one particular spot.

"When the enemy came yelling from the woods, the entire regiment fired at once. It was our first battle—we'd only fired our muskets on drill before that—but we stopped them, and we reloaded as fast as we could and we fired again. But they came on again, and then Colonel Appler cried, 'Retreat! Retreat!' and ran back toward the creek. Many of our boys ran with him, but I stayed with my company. The officers who didn't run away tried to form a new line, right about here." Stanley drew a long, invisible line through the hayfield with his cane. "The command was given to fire at will, and it was just then that I felt a sharp pain in my left arm. I looked down and saw the blood."

Willy reached up and patted Stanley's left shoulder.

"Gilbert used both our kerchiefs to bind it tight. 'You're done,' he said, 'the surgeon's back by the church.' I couldn't lift and steady my rifle, so I was of no more use that day. The officers had told us to always face the enemy, even while retreating, and talk around the campfire was the worst thing that could ever happen to a soldier was getting shot in the back. So I tried to walk backward as I passed through our tents toward the rear, keeping my face toward the enemy, like I was told." Stanley lifted his cane to "arms-at-the-ready," as if he was carrying a rifle and hobbled backward a few steps.

"No more, Stanley," Anna said. "Can't have you falling."

Stanley about-faced and led Anna and Willy back toward the road near where they had left Duke and Earl. He stopped about twenty feet before reaching the road and tried to make his words sound matter-of-fact. "This is where I got shot in the chest."

Anna trembled visibly, but Stanley went on. "There were lots of tents out there, Willy, and I couldn't see much of the enemy, so I think it was a stray shot, but it knocked me on my back just the same. I thought I had been killed, so I just lay there, but a few minutes later our boys were getting it bad, and they were falling back. I had to move or find myself in the middle of it again."

Stanley led Anna and Willy across the road. "You see how the ground slopes down steeply for a few yards and then less so toward the creek? I thought the bank would protect me from the fire of the enemy, but that's also where the mule teams were being hitched, and the mules were very nervous because of all the firing going on. The officers didn't say one word about mules during drill, so I got too close and got kicked." Stanley pointed to the grass-covered earth near the bottom of the slope. "That's where I fell, and that's where I was when your brother found me."

"And that's where Mama found you," Anna said, her voice wavering.

"Yes." Stanley walked down to the place he had lain and sat down cautiously on the grass. Anna and Willy likewise sat down, the three facing one another in a close circle. "The fighting grew hotter and hotter," Stanley said, looking at Anna and Willy in turn. "For a while I was between the lines, with our boys across the creek and the Rebels up by the lane. A battery of our artillery was up on the ridge across the creek pounding away at them. Lead and iron filled the air and struck the ground all around me. A bullet hit the buckle of my belt and I knew I would soon die."

Stanley paused. He breathed deeply of the clean, fresh air, and let the breath out slowly.

Willy grabbed Stanley's hand. "What happened then?"

"Then...." Stanley's voice broke. His own eyes now welled with tears. "Then I cursed God."

Willy looked awestruck. "You did?"

"Yes, I did. I cursed God for every bad thing that ever happened in my miserable life and then I cursed him all the more for the miserable death I would soon suffer." Stanley lowered his head and closed his eyes. He brushed his shirtsleeve quickly across his face. "And then in all my cursing, I realized that I was speaking to a God I had never spoken to before, I guess because I was never convinced he was really there. And then I just...I just prayed. For the first time in my life, I think. 'Lord, help me!' was all I said. Again and again I cried out, not knowing for sure who or what I was praying to."

Stanley opened his eyes. Anna's tears flowed freely now and she made no attempt to conceal them. Willy dabbed at his own wide, unseeing eyes with his shirtsleeve.

"A few minutes later," Stanley went on, "our boys began to fall back again. The enemy advanced. More than once men stumbled over me in the rush, and several fell dead close by, and then a boy in a red-checked shirt and brown cloth jacket, and wearing a small, funny-looking straw hat, stopped and offered me a drink of water. Then he ran to the creek and filled my canteen."

"That was Aaron," Willy said. "God sent him."

"Maybe," Stanley said, "but *why* would God send him, and why did I live until your mama and Levi came? Why would God spare me and not someone like Aaron?"

Anna spoke quietly through her tears. "Mama and Papa told us ain't right to question what God done. Ain't that so, Willy?"

"Yep. I ain't asking why God saved you," Willy said, "but I'm glad he did, 'cause you been like another brother."

Anna laid her hand on Stanley's arm and smiled. "I see how

it pains you when you talk of it, and it pains me to hear it, but I had to know, Stanley. I had to know what sort you are, if you're what Luke says, or if you ain't."

"And?"

Anna's hand tightened on Stanley's arm. "You ain't what Luke says."

"So are you starting to think of me as a brother, too?"

"Oh." Anna lowered her eyes. Her fingers released their hold on him, but she did not remove her hand. "No," she said, looking at the ground, "I don't think I'd ever take you for a brother."

"Know what Shiloh means, Stanley?" Willy asked.

"Talk was when we got here that it meant 'place of peace.'"

"Yep. Strange thing so much killing here."

"Yes, very strange," Stanley said. He looked down at Anna's hand still resting on his arm, then covered it with his own. "Are we at peace?" he asked, once again lost in her bright eyes.

"Yes," Anna said. "That's a good word for it. Peace."

"Show us where Mama found Aaron," Willy said.

The three stood and walked toward the small, gently flowing creek. Willy splashed through the stream, but Anna stayed by Stanley's side as he felt his way slowly across.

"I first noticed him about midday," Stanley said. "He was by this large oak, facing toward the creek, and I knew he was the one who had filled my canteen."

Willy reached out both of his hands to touch the tree. Inch by inch, he moved around it, his fingers measuring its girth, sensing the texture of the bark, probing every fissure, every knob, and every hole and scar made by iron or lead within his reach.

Anna fell to her knees beside Stanley, exactly on the spot her brother had lain. For a time she remained quiet and still. Then she wept. Stanley lowered himself to his right knee and laid his cane on the ground before him. He put his right arm around her shoulders to comfort her and she leaned heavily against him; only his strength kept her from collapsing altogether. And when she trembled in her sorrow, her trembling ran through him; every weeping sob and shudder he felt, more than if they had been his own.

Willy came close, his face streaked with tears. "Thank you, Stanley. I can see it now."

Anna wiped her own face with her hands and looked up at Stanley. "Yes, thank you. You won't never know—"

Stanley enfolded both Anna and Willy in his strong arms. "But I do know."

CHAPTER 36

A NNA HAD ALWAYS ENJOYED THE RIDE TO THE INDIAN Mounds, but now it held as much sorrow as pleasure: The way led past Shiloh Church, or more precisely, the site upon which Shiloh Church had stood. Almost nothing was left of the simple log structure. Stanley remained astride Duke, but Anna and Willy dismounted. She took her brother by the hand and led him around the ruins, describing in great detail how what he had once known as the house of God was now only a pile of charred fragments.

About a mile up the Pittsburg-Corinth Road toward the landing, Anna turned Earl off onto a narrow trail. "This trail goes to the river," she called back over her shoulder to Stanley. "Almost missed it, what with the trees blasted and all. Stays on high ground and there's ravines right and left."

So much had changed since the last time Anna had ridden to the mounds. The signs of the recent battle surrounded them, and had since they'd neared Shiloh Branch—trees bearing wounds or shattered to splinters, devoid of greenery, dead. They passed the wreckage of war: broken-down wagons, discarded tents and clothing, the occasional spiked cannon. She looked right and left, half-expecting to see rotting, ravaged skeletons amid the woodlands and thickets. But she saw none, and the signs of warfare lessened as they neared the river.

Anna reined Earl to a halt beside a low flat-topped mound of earth. "That's the first mound," she said. "We walk from here." Anna took Willy by the hand and led the small procession toward a larger mound that lay bathed in sunshine about a hundred yards ahead. Beyond, an opening in the trees revealed the broad flow of the river.

"All I know about this place," she said, "old Mr. Chalmers told us when we was little. Used to be a village, hundreds of years ago maybe, and these smaller mounds was where the important Indians had their huts. That big mound is where we're going, and the chief had his hut on top, right over the river."

Anna and Stanley tied the horses to saplings near the base of the large grass-covered mound, which was perhaps ten feet high, almost square in shape, and its four sides were inclined at an angle to allow access to the summit from any direction.

Anna reached into Earl's saddlebag for her book. "Go on up and wait for us, Willy, and don't go straying near the edge. Can't have you toppling down and getting yourself hurt."

Anna reached for Stanley's hand to help him climb, but after only a step or two, the treacherous footing on the steep, grassy incline caused Stanley to let go of her hand.

"I'm sorry, Stanley, I forgot how steep this was."

"I think I can do it," he said, "and if I fall, at least the ground is soft." Using both his cane and his free hand, he pushed and clawed his way up the slope a few inches at a time. Finally, with one grunting, straining push, Stanley reached the top of the mound. Anna took his hand again and, after pausing to clean away as much torn grass and clinging earth as she could from his fingers, she led him toward the edge of the mound that overlooked the gently flowing waters of the Tennessee River.

"It's so quiet here now," Stanley said. "When my regiment arrived here, the steamboats were crowded up to the landing, officers were yelling orders above the sound of the engines, and steam whistles were blasting. That was Sunday, March 16th—almost three months ago, but it seems much longer."

"The war's almost killed this place," Anna said, her voice tight and snappish.

"I'm sorry about that."

"I know it ain't your fault, Stanley. You was just doing what you was told, and I'm trying hard not to hold any of it against you." She had seen the looks and heard some of the hateful words at meeting. Mama was trying her best to make light of it, but could folks hereabout ever allow themselves to think of Stanley as anything other than a stranger—or worse, an invader of their homeland?

"From here north is prob'ly all in Yankee hands," Anna added, "but I don't know about down Mis'sippi and 'Bama way, so I don't figure much trade's going up or down. I heard Mama and Levi talking about sending our goods halfway across the county to Selmer come harvest time, if it don't get better on the river, and that'll be a lot harder than bringing them to the landing here."

"You know I'll help," Stanley said.

Anna's reply was barely audible. "I know. If you're still here."

"So, Willy," Stanley said, mussing the boy's already unruly hair, "what do you think?"

"About what?"

"About me being here."

"I already told you, Stanley."

"Yes, but I think you should tell your sister."

"I think God brung Stanley here to help me and Mama and Levi, and it ain't no use talking about him being a Yankee no more."

"If Willy's right," Stanley said, "then I guess I'll be around a while longer."

Anna lowered her head to hide her smile. "We got to start

reading and head back home while it's still light." She offered the book to Stanley. "You read, at the bookmark."

The three sat near the edge of the mound facing the river. At first Willy was interested in Stanley's reading, from time to time asking a question or two that Stanley was glad to answer. The boy exclaimed in wonder when Stanley read of Hawkeye's skill with a rifle, but as Stanley began to read Magua's sly arguments before Chief Tamenund for regaining custody of the lovely Cora, Willy lost interest and was soon sleeping peacefully upon the grassy mound.

Anna moved closer to Stanley. She watched how his lips formed the words, how clearly he spoke them, how pleasant they were to her. She listened to every nuance, every inflection of his warm, low voice; she shut her eyes and allowed his words to draw the scenes upon her mind. Anna trembled at Tamenund's fateful judgment that doomed Cora to life with the despised Magua, and her stomach tightened uncomfortably when Stanley read how Hawkeye and the handsome young Delaware, Uncas, fought without success to save Cora.

When Stanley began to read of the final chase through the cave, Anna drew even closer. She laid her head against his shoulder and not only heard the words as he read, but also felt them resonate within him, within her. She opened her eyes and watched her own tears fall one by one on the sleeve of Stanley's shirt as he read about Cora's brutal murder and Uncas's death at the hands of the evil Magua.

Stanley closed the book and laid it on the grass. Anna's sniffles continued for several more minutes. "What do you think?" Stanley finally asked.

"Another sad ending," Anna said into her own shirtsleeve as she dried her tears.

"What about Cora and Uncas? He certainly was devoted to her. What if they'd both lived?"

"But she was white and he was Indian. It would never do."

"Ah, but I've heard of white men taking Indian women as wives."

"Yes, but—"

"That first camp meeting, Pastor Blackwell read something from the Bible that I can't forget. 'There is neither Jew nor Greek—'"

"'—there is neither bond nor free,'" Anna added, "'there is neither male nor female, ye are all one in Christ Jesus.' Yes, I've heard it before, but an Indian and a white woman?"

Stanley reached for Anna's hand. "So what do you think about north and south?"

Anna's eyes widened, but she didn't look away. "You mean what about a Yankee and a Rebel?"

"Yes. Is it possible for them to be one?"

The sincerity of Stanley's words was written in his eyes. Deepest pleasure filled her, light and warmth and joy such as she had never known. But then her stomach churned uneasily and a dreadful and powerful chill descended upon her.

Anna looked away at the river below, knowing her own brimming eyes would give her away. Then she slowly pulled her hand away from Stanley's. "I think it's time to wake up Willy."

CHAPTER 37

———

*T*HE THREE EMPTY CHAIRS AT THE SUPPER TABLE HAD SPOKEN to Luke clearly enough: His sister and brother had spent the entire afternoon in the company of that vile Yankee—and Mama had known all about it because their places weren't even set. She gave no hint of where they were or what they were doing, and when he'd tried to goad Li'l Davy to ask Mama about it, the boy just shook his head and took another bite. But the particulars didn't matter.

They had sneaked away right after dinner—Luke had seen them go. The interloper had been astride his Duke—no permission had been asked or given. Sure, that Yankee seemed pleasant and agreeable, but Luke knew better. What was wrong with everyone else? Why was he the only one who saw the truth?

They would have to return by nightfall. From where he now sat among the dark shadows of the veranda, it would be impossible for them to slip past him. Indeed, within twenty minutes of taking up his solitary vigil, he heard the soft clip-clop-clip-clop of hooves upon the lane.

Luke watched as the dark forms of Anna and Stanley rode slowly into the yard side by side. Duke and Earl stopped before the wide doorway of the barn. Willy slid quickly to the ground and shuffled toward the house. Anna dismounted and held Duke while Stanley maneuvered that crippled left leg over the horse's back and down to the ground. Anna reached out to steady the Yankee—she actually *touched* that Yankee! And not the simple, fleeting touch of a helping hand, either. Her hand lingered much too long on that Yankee's back before she walked into the barn and lit a pair of oil lamps.

Anna and Stanley led the horses into the barn. "You were right," Luke heard Stanley say, "walking them up the lane. They're not winded at all."

Luke stood and walked silently across the veranda, careful to avoid the several squeaking floorboards he knew would betray his presence. King George III had been eyeing him, and with Luke's first step in his direction, the cat jumped up and disappeared around the corner of the house. Luke crept across the yard to the barn, but he didn't peer inside; he knew what was going on. Instead, he crouched beside the doorway and listened for his opportunity.

"Take the bridle off first. Then put the halter on and tie Duke off." Anna knew what she was doing. Proper care of the two stallions after a long ride was important.

"Now the cinch. You need help with that saddle, Stanley?"

"No, Duke and I are good friends now, and besides, it should be the man who helps the lady with her saddle."

Luke heard the normal sounds of saddles and blankets being removed and stowed, the horses being rubbed down with cool, wet cloths, and their hair brushed smooth. Then Luke heard his sister telling that Yankee how to check each hoof to make sure no stones had been picked up. Didn't everybody know that? And through all the work, they chattered on and on about people with strange names, like Hawkeye and Cora and Uncas, a foreign language to Luke, who could make no sense at all of it; it might just as well have been Latin. And when they laughed together, he found nothing amusing enough to draw even a smile. Indeed, he found that the more banter that passed between his sister and that Yankee, the more his stomach roiled with disgust.

Luke peered around the corner of the doorway just in time to see Stanley lead Duke into his stall. "He's got plenty of water for the night," the Yankee said.

"Same here," Anna replied, "and they been eating grass all day, so they'll be good 'til morning."

Anna and Stanley closed and bolted the stall doors, almost in unison, and Luke found this annoying. Anna leaned back against the pillar between the two stalls and crossed her arms in front of her. Had either of them looked his way, Luke knew, he would have been clearly visible in the lamplight, but it was plain that they had eyes only for each other.

"Stanley, I need to ask you something before we go in."

Stanley turned to face Anna. "Anything."

"Way I heard it from Mama, you was well put back in Ohio, but you had a bad rearing and no churching to speak of. Even so, you ain't mad about any of it. Fact is, you're calm and still on the inside. And Luke's had good rearing and good churching, and like I said before, he's turned wicked and hates most everything, not just you. I'm just trying to sense it out, that's all."

Luke's ears burned, as did his eyes when he saw the Yankee smile at his sister, and all the more so when he saw how Anna's bright eyes gazed steadily at Stanley when he began to speak.

"When I lived in Ohio," he said, "I could have been like your brother. Looking back on it, I did hate my aunt and uncle, and I remember thinking how happy I would be if they died. I'm not proud of that, but how's a boy supposed to feel about not being wanted or cared for? And hearing them telling their friends how charitable they had been toward me? And how they had spared no expense for my schooling?"

Anna's gaze never left the Yankee's.

"But I've seen how your mother loved Aaron, and she loves Luke just the same, so I don't understand why he's so filled with hate and anger."

"He's likely still grieving over Aaron and Papa."

Stanley nodded. "As you are. But you aren't filled with hate. I used to think it was just me Luke hated, but it isn't. It's also the Jacksons, and I've seen how he treats your mother, and you, too, Anna." Stanley reached out and touched Anna's bruised right cheek. "If someone loved me the way your mama loves Luke, I would be happier than I've ever been."

Luke's hand closed on the hilt of the knife. He imagined how he would plunge the blade into the Yankee's chest, piercing his heart. The blood would gush out, the Yankee would fall to his knees, and Luke would see the light leave his eyes. But they were standing so close. How could he do what needed doing without hurting his sister?

Perhaps the Yankee's back. They were so enchanted with each other, he could sneak up and bury the knife to the hilt. But the Yankee was big, that was sure. And a strike to the back might not find his heart; it might kill him, but it might not. And Anna might see him as he approached...

"They kept an account of all they spent on me so I could pay back every penny," that Yankee droned on. "If I had stayed there, I probably would have become like them, and since they had no children of their own, I probably would have inherited their entire estate."

"You'd have been rich."

"But something told me that life was not for me, so I enlisted. On board the river steamer to Portsmouth, and then on the train to join the regiment in Jackson, I kept thinking that I now had a chance for a new life, a better life."

"So, is it better?"

"Yes."

"So what you thought was bad, you almost dying, maybe God was being good to you."

"Maybe. I've been turning that one over and over in my mind, but I haven't been able to figure out why God would want to be good to me."

"That's what grace is, Stanley." Anna took both of his hands in hers, and Luke clenched his teeth. "I been thinking," she said, "all the way home here from the mounds, about what you said, and I'm thinking it might could be. I mean the Yankee and Rebel part. Could be God brung you here to us, to help us, you know. And to me, too."

"You mean *for* you, Anna?"

The neck. Slitting the Yankee's throat would be very satisfying, but it would require too much care, and too much time. Still, a single quick slash at that boy's neck could well be deadly.

Anna's words came in a rush. "I'm saying that I'm still sorrowful over Aaron and Papa, and I'm mindful of them all the time, but I think I'm happier than I ever can recall. And I'm saying I think you're the reason." She paused for a moment, then went on more slowly. "And I'm saying I been thinking less and less on what should keep us apart."

Stanley cupped Anna's face in his hands and leaned down close. "You know," he said, "we've not been on speaking terms two months yet."

Laughter echoed throughout the barn.

"That's what I mean," Anna said, "about being happy."

Stanley and Anna grew very quiet then. They stood close, almost touching, looking at each other. Even in the soft lamplight Luke saw something powerful pass between them, and he hated it. *Fools! It can never be!*

"I will have to speak to your mother," Stanley said. "She has to give her permission if I'm to court you."

No! Every muscle in Luke's taut, wiry frame screamed against it.

Anna leaned even closer toward Stanley. Her voice was a hoarse whisper. "There's nothing I would like better. But I don't know if she will. I'm so afraid—my insides is all balled up 'cause I know it'll be real hard. Luke and lots of other folks hate you just 'cause you're a Yankee. But if it's God that brung you here, then I'll have to learn to leave all that to him."

Luke couldn't contain himself any longer. He leaped through the doorway. His raised blade glinted in the lamplight. In one swift motion he shoved Anna aside and thrust the hunting knife downward toward the side of the Yankee's neck. But pushing Anna away had thrown his balance off and caused the blade to miss its mark. The knife plunged into Stanley's chest, just below his left shoulder.

Stanley stumbled backward. Luke drew the knife out and raised it high again. An angry, piercing cry, like that of a grievously wounded animal filled the large barn. *Anna—you oughtn't to scream so. He's just a Yankee.*

And now there she was, wild-eyed, defiant, standing before him, shielding the Yankee, who had collapsed to the hay-strewn dirt floor. He tried to push her aside, but she stood firm.

"Stop, Luke!" she screamed. "Let him be!"

Luke dodged to the right, looking for an opening to strike again, but Anna blocked the way. Luke feigned right again, then back to the left, but his sister matched his every move.

Just as he gathered his strength to lunge yet again, firm hands gripped his upraised arm from behind. He whirled around and came face to face with Mama.

"What have you done, boy?" she asked, her voice a bare, hard whisper.

The knife, dripping with Stanley's blood, slipped from his fingers and fell to the hay-covered floor. Luke looked over his shoulder. Anna knelt beside the Yankee, leaning heavily upon his chest, her hands pressed together, blood seeping through her fingers—Yankee blood.

Luke had won. He was the victor and the Yankee was dying. There was no stopping it. He whooped with delight and ran out of the barn into the dark night.

CHAPTER 38

ANNA BRUSHED A STRAND OF STANLEY'S DARK HAIR AWAY from his face. "It's getting long, needs a cutting. I can do it, if you like. Do Willy's and Li'l Davy's all the time. Used to do Luke's too, but don't think he'll let me now."

She hadn't left Stanley's side, except for the occasional moment or two when she left him in Willy's care, since they had carried him up the stairs and laid him on the bed. There had been so much blood that she had thought he would die right there in the barn. All she had been able to do was press her hands tightly over the deep wound and watch his blood seep between her fingers, with every passing second tearing her heart slowly to pieces. An eternity had passed before Levi had stoked up the fire, heated a branding iron to red hot, and staunched the flow by searing the poor boy's flesh.

Stanley had been conscious throughout. His cries still echoed within her.

She sat on the edge of the bed, at Stanley's right side, gently stroking his flushed cheek. "You feel warm. A fever, I think —your hair's all sweaty." She took a cloth from the water basin beside the bed and, after she'd rinsed and wrung it, bathed Stanley's face with its coolness.

She kissed his forehead lightly. "Can't you please wake up?"

He's a blessing, Lord, a good and perfect gift from you. I shoulda seen that sooner.

"Your soft blue eyes—I ain't never seen nothing but fondness when you look at me. I was blind at first. It would sure be a blessing to see those eyes looking at me again."

Anna put the cloth aside and took Stanley's hand in hers.

"Here you are again, trying your best to die in our house. I weren't much good before, and I gave you more grief on top of it all—bless you for forgiving me. But I'm here now, and I ain't never leaving. Now, don't you go and leave me. You're *my* Stanley now."

Would you give him to me just to take him away so soon?

She pressed Stanley's hand against her face.

Has this all been for nothing? Will you allow evil to win? And have you just left Luke to his own reapings?

"I shoulda seen it. I knowed Luke was riled when I left him by the creek, but I thought he'd cool down. I thought him hitting me was the end of it, and I was happy about it. It's my fault he done what he did. I stuck that hornet's nest."

Have mercy and spare this good boy again, Lord.

"Wake up, my dear, dear boy," Anna said, kissing Stanley's hand again and again, tasting the salt of her own tears. "Don't die or I'll hate you forever. No, you know I wouldn't. Wake up so I can tell you real and true."

————

Stanley opened his eyes. The light coming through the window was the dim and diffused glimmer of evening.

He was alive.

His mind was clear, and there had been no recurrence of the horrible nightmare. The pain in his chest was sharp, constant, and powerful. And once again, his left arm was bound tightly. He didn't try to move it.

His right hand felt warm and damp. He turned his head.

Anna sat in the chair next to the bed. She had enfolded his hand in both of hers and leaned over the edge of the bed to rest her head upon them. Her face was turned away, but she appeared to be asleep. The dampness he'd felt came from her tears, and for an instant Stanley recalled the terrible river of tears he had heard in his dream. But Anna's tears were far different. Miss Don't Matter had wept for him—Stanley wanted to chuckle a little at that, but didn't—and each of her tears warmed Stanley through and through.

Slowly and carefully, so as not to wake Anna, he extracted his hand. He put it gently upon her head and began to stroke her hair lightly. Never before had he felt anything so soft and smooth. He had heard the saying "smooth as silk" from Aunt Bess, and although he had never touched any silk that he knew of, it could not have been any finer.

"My dearest Anna," Stanley whispered into the gathering gloom. "My Flower of the Woods."

"What's that you called me?"

Anna's soft voice startled Stanley. "You're awake?"

She raised her head and looked at him. "Ain't that what I should be asking you?"

"Yes, I'm awake. About ten minutes, I think."

Anna struck a match and lit the candle on the small table beside the bed. Then she sat on the edge of the bed and pressed the palm of her hand to Stanley's forehead. "What's that you called me?"

Stanley laughed softly. "It's from *The Deerslayer*. When the Hurons captured Hawkeye and were going to kill him, Judith marched into their camp in her best dress and boldly defended Hawkeye before Chief Rivenoak. Do you remember?"

Anna nodded slowly. Her eyes widened.

"The chief gave her the name Flower of the Woods because of her beauty and her bravery." Stanley marveled at how the candlelight highlighted the green hints in her eyes. "You reminded me of Judith last night in the barn."

"Which was it? The beauty or the bravery?"

"Both, of course."

"So I'm your Judith?"

Stanley thought Anna's eyes sparkled even more. "Well, no, but—"

"What was that other thing you called me?"

"I didn't know you heard that."

"I heard. You said 'my dearest Anna.' Do you really mean that, Stanley?"

Speak your heart, he had told Willy. Stanley reached for Anna's hand.

"Yes, if I may be so forward. I've never called anyone 'dear' or 'dearest,' but from the moment Willy told me your name, you have always been 'dearest Anna' to me."

"From the very first? And me being so ornery?" Anna shook her head slowly. "But I think I like it, your dearest Anna and not your Judith. Are you hurting much?"

"Yes, but it's all in the shoulder. I've had worse."

"I'm sorry, Stanley."

"What for, Anna?"

"For what Luke did to you and I couldn't stop it. I told him over and over to let you alone. But when that knife"—Anna took a deep, trembling breath—"when Luke stuck that knife in you, I felt it right here, too, like I been stabbed. And when that iron set your flesh all black and smoking? Oh, my...."

She raised Stanley's hand to her lips. "You spoke true to me, Stanley, so I'm going to speak true to you. That's when I knew how I'd feel if you died, or if you went away. And when you was asleep, I prayed God not to take you away."

Such sweet words Stanley had never imagined. "Then, dearest Anna, I shall pray the same. Now, since you mentioned it, what *are* my prospects for this life?"

Anna giggled quietly. "My, how nice you talk, even when you're laid up. When Mama was up here after she come home from meeting, she said the knife spilt lots of blood, but didn't cut nothing too important. Cut you two, maybe three inches deep and one wide. The wound was uncommon clean 'cause of the hot iron Levi used. And Aunt Min done a poultice up with herbs, marigold, I think, maybe comfrey and other stuff, don't know what all, but she says it helps with the festering and the swelling."

So Levi had saved Stanley a second time.

"And I'll tell you another thing Mama told me," Anna added. "We was talking and I told her you forgave me for hating you and wishing you dead, and she said, 'Many folks never forgive when they been done wrong, so I can see there's much you'd find likeable about this boy.'

"And I say Mama was right," Anna said, her joyous words matching her beautiful smile. "Oh, I clean forgot. You look hungry, and you ain't had nothing to eat since yesterday dinner. Let me just go downstairs and fix you something, and I'll be back in a couple of minutes."

Stanley lay in peaceful contentment, feeling the warmth of her tears and the softness of her hair, hearing her tender words, counting the moments.

CHAPTER 39

THE NEXT MORNING, WHEN BREAKFAST WAS DONE AND SHE had read Scripture and prayed for the day, Davina paused for a few moments, after the children were dismissed from the table, to offer up her own silent prayer for what she was about to do. Then she stood, went to the foot of the stairs, and with an audible sigh, began to ascend the twelve steps.

Stanley was sitting up on the bed. His eyes were bright and alert. "Good morning, Mrs. Matthews."

Davina tried to match Stanley's cheerfulness. "Good morning, Stanley. I've come to check on how you're doing." Davina held her palm to his forehead; his fever was down. The bandages that covered the healing poultice and held his left arm motionless were clean and white.

"I think I'm on the mend, Mrs. Matthews, but I didn't get much sleep last night."

"Oh, was the pain very bad?"

"Sometimes, but mostly it was just my own thoughts keeping me awake."

"Oh." *Thoughts about Luke, no doubt.* Davina sat in the chair beside the bed. "Min says that poultice is going to heal you up right fine and that we got to change it every second day. The pain should get less every day—tell me if it don't—and then it'll start itching, and when it does, we'll take the bandage off and all you'll be left with is an ugly scar—another one, I should say."

Stanley's soft laughter encouraged Davina to speak her mind. "That's a terrible thing my boy done to you, and I'm sorry."

Stanley seemed to be thinking it over. "Thank you, Mrs. Matthews, but it would be better if he was the one saying it."

"That's true enough. Stanley—I fear for my boy. Luke's had a hard time of it, losing his papa and his brother, and he used to be a sweet boy, near as sweet as Willy, and I pray every day that I'll see that sweetness in him again."

Stanley laid his head back on the pillow and stared at the rafters. "But a sweet boy doesn't stick a knife in someone who's done him no harm."

"That's true, too, Stanley, and I know that when you've gotten your strength back you could go after him, and hurt him real bad, if you want to. Maybe even kill him. And I don't doubt that if you'd known he was coming at you, you'd have killed him right there in the barn, but I thank God you didn't."

Davina leaned forward and gripped Stanley's right arm firmly just above the elbow, forcing him to look at her. "Stanley, I'm asking you to not go after him, not now and not ever. 'Vengeance is mine,' the Lord said, and I pray you'll leave this in his hands."

Stanley's only response was a single nod of his head so slight that had Davina's gaze wandered at all, she would have missed it.

"Me and Anna have talked, and I can see how she's taken with you, and how you done forgave her for being so mean to you at first. I was hoping you might find it within yourself to forgive Luke."

A faint smile formed on Stanley's face. Davina relaxed her hold on his arm.

"I'm glad you mentioned Anna, Mrs. Matthews," he said. "It's thoughts about both Luke and Anna that kept me awake much of the night."

Stanley paused long before finally saying, "Mrs. Matthews, I would like your permission to court Anna."

Davina's breath caught in her throat. She sat back in her chair and crossed her arms in front of her. "How can you ever—"

"Please, Mrs. Matthews, let me finish."

Davina stiffened and sat upright in her chair. Weeks ago, maybe just days ago, his direct tone would have offended her, but now she heard only an earnest plea. The serious look in his eyes confirmed it. "All right, I'm listening."

"During the night," Stanley said, "I thought it would be a grand gesture to forgive Luke, as you've just asked me to—and then use it to my advantage in winning your permission to court Anna. The Stanley you found on the battlefield that night might have done that. But I'm not that boy anymore."

Davina wanted to argue, but she had to admit that Stanley had proven the truth of that again and again. *If any man be in Christ, he is a new creature. Perhaps.*

"I'm not sure who I am anymore, or what I might become someday, but I do know that treating people like that would be wrong. I knew the Lord's Prayer before—said it every day in school. Now, I know I should forgive Luke. I'm willing to do that right now, with or without your permission."

"What about the other thing I asked?"

"You mean getting even with Luke?"

Davina nodded.

"That's got to go along with it, Mrs. Matthews. I can't say I'll forgive him and then try to get even. I admit that, during the night, I thought of a dozen ways to take my revenge, and some of them were very tempting. But my thoughts always came back to Anna."

Davina thought Stanley's eyes were brighter now, perhaps showing the faint trace of a tear. His voice thickened just a little.

"Whenever she looks at me, I see her happiness, but I also know that I'll always remind her of the terrible night you brought me here. I can't help that. She knows I couldn't have caused Aaron's death, but if Luke's blood is on my hands, that would always come between Anna and me, and I can't allow that to happen. Luke will never have anything to fear from me, and I'm willing to tell him that, too."

Thank you for hearing me, Lord. Davina could have asked for no more. She'd felt compassion for this boy from the start, but compassion is one thing, and love's another. She had told herself over and over that she couldn't feel love for this Yankee. She had even told him that once. Now the churning within her spoke louder than her words. Her own eyes began to moisten. "About my permission…"

"Please, Mrs. Matthews, don't decide now. All I ask is that you take time to think about my request. But now that I say that, it sounds like I'm trying to bargain with you again."

"Maybe," Davina said, her voice soft and wavering, "but just a little."

An hour later, Mrs. Matthews marched Luke upstairs to Stanley's room and stood behind him to prevent his escape. Luke slumped carelessly against the frame of the open door.

Stanley was sitting in the wooden chair next to the bed. Despite the sharp pain, his mind was clear. "Good morning, Luke."

Cold, tortured eyes stared back. "Whatdya want?"

Stanley fought the disgust he felt. He kept his voice gentle but firm. "Why did you try to kill me, Luke?"

"Ain't it obvious? You ain't gonna shame Anna. I won't have none of it."

"But I didn't—"

"Saw you myself, you touching her and carrying on, and if I didn't stop it, you woulda kissed her. I won't have none of it."

"I would never shame Anna in any way."

"I bet you're thinking to marry her."

"We haven't spoken of that yet."

"Yet? I knew it. I see it plain as day. It's all part of your plan. You horn your way in here, and then make everybody feel so sorry for you, and then it seems you're not such a bad sort, and they start liking you, and then you got my own sister going all sheep-eyed on you."

"That's enough, Luke," Mrs. Matthews said from behind her son, but her interruption only seemed to remind Luke of another point he needed to make.

"And you been working so hard," Luke added, "Mama can't do without you. For sure you're earning your keep, working away like one of them blacks. But like them blacks, you can't never be a Matthews. You think you can be one by marrying Anna? And you think you'll be master of this place? You must be crippled in the head and ain't no cane a help for that. Ain't never gonna happen. Mark my words. Try as you might, you'll never be a Matthews. Never!"

"You're right," Stanley said, his gentle tone now gone. "I'll always be Stanley Mitchell."

"Enough," Mrs. Matthews said again. She laid a hand on Luke's shoulder from behind; he shrugged it off.

"I ain't done," Luke said, never taking his dark eyes off Stanley. "You got me here, Mama. And now I'll say my piece." Luke crossed his arms defiantly and glared down at Stanley. "And so what now, Mr. *Yankee* Stanley Mitchell? You leaving for good? Or maybe you're fixing to get even with me?"

Stanley pursed his lips and shook his head. "No, Luke, I don't want to leave, but just so we're square on this point, I don't want to be master of this place, either. I don't think farming suits me. I asked your mother to bring you up here because I have something to say to you."

"Best get to it. I got stuff to do."

Stanley's neck muscles tensed at Luke's hostility. He wanted to voice his own pent-up contempt for the boy, but only peace between himself and Luke—hateful, angry Luke—could make a life with Anna on Matthews Hill possible. "I won't try to get even with you," Stanley said, his voice calm and steady. "Not now, not ever. You have nothing to fear from me, and I want your mother and Anna to know that, too."

"Yeah," Luke said, "more of the same. Just trying to make them like you more."

Stanley shook his head. "No. It would have been a simple thing to take you to pieces, and don't think I wasn't tempted to. I will defend myself if you try it again. But your blood would come between Anna and me, and *I will not allow that*. Do you understand what I'm saying?"

Luke didn't reply.

"And there's one other thing."

Luke snickered. "Get it over with."

"I also forgive you for hating me and for trying to kill me— not because I want to, but because I must. This must not stand between Anna and me either. I will also try not to think evil of you, and maybe someday you will come to believe that I am worthy of your sister."

"Never!" Luke shook his head in amazement and turned to face his mother. "You just don't see it. Ain't never gonna happen. Only cure is for him to leave—or die."

When Luke pushed past her, Mrs. Matthews made no move to stop him. He bounded down the steps and out of the house. With a shrug, she stepped into the room and sat on the edge of the bed so that she was face to face and eye to eye with Stanley.

A long moment passed. Neither moved. Neither blinked.

"You don't make it easy, do you?"

Stanley cocked his head a little to the side. "Mrs. Matthews?"

"You had me awake most of the night thinking of a score of reasons to say no." She spoke in a mildly scolding tone that, as she continued, softened and became the motherly voice Stanley had often heard her use with Willy. "The way you spoke to my boy just now, and the devoted way you are about my Anna? I just can't say no to you. But I can't say yes either."

Mrs. Matthews began to shake her head slowly from side to side, and Stanley thought his cause was lost.

"You're still so young," Mrs. Matthews added. "Still children. And the folks hereabouts? Their tongues will be set a-wagging for sure. But I will tell you this, Stanley. If your mother was alive, she'd be most pleased with the young man her boy's becoming. Thank you for what you done for my girl, taking her to Shiloh and all. She's come to life again, and I know you're the reason. So like I said, you don't make it easy." Her voice dropped to a whisper. "My dear, dear Ben, I wish you were here. You'd know what to do."

Mrs. Matthews stood and went to the door. Stanley wiped his eyes with the sleeve of his shirt. "I'll be praying and thinking on this a lot, Stanley, and then I got to leave it be in the Lord's hands."

CHAPTER 40

*L*UKE RODE DUKE AT A SLOW WALK PAST THE LARGE OAK beside the cemetery, his eyes fixed on the small white cross that marked Aaron's grave. Then Duke began to plod down the gentle slope toward the creek. Luke had thrown the saddle on his horse, something he didn't usually do for a short ride, and while he hadn't set out for a long ride, he was definitely looking for some remedy for the bitterness that rumbled within him.

Perhaps the creek—fishing had always helped his sullen moods pass. But even as he dismounted, Luke knew that today, he would find no relief in fishing. He laid his rod aside and stared down at the slow water. He knew every bend and pool of Owl Creek downstream to where it flowed into Snake Creek, but he had never followed the creek upstream, west and north all the way to its source.

Luke mounted Duke again and steered the horse at a slow walk along the narrow strip of untilled land that lay between the huge field of Indian corn and the creek. The corn ended at the Stantonville Road, as did the Matthews property. Luke crossed the road and continued riding along the creek.

Several miles farther and about an hour and a half later, little more than a trace remained of Owl Creek within deep woods. His route had skirted several fields, and Luke thought he could identify most of the owners, so he thought he knew generally where he was. He checked a nearby tree for telltale moss and lichens and then turned Duke northward. A few minutes later, they emerged from the woods and saw a narrow lane.

Now Luke knew exactly where he was. A few miles to the right lay Stantonville, and a few miles beyond that village, home. To the left lay Purdy, the county seat, where he had ridden that dreadful Monday, right after he had finished spading earth over Aaron's coffin, to fetch Dr. Comstock for that Yankee. Luke turned his mount toward Purdy.

The nerve. The impudence. That was a word Luke had read somewhere, the kind of word that Yankee would throw out just to see who he was smarter than. *And then he'd explain with even more big words, like we was all simple.* And the forgiving? What was that all about, but to impress Mama? It sure seemed a great success. He sure could speak good, that Yankee, had to give him that, like some lawyer or preacher. *Nope. I don't need forgiveness.*

He reined Duke off the road into a wheat field of many acres and kicked the horse to a gallop. Gopher holes were common in such fields, but Luke gave no thought to what could happen if Duke stumbled into one of those holes. Now Luke knew what he would do. The remedy would be found in Purdy.

That Yankee will never marry my Anna. He'll never be a brother to me. Never.

Duke was thoroughly winded when Luke galloped into the village. He reined up in front of the general store, jumped down, and tied Duke to a post next to the watering trough. Then he walked a few buildings down and entered the Kincaid Hotel.

A heavy, balding man with gray hair sat in the barroom, almost hidden at a corner table to the right of the door. Before him on the table was a bottle of rye whiskey and a half-full glass —just the sort of man you needed to sheriff a sleepy out-of-the-way county seat. He looked Luke up and down. "A few years shy of being lawful in here, boy."

Luke hated that word when it was used on him, especially

when Mama said it, and how she said it, always with a hint of belittling. He tried to look pleasant and keep his dark mood out of his words. "I'm just looking for LaVache, sir."

"Who's asking?"

"Luke Matthews, sir."

"Ben's boy?"

"Yes, sir."

The sheriff shook his head, causing his jowls to wobble like a rooster's wattle. "A shame when I heard about your pappy, and my sympathies about your brother. Now, who's this you're looking for?"

"Mr. LaVache, the slave trader."

"Oh, him. Seen him hereabouts, but I don't track his comings and goings, boy. What you want with him?"

"We got a—a thing going on down to Matthews Farm. A negro thing, sir."

"They causing a stir, are they, boy?"

"Uh, no sir." If the sheriff came calling, that would spoil everything. "Just something my mama needs to see LaVache about."

"Hey, Harv?" the sheriff called out to the barkeep, the only other person in the barroom. "Know where that slave trader LaVache is at?"

"No, but Al Dickson, down the general store, he oughta know."

Luke thanked the two men and walked back to the general store.

"Oh yes, Jean-Baptiste used to be reg'lar about his traveling," Mr. Dickson told Luke. "Said he liked folks to count on him showing up every now and again right reg'lar like. Come through here every six weeks or so, he would, and take a room down the Kincaid. Thursday night mostly, then he'd set out early Friday. But it ain't likely no more."

Luke's remedy began to slip away. "Why's that?"

254

"Ain't you heard? Memphis is gone to them Yankees, just like Corinth. And about ten days ago, a whole bunch of them Yankees marched up the railroad a few miles west of here and took Jackson up in Madison County. Just ain't good for business, young fella, least not Jean-Baptiste's kind."

"So he won't be passing through anymore?"

"Maybe, but not reg'lar no more. Got a note from him, I did, a week maybe ten days ago now. Yep, said he was moving his haitch-queue to Somerville—"

"Haitch-queue? What's that?"

"His headquarters, young fella." Mr. Dickson bent down and rummaged around under the counter. "Ah! Here it is." He straightened, waving a small sheet of elegant letter paper. "'Please note that recent events have compelled me to abandon Memphis and relocate my residence, at least temporarily, to Somerville. Please forward all correspondence to Hotel Fayette, Somerville. Will call soon to settle account.' You could leave him a note, young fella."

"How far's Somerville, Mr. Dickson?"

"It's between here and Memphis, two counties over west there."

Too far to ride, but a note might do. Simple. Easy. And LaVache might come any day to settle his account. Perhaps he could settle that Yankee's account, too. "What does it mean 'will call soon?'"

"Could be days, could be weeks. But he'll come by to pay what he owes. Jean-Baptiste is good that way."

Luke borrowed pen and paper from Mr. Dickson.

Dear Mr. LaVash,

Mama lied. That Yankee ben here all along and he ben making trouble. Gonna take this place for his, if sumbody dont stop it. He ben making frens with the blacks and talking like they gonna be free. Likely Mama will go soft and let them go, don't know when. And that Yankee ben chasing after my sister Anna and now shes gone soft on him and they ben thinking on being wed. It aint right. Tried to kill him myself but hes big and strong and it didn't take. Need help soon.

Luke Matthews

Luke smiled as he read his finished note—just the thing to get the slave trader's attention. What was more, some of it was even true, particularly the part about Anna. Within ten minutes Luke handed the shopkeeper the neatly folded note. "Could you see that Mr. LaVache gets this, Mr. Dickson?"

"Anything I should know about, young fella?"

Luke shook his head. "It's nothing, just a little business Mama needs him for."

Mr. Dickson found a small envelope and, after scrawling *J-B LaVache* on it, sealed the note inside. "Before you light out of here, is that your horse outside?"

"Yes, sir."

"Looks all tuckered out, all lathered like that. You musta been in a awful rush getting here." He handed Luke a newspaper from under the counter. "You know how to read?"

Luke nodded.

"Then you go out and read for a spell. You rest him good before setting out again, or you'll break him down for sure."

"Yes, Mr. Dickson."

"And that paper's a special one. Old news on the front, printed in Memphis like always. Then the Yankees came and the newspaper skedaddled to Grenada, down there in Mississippi, and that's where the new news on the back was printed. See that?" Mr. Dickson pointed to the top left corner of the page.

"That's kinda interesting, being printed in two places. Thanks, Mr. Dickson. I'll bring it back when I'm done."

Luke sat on the bench next to the door. The newspaper seemed full of bad news—an extensive account of the fall of

Corinth, a list of Confederate steamships destroyed during the fall of New Orleans, and a report that Cumberland Gap had fallen into Federal hands as well.

Luke turned the paper over and read of the fall of Memphis. He soon found himself trying to read through blurry, tear-filled eyes. It had taken a small fleet of Union gunboats just two hours to destroy or capture all but one of the Rebel vessels that defended the city. And when he read the short note from Commodore Davis to Mayor Park demanding surrender of the city, Luke could only shake his head in disgust.

The news from the east was little better. There had been a defeat near Richmond and there was a new commander, a man he had never heard of before—Robert E. Lee.

Duke was rested and watered now. Luke returned the newspaper to Mr. Dickson, then mounted and turned the horse toward home. He would stick to the roads and save his horse. The pace would be slow, but he would smile to himself all the way home, because within days, at most a few weeks, that Yankee would finally get what was coming to him, and Luke's life would get back to normal again.

It wasn't what he wanted, having to wait, but it would have to do. Still, it was something to hope for, like when you dropped a nicely wormed hook in Owl Creek. What a great day that would be when he wouldn't have to set eyes on that Yankee, always there in Papa's chair for breakfast, dinner, and supper. No more charming Mama, no more sweet-talking Anna, no more of them secretly looking at each other and meeting who knows where, no more book learning, no more taking his horse out, no more reading with Willy.

CHAPTER 41

_D_AVINA HAD BEEN IN THE CEMETERY FOR MORE THAN AN hour, at times rising from the setting rock to stretch her legs. Solitude here had calmed her often during the past couple of months. Ben's remains weren't within a hundred miles, but just touching his memorial brought him nearer. She had often poured out her heart to the Almighty with one hand on Ben's stone, and answers to her troubles usually became clear. But the clouds that had suddenly closed in Saturday night in the barn hadn't parted by Friday morning.

Her own Luke had tried to kill another boy, and it grieved Davina deeply to think that her own flesh could conceive of such a thing, let alone carry it out. Sure, Stanley was a Yankee, but he had proven time and again he was no enemy. He was a Yankee by an accident of birth more than anything. But could she pledge her daughter's hand to him? Could it ever be possible for a Yankee to find a home among them? She'd seen the way Anna and Stanley looked at each other and how easy they were together. It was clear where their relationship was headed. "I think I know just what you'd say if you were here," Davina whispered to herself.

"A man ain't what he is, but who he is," Ben had told her once shortly after they were married.

Davina had looked at him, her head tilted a little to the side. "Whatever do you mean?"

"What's on the outside is what he wants you to see, and that can be anything. But what's on the inside where nobody can see is who that man is for real."

Ben had lived by that creed, and that was why he came to have a great deal of respect for Levi. The slave worked hard, he had skills, and he always spoke the truth. Ben thought those three qualities were the most important for any man. And the more she thought about it, the more she knew that Ben would have come to respect Stanley Mitchell, perhaps even with growing fondness. And that's what made it all so hard.

Movement in the lane caused her to look up. Stanley was walking slowly past the cemetery. He carried a garden hoe and a bucket awkwardly in his right hand, while he tried to use the cane with his left. He winced with each slow, careful step.

"Stanley," Davina called out, "what have you been at this hot morning?"

He turned and approached the gate. "Just weeding the bean patch."

Davina stood and walked to the gate. "Oh, my poor boy, you look all done in." He was red in the face and dripping sweat.

"Yes, Mrs. Matthews. I was just going for more water."

"What? You're still mending. You shouldn'a been out in this heat at all. What made you think that was your job?"

"It needed doing and I thought I could do it, but it's harder than it looks." He set the hoe and bucket down beside the gate. "I think maybe I've had enough for today."

"No maybe about it. We've got Levi's bunch to do that work. You just come in here and set under the shade a spell and cool down." Davina held the gate open for him. "Then we'll go down the house. It's almost dinnertime."

Davina returned to her seat on the rock, and Stanley sat beside her. He took off his hat and mopped his brow with his kerchief.

His heavy breathing quieted. "'My poor boy.' You've said that to me several times, Mrs. Matthews."

"It's just a saying."

Stanley nodded slowly. "So it doesn't mean anything?"

The question made her a little uneasy. "No, it means I'm concerned about you, Stanley. You know I care for you."

"Why did you bring me here, Mrs. Matthews?"

"What kinda question is that?" Davina heard an edge of irritation in her own voice. "I done told you why—it was because I'm a Christian woman."

"It's just that I've been thinking. About my life before the army and my life now, and how your taking pity on me changed everything. Would you still have put me in your wagon if I hadn't—"

"Can any good come of that kinda talk?" Davina sighed deeply. Stanley deserved a better answer. "Perhaps we *should* talk of it. Truth be told, I'm glad now I brung you here—but I've wondered the same thing myself."

Davina took Stanley's large sweaty hand in her own. "'Thou shalt love thy neighbor as thyself.' That's what Jesus said. And then somebody asked him, 'Who is my neighbor?'"

"I've read that story."

"Well, Stanley, that story's been on my heart since I brung you here, and I been troubled by it. That Samaritan man helped the other out of love, not 'cause he had to."

"Why does that trouble you, Mrs. Matthews?"

"Well, I can't rightly say I was loving you when I brung you here. That Samaritan man—I shoulda been like him."

"But the Samaritan didn't find his own son dying, too," Stanley said, using the tail of his shirt to wipe his hickory cane up and down, removing a thin layer of dust from his morning exertions. "Your saving me was nothing *but* kindness and mercy, like Levi making this walking stick for me. And, Mrs. Matthews—I don't know how else to say this—when you say things like, 'my poor boy,' even though you think it's just something you say, when you say it to me, I feel...loved."

Davina felt her heart flip within her. She stole a glance sideways at Stanley. A tear, not just another droplet of sweat, slid down his face.

"But there's something else," Stanley went on, "something I didn't see coming—don't even know when it first happened. I tried not to—but the truth is—is it wrong of me to think of you as my own mother?"

Davina drew Stanley into a warm embrace. "There, there, my boy. It ain't wrong. Your feelings is your own, and can't nobody tell you what they should be."

Davina held him tightly for a few moments, fighting her own tears, and then released him. "When you talk like that, you tear at my heart, young man. I was thinking about my Ben when you come up, and I think he would have been quite fond of you. And the truth is, I've grown fond of you, too."

Stanley opened his mouth to speak, but Davina shook her head. "Let me tell you one more thing, Stanley," she said, struggling to steady her voice. "Did you hear the last thing Aaron told me before he died?"

"No, ma'am."

"He pointed at you and said, 'Woman, behold thy son.' Jesus said that to his mother from the cross. That night, I thought loving you as a son would be impossible, but it wasn't, not with God."

Stanley wiped his eyes with his shirtsleeve.

"You and Aaron would have got on well, I think. My heart tells me you should court my Anna, but my head keeps bringing up a host of reasons why it's impossible."

Stanley dabbed his eyes again and looked at Davina. "What reasons, Mrs. Matthews?" he asked, his tone innocent and inquisitive.

Davina stood and started for the gate. "Let's start walking

down the house." She picked up the bucket and the hoe. "I'll take these so you just have to worry about your walking."

They walked slowly down the lane side by side. "I'm wondering about your prospects," she said. "A boy setting out to court a girl, he's got to have prospects. I'm concerned about your lame leg. What kinda prospects you got for keeping a family?"

Stanley chuckled a little. "It's only been since coming here I've been thinking that I might have a life to live, so I haven't thought much about it. I do like teaching Willy, though, and I love books, so perhaps I should become a schoolteacher."

"Hmmm. Lord knows we need good teachers hereabouts. You'd need to go to university. Up north, prob'ly."

"No, ma'am, there's nothing for me there. I feel like I'm part of a family here, and I don't want to go away, not for a long time anyway, and not unless you wish it, Mrs. Matthews."

"I don't wish it, Stanley, not anymore. A college in Nashville, after the war, or maybe down Mississippi way." Davina turned toward Stanley. "What about the army, Stanley? Don't you need to put things right? And what would they think of you living here in Tennessee?"

Stanley frowned. "I haven't thought much about that either, Mrs. Matthews. Maybe I just didn't want to."

"Your fighting days are done. Maybe you *could* get a discharge. But how would you go about it?"

"I don't know, Mrs. Matthews."

"Your army's just down the road a dozen miles or so. Maybe we could…" But Davina didn't know any more than Stanley did about it. "Trust the Lord with that, Stanley. I just wouldn't want them to think you're a deserter, and I wouldn't want my daughter getting too fond of one, either."

Stanley nodded. "I agree, Mrs. Matthews, Anna deserves better."

"And there's Luke. How would he be with you taking up with Anna and all? There'd never be peace in this house."

"I can only promise you that I will try to be as peaceable with Luke as I can, for Anna's sake. And yours, of course."

"I do hope that's enough." Even as she spoke Davina doubted it would be.

"Anything else?" Stanley asked.

"Yes, one more thing. Scripture says, 'Be ye not unequally yoked together with unbelievers.' Do you know what that means?"

Stanley stopped and looked at Davina. "You want Anna to marry a Christian man."

"Indeed I do. Are you a Christian, Stanley?"

"I think I am, sometimes, but I can't say for sure. I've been reading the Bible more than just with Willy and the Jacksons, and I understand a lot of it, but some of it just doesn't make sense."

"Such as?"

Stanley resumed his slow pace down the lane. "Well, whenever you pray, you say, 'Our heavenly Father,' like the Lord's Prayer."

"God *is* our Father. When we believe in Jesus he makes us his children."

"Levi prays the same way. Is God their Father, too?"

"Of course he is."

"Then it seems to me that Levi and Min are your brother and sister."

Davina let go of Stanley's arm and turned to face him in the middle of the lane. "What are you trying to say, Stanley? We love the Jacksons."

"Like neighbors?"

"No! Like they're part of our family. Ain't that obvious to you? We give them food and shelter and clothing, and if one of them is sick, we send for the doctor, just like we done for our own —and for you, I might add. And we never beat them, never ever!"

"But are they free, Mrs. Matthews?"

"You know they ain't."

Stanley turned down the lane again.

Davina quickly caught up. "Ben and me got Levi and Min baptized as soon as a preacher came round to do it, and all of their babes, too."

"But what I don't understand, Mrs. Matthews, is how some Christians can keep other Christians as slaves. It seems that whites and blacks are the same before God in heaven, but not here on earth."

Davina felt the color rise in her face. "It's been this way since forever, the blacks working for the whites. You think we oughta change the way we do things?"

"That's not for me to say." Stanley stopped at the gate to the farmyard. He looked down at Davina, his gaze direct and earnest. "A little while ago a Tennessee woman said she was fond of a Yankee boy. I think that could have come only from God, and I believe you when you say the Jacksons are like family to you. But I have one more question. Is it true that you could sell any of them at any time?"

The gentle way he spoke took Davina unawares. "Oh my." Davina closed her eyes for a few moments before she replied. "I think you understand a whole lot more than you let on, and it scares me some. I never would sell any of them."

"But could you?"

Davina looked down. "Yes."

"I couldn't live like that—always worrying about crops failing, and maybe being sold to pay the debts."

It seemed to Davina this boy wouldn't stop until her entire world was turned inside out. And it irritated her. "I said I never would, and you can believe that, too. And need I remind you that you're still a guest in my house?"

"Ma'am, I remind myself of that many times each day, and I thank you for it, but you could still send me away with only a word, just like the Jacksons."

Davina stared up at Stanley for a long, painful moment. Then she lowered her head and shook it slowly from side to side. She had felt so full of emotion when he told her he thought of her as his mother. And she *did* love him, almost like one of her own. The tall Yankee boy was right, and it troubled her deeply.

She turned toward the house. "You do make it so very hard," she said back over her shoulder. "What am I going to do with you?"

CHAPTER 42

*L*AVACHE AWOKE EARLY. AFTER WASHING AND DRESSING, he retrieved a small leather pouch from his satchel and took his gun belt from the back of the straight-back chair where it had hung untouched for the last two weeks. Then he crossed the small room to the table by the window and sat down.

It was a familiar ritual, one he always performed with the utmost care and never rushed. He slid each of his Remington 1858 pistols from their black, silver-studded holsters and laid them on the table. Then he opened the leather pouch and removed a box of cartridges, a box of caps, and two extra cylinders.

LaVache removed the cylinder of the first pistol and held the gun up to the early morning light and inspected the barrel and the firing mechanism. Then he checked the six chambers of the cylinder. Each chamber held a powder-and-ball cartridge. At the rear of each chamber was an unfired percussion cap. He reinserted the cylinder into the pistol and, using the loading lever, checked that each ball was seated properly. Then he cocked the hammer and spun the cylinder.

Satisfied, LaVache removed the cylinder again, laid it on the table beside the holsters, and inserted one of the extra cylinders. Using the lever again, he pressed six fresh cartridges into the chambers and placed a new cap on each of the studs.

LaVache repeated the entire process with the second revolver

—first checking the loads of the cylinder before removing it, then loading the extra cylinder with fresh ammunition. When he was done, he strapped the pistols to his hips and slipped on his frock coat. One of the extra cylinders went in the left pocket of the coat, the other in the right. If pressed, he could now get off twenty-four well-aimed shots in under a minute.

After breakfasting at the Fayette, LaVache walked down the street to the livery. His wagon was almost unrecognizable. Chet Adams had painted it green, a color LaVache hated, and given it only a single coat. In places, remnants of old black pigment showed through the green, creating a hideous, mottled appearance. Even so, LaVache grunted with satisfaction when he saw it. Even in brilliant sunlight, no trace of the gold lettering he had taken such pride in remained.

Chet had also installed four large wooden hoops over the top of the wagon and draped an old piece of canvas over the hoops to cover the wagon.

"I told you to use new canvas, Chet," LaVache said. "I don't want any holes to let the rain in."

"It's new, Jean-Baptiste," Chet said, smiling with obvious pleasure. "You also said you wanted it to look like a regular farm wagon, so I had Mildred sew them patches on, and then I mixed up some turpentine with some black soot and just splattered it with a brush. Looks kinda like mildew, don't it?"

"It looks like it's years old, Chet. Good work." LaVache looked inside the wagon. The bed was covered with a thick layer of straw. "What's that for?"

"I laid them chains on the floor and covered them up. Shouldn't be nary a rattle."

"That was good thinking, too, Chester."

Chet showed LaVache the hidden compartment he'd built on the underside of the wagon. It was built down the center of the wagon, about three feet in length and one wide. The end facing the rear of the wagon was hinged. A heavy hasp and lock secured it.

"Here's the key," Chet said. "Best not lose it, be hard to get another."

LaVache gave Chet an extra twenty dollars and the two men shook hands.

LaVache arrived at the bank a few minutes after eight o'clock. Ten minutes later, he threw a small sack under the seat of his wagon, climbed aboard, and drove out of Somerville toward the east. As soon as he was sure he was unseen, LaVache pulled the rig to the side of the road.

He removed his gun belt and placed one of the pistols under the seat—just in case. Then he crawled under the wagon and stowed all of his Confederate dollars, save for a few hundred he would need for expenses, within the hidden compartment, along with his gun belt and the second pistol.

An easy drive would bring him to Bolivar by tomorrow noon, Selmer by Wednesday evening, and Purdy on Thursday. He had accounts with shopkeepers in those three towns, and he meant to square every account before leaving Tennessee, perhaps forever.

CHAPTER 43

TUESDAY EVENING AFTER SUPPER, ANNA AND STANLEY SADdled Duke and Earl. Though still warm and humid, it was cooler and more refreshing outside than inside the house. This quiet time at the end of a hot summer's day had often found Anna riding along the lanes and through the fields of Matthews Hill. Much to her surprise, Luke hadn't so much as scowled when he heard their plans for the evening.

"We'll follow the fence line," she told Stanley. "Maybe a half hour to go all around the pastures, if you're up to it."

"I'm feeling much better, thank you. Min says only two more days with the poultice. It itches a lot sometimes, and I can't tell if it's the stuff she puts in it or the healing. So I can ride, but I don't think I'll be spending any time at the wood pile just yet."

As if to demonstrate his improving health, Stanley offered his hand to help her climb aboard Earl, and then mounted Duke on his own.

They rode slowly side by side and in silence to the northwest corner of the fence. Anna turned Earl so she faced Stanley. "Mama was all knotted up about giving you permission to court me, you know. She's been fretting and sighing and praying for a week like I never seen, and she been tossing all night too. And then she said you and her talked on Friday, and then this morning she said it was all right. I'm kinda curious what you said to her."

"I'm curious, too. At the end of our talk she was rather upset with me, and I thought I was done for sure."

Anna sat staring at Stanley, waiting for him to say more.

"Maybe it was the way we talked," he said finally. "Like a real mother and son would. At least that's how I think of it."

Anna was stunned. She had hoped, even prayed, that Mama would find a place in her heart for Stanley, and she dearly wished to believe it.

When she found her voice it was soft and a little shaky. "What do you mean?"

"Well, Anna, she spoke to me about things a real mother would talk to her son about—she even said she had grown quite fond of me. She told me I should try to get a discharge from the army so I can't be called a deserter."

"Mama told me that part. At first I was mad about it, but it prob'ly needs doing. I can't help being afraid for you."

"So am I a little, but I think I need to be finished with that if I'm to live here."

Anna didn't miss Stanley's meaning.

"And there's one more thing," he said. "I listened—or at least I think and hope I did—I listened to your mother like a son would. And spoke to her that way, too."

"What way do you mean?"

"With respect—and love, I think. I do know that I love your mother, and no matter what happens between you and me, Anna, I will always love her. For everything she's done for me. And for who she is."

The last tattered remnants of the misery clouds that had hung over Anna's life for the last several months suddenly vanished. As they turned without another word and rode along the fence line at the western edge of the pastureland, Anna felt nothing but peace and contentment, and such joy as she had given up all hope of knowing in this life.

She halted Earl again at the southwest corner post. "You said Mama was upset. Why?"

"Maybe you should ask her that."

"But I'd like to hear it from you, Stanley," she said, with a hint of mischief.

Anna sat motionless as Stanley recounted how he had talked with Mama about what it meant to be a Christian—and about the Jacksons. The more he talked, the more Anna knew why her mother had been upset.

"Why'd you ever speak to Mama like that?"

Stanley leaned forward, both hands on the pommel. "Maybe because a white woman and a black man took equal parts in saving my life, and when your mama and Levi carried me to the wagon, I didn't care that one of the shoulders I leaned on was white and the other black."

Anna gazed steadily at Stanley. His eyes seemed to reach out for her, to capture her, to plead with her.

"I used to think of the Jacksons as just simple, hard-working folks," he went on, "but very different from me, strange even. But now I think of them more like family, an uncle and aunt maybe, with a bunch of cousins, and I began to think how I would feel if I was a slave."

Anna thought she knew what Stanley was going to say next. She shifted uncomfortably in the saddle. "It'll never work," she said, shaking her head vigorously.

"Why not?"

"Just ain't practical. Every body's got its place, some to be masters and some servants. It's the natural way of things."

"It's *not* natural, I say. It's tradition. Your mother said it's the way things have always been. Down here maybe. But there are lots of freed blacks up north. Some of them have their own businesses and have become very rich." Stanley stroked Duke's neck, then looked at Anna again. "Wow!"

"What?"

"Your eyes are beautiful when you get fired up, facing the setting sun the way you are."

"You're just trying to change the subject."

"No, it's true. I've never seen eyes like yours. They have that deep brown ring around the black center and then a ring of grayish green around the outside, and when you get your blood up, the green parts really shine."

"Couple hundred years ago these eyes mighta got me hung for a witch."

"You *are* bewitching."

"You're just being stupid now. If you weren't already hurting, I'd—you're trying to make me forget what we was talking about!"

"No, Anna, I'm just telling the girl I'm courting, with her mama's permission by the way, that I would be a happy man indeed to see her enchanting eyes for the rest of my days."

"Oh." Anna felt a deep flush redden her face. "Fine, sweet words. What can a girl say, except… except…how would we live without Levi and his bunch? Git, Earl!" And with a quick flick of the reins she galloped down the fence line.

Stanley caught up with her at the next corner post. "And what about the farm?" she asked. "Who'd do all the work?"

"This is their home, too. They don't know anywhere else. Don't you think they would stay, and work all the harder if they were free rather than slave?"

"You make it hard, you know."

"Your mother said the same thing. But think for a minute, Anna. If you were a slave, what would make you happy?"

Anna's gaze dropped to the reins in her hands; her grip tightened; she watched her knuckles whiten.

"What would make you sad, Anna?"

Stanley's words were soft, but their meaning was hard upon her ears.

"What would you hope for?"

How she wished he would stop.

"What would be your greatest fear?"

Question after question, and she had no answers.

She couldn't hold back the tears, and then Stanley was standing next to Earl, reaching up, helping her down, gathering her into his arms, speaking not a word until her sobs subsided and he had dried every tear.

"I'm sorry," Anna said. "Don't know what came over me."

He brushed a strand of her hair away from her face. "It's almost dark. We should head back. After we take care of Duke and Earl, I'm going over to the Jacksons' cabin to read Scripture. Would you like to come with me?"

Never once had Anna wanted to visit that small cabin in the woods. Now she just needed time to think. "You ain't letting go of this, are you?"

Anna remounted and let Earl set his own pace as they rode toward the barn in silence. She'd said it to herself a hundred times in the last weeks—*he always makes it so hard*. But that was Stanley: All that was good and decent and strong in him made everything else so hard. But those things also drew her closer to him every day.

"Yes, I'll go with you, Stanley," she said, after they had dismounted and were walking Duke and Earl into the barn. "But only to keep them hogs off you."

CHAPTER 44

———·——

*S*HORTLY AFTER THREE O'CLOCK IN THE AFTERNOON OF Thursday, June 26, LaVache drew his wagon to a halt at the south end of Courthouse Square in Purdy. The square was the town's most unique feature. It resembled the Metairie horse track he had visited on several occasions when business took him downriver to New Orleans—an oval about half a mile long and a hundred yards across.

Only a month before, on his last visit to Purdy, he had halted his team at exactly this same place. He had checked his pocket watch and the moment the second hand struck twelve, he had given the whip. As he had often done, he raced up the eastern side of the square, past the McNairy County Courthouse, the Masonic Lodge, and the cluster of businesses that lined the street. Then he had driven the team hard around the turn at the north end and sped down the western side of the square. In a cloud of dust he'd pulled up in front of the Kincaid Hotel, near the south end of the square. One minute and thirty-four seconds to cover three fourths of a mile—almost thirty miles an hour. His previous best had been a minute forty.

LaVache had always loved making a grand entrance, but those days, he feared, were gone forever. He spoke a soft "Gid-dap" and turned the two chestnuts toward the western side of the square, the shortest route to the livery that was just a short walk from the Kincaid.

At the general store, Alfred Dickson jumped from his seat behind the counter the moment LaVache entered. "Jean-Baptiste, it's good to see you again. Got your note and got one for you, too. From the Matthews boy down other side of Stantonville."

LaVache opened the sealed envelope and read the note. Then he refolded the paper slowly and replaced it in the envelope. Without looking, he absently slid the envelope into the pocket of his trousers.

A woman—a good southern woman—had lied to him to protect a Yankee. He had heard of slave uprisings in other places, but never in any of his counties. And the girl? As the Matthews boy had said, that just wasn't right.

"Something wrong down there?" Dickson asked.

"Nothing that can't be put right tomorrow," LaVache said. "I need supplies, though—feed for the horses, food for me. My usual kit should do, but I'll need enough for a week, and throw in a lamp and some oil. I'll pick it up first thing and settle my account."

That evening, LaVache took his supper at the Kincaid, but the bar was entirely too quiet for him. It drew its clientele from among the more prosperous citizens of Purdy: the lawyers, the doctors, and the shopkeepers, some of them Union people. After sundown he walked up the western side of the square to Turkey Jack's Saloon. No Unionist would ever set foot in the place for fear of his life.

He stepped up to the bar and ordered a bottle of whiskey with three glasses. "I'm looking to hire two men for a day's work tomorrow," he told the barkeep. "They must be loyal to the cause, good horsemen, and handy with a pistol."

"Most of these men would fit the bill," the barkeep said, "but there are two of Forrest's men that come in about this time. Take a table and I'll send them over."

Shortly after nine o'clock, two men entered the saloon. LaVache had seen them around town on previous occasions, but he had never had any dealings with them. The barkeep spoke briefly with them and pointed in LaVache's direction. LaVache poured four fingers in each glass as the two men ambled across the room.

The slightly taller and thinner of the two said, "I know you. You're that slave trader from Memphis." He grabbed LaVache's hand. "Name's Jim Dillon. Just call me Dill. This here's Jim Tyson."

"Jean-Baptiste LaVache. Please sit."

The two men sat and lifted their glasses. "Thanks, mister," Tyson said. "Earl says you got a job for us."

LaVache nodded. "Tomorrow, if you're right for it." Dill and Tyson appeared to be in their late twenties or early thirties, and both smelled heavily of horse. "How is it you boys aren't off fighting in the war?"

Dill and Tyson looked at each other. "I guess we can trust you, Mr. LaVache," Dill said, "given your line of work and all. You might say we scout the scouts."

"You what?"

The two men laughed. "There's a lot of Union folks in McNairy, Mr. LaVache." Dill took another drink of the whiskey. "One's the richest man in town, Mr. Hurst. In prison for a traitor in Nashville he was, until the Yankees took it. Now he's getting up a mounted band of scouts, a militia kinda, and they go out scouting for the Yankees. Me and Ty, we sorta keep an eye on them for Colonel Forrest."

A local band of armed Unionist militia was something he hadn't planned on. "So where is Hurst now?" LaVache asked.

"Don't rightly know," Tyson said. "We thought they was riding north to meet the Yankees in Jackson, but they gave us the slip. That's why we're in town—trying to pick up the scent again."

LaVache took a sip of his whiskey. "Then I take it you boys won't mind helping me deal with a little trouble tomorrow?"

"What kinda trouble, Mr. LaVache?" Tyson asked.

"Yankee kind. I know where there's a Yankee that's been holed up for almost three months. You interested? Twenty apiece for the day."

Dill and Tyson nodded eagerly.

"All right, then," LaVache said, "here's how I see it."

CHAPTER 45

*I*T WASN'T THE SORT OF DAY ANNA HAD HOPED AND PRAYED for. No sunlight beamed through the window, and it had rained heavily overnight. As she dressed for breakfast, she couldn't help thinking that her plans for the day were ruined. The trees were still dripping; the clouds still hung heavy and low. It looked as if the rain might start up again at any moment.

"It ain't normal," Mama had said the evening before. "The boy should be the one asking the girl to a picnic."

"But you know there ain't nothing normal about me and Stanley, Mama."

Mama had laughed at that. "Go ahead, girl. In the morning tell Min you'll need a basket."

Stanley was delighted when Anna suggested they have a midday picnic down at Owl Creek. By noon, the day had brightened. The clouds had parted in places, and the late June sun was beginning to shine through. The morning had been cool and damp; the afternoon promised to be hot and oppressive.

After washing at the well and going upstairs to put on a clean shirt, Stanley met Anna on the veranda by the door to the larder. On her arm she carried a wicker basket filled with delicious food Min had prepared for them. Hand in hand, they strolled up the lane toward the crest of Matthews Hill.

Anna gave Stanley's hand a small tug when they came abreast of the graveyard. "I think you and Aaron woulda got on well."

"Would you like to stop, Anna?"

"No, not today. It's just something I been thinking about." And sometimes those thoughts saddened her, but only sometimes. "So you're going to Corinth with Levi tomorrow?"

"Yes. Leaving at first light."

"I told you what I think about it. The army might not let you out, even with your second wounding."

Stanley shrugged. "It's a chance I have to take."

The sweet potato field was lush and green, and Anna remembered Stanley's part in that. The fields, the house, the barn—they would all seem so empty without him. "But if they keep you," she said, "I won't see you for maybe a long time. And what if you're killed? I hate this horrible war, always pulling people apart."

They walked in silence the last fifty yards to the creek. Anna removed a neatly folded woolen blanket from the basket. Stanley helped her lay it upon the still-damp grass. Then they laid a tablecloth about six feet square on top of the blanket.

"Your mama and Levi, and Willy, too, in his way, have told me over and over to trust God," Stanley said. "I guess I have to. I don't have any choice."

"It's not just you, Stanley, it's *we*—me and you. *We* don't have any choice."

Stanley took both of Anna's hands in his and blessed the meal, just as he had heard Mrs. Matthews and Levi do many times. Then he asked God to help them trust him, no matter what happened tomorrow.

The first plate Anna removed from the basket held several eggs, sliced in half, the centers of which contained a creamy yellow filling.

Stanley took a small bite. "That's wonderful," he said. "I've never had anything like it." As he finished the first, he reached for another and crammed it into his mouth.

"Min calls them the devil's eggs 'cause they're so tempting. She boils them and takes out the yellow middle part, and she makes up this white, creamy stuff and adds some spices she won't let on to nobody. Then she stuffs it back in the eggs. She only makes them up for special days 'cause it's hard work."

Min had also prepared roast chicken, freshly baked cinnamon bread, and a plate of her greens with onion and fatback. Anna and Stanley passed back and forth a jar of cool, sweet tea.

When the meal was done and the basket—much less weighty now—was packed, the two sat side by side, hand in hand, on the bank of the creek. "I'd like to stop time just now, Stanley," Anna said. "It's so peaceful, can't hear nothing but the birds and the water in the creek."

"And a breeze playing through the treetops now and then."

Anna smiled. "You always been fine with the words. Wish I was. Has your second wound done healed?"

Stanley moved his left shoulder around, testing it. "There's still a pang now and again, but it's not a bother. This might sound odd, but it's a wound I'll always be thankful for."

"Now, that makes no sense at all, Stanley."

Stanley lifted Anna's hand to his lips and kissed it softly. His pleading blue eyes pierced her deeply. "Are we closer now than before?" he asked.

"You know we are."

Stanley wrapped a strong arm around Anna and drew her close. She laid her head upon his chest and he began to run his fingers through her long, fine hair.

"I love you, Anna."

Anna lifted her face toward Stanley. "I—"

The touch of his finger to her lips silenced her.

"I couldn't leave tomorrow without telling you. When I awakened after Luke—I wanted to tell you then, but I was too afraid, I guess. A beautiful, courageous girl fought for me, and when I awoke I saw that same girl clinging to my hand, and she had been weeping—for me. Do you know how amazing that is?"

Anna nodded silently but didn't take her eyes from Stanley's. And when Stanley bent his head down toward her, she didn't pull away. She welcomed his warm, soft lips upon hers.

"My first kiss," Anna whispered against Stanley's lips when they parted. "And quite nice, I think." She kissed him again, long and lingering. "I love you, too, Stanley. Fought it for a while, you know I did. But then I just gave up."

Their laughter mingled with the rippling waters of the creek below and rose to the canopy of leafy greenery above.

Stanley grew quiet and serious again. "Anna?"

She brought her face close to his. "The army?"

Stanley touched her cheek gently, where Luke had struck her. "You know I must try."

Anna nodded slowly. "But if you ain't back with Levi tomorrow night, my heart'll be broke."

"As will mine. But it will probably be for only a few days, or a week or two, until they get all their papers in order. At worst I might have to return to Ohio to be discharged, and I can write letters to you in the meantime."

Stanley raised himself from the bank of the creek, held out his hand to help Anna up, and led her a few yards away from the creek. "I have something to give you and I wouldn't want to lose it in the creek." He reached into the pocket of his duck trousers and took out a small cloth-wrapped bundle.

Anna was instantly curious. "What's that?"

"In school," Stanley said, "I learned that in some cultures, it's customary for the man to give the parents of the young lady he wishes to marry something of value."

Anna's breath caught in her throat. She swallowed hard. "Like a...a bride price? Mr. Chalmers said the Chickasaws used to do that."

"Yes. In other cultures, the price would be given directly to the bride. I hold in my hand all of my worldly possessions. It's all I have to offer as my bride price, and now I give my all to you."

Anna couldn't speak. She smiled at Stanley with joy-filled, tear-filled eyes and received the small bundle in her own trembling hands, cradling it tenderly, treasuring it before she even knew what the bundle contained.

The simple knot in the string yielded easily to her shaky fingers; she pulled the cloth carefully aside.

"Oh, my darling Stanley, you sure know how to make a girl cry." Anna picked up each of the six shiny brass buttons in turn and held them close to her face. She did likewise with the belt buckle. Her fingers traced the large embossed letters and explored the impression made by the musket ball, first on the front of the buckle, then on the rear. Lastly she picked up the ball that had pierced his chest and held it high, watching how it gleamed in the sunlight that filtered down through the trees above. Then she pressed it to her lips.

Anna folded the cloth tightly around the priceless gifts and tucked the small bundle away in her own pocket. "I'll always see you in them things," she said, drawing close to Stanley and looking up at him.

Stanley cupped her face in his hands. "I can't ask you to marry me, my dearest Anna, not yet, anyway. But I do make this pledge to you. No matter what happens after Levi and I drive down the lane tomorrow morning, I promise to find my way back to Matthews Hill as soon as I am able—and to you, Anna, if you'll have this lame Yankee, and if the Lord allows it."

"What do you mean 'if you'll have this lame Yankee'? We're done with lame and Yankee, too, ain't we?"

"We are."

"Then I can only pledge you back with all me, 'cause I ain't got any buttons I can spare. Deal?"

Anna extended her hand to shake on it, but Stanley wrapped her in his arms and held her tightly, and the deal was sealed with another long, passionate kiss.

CHAPTER 46

*D*AVINA FELT AT PEACE FOR THE FIRST TIME IN A LONG TIME. There was still plenty to do, and the prospect of a long, steamy afternoon ahead, with air so thick it drained the body just to move through it, made her unwilling to move a single muscle. The best place to be on such a day was right where she was, seated in the shade of the veranda, where gentle breezes tickled wisps of her hair, or rippled over the damp skin of her neck.

Rest in the Lord, and wait patiently for him, Davina had read that morning after breakfast. Her daughter and a Yankee boy—she was resting in the Lord for that decision. And when Stanley left for Corinth in the morning, she'd be resting in the Lord then, too. If the army kept him, she'd miss him for sure. The gaping hole where Ben and Aaron had been wasn't gone, not by a long shot, but it was shrinking a little day by day. She had told Stanley she meant to do good by him, and she had, but she knew that he had done just as much good by her.

Across the yard Levi and his oldest, Jeremiah, were cleaning out the stalls of Duke and Earl and the two mules—a chore they usually did together every Friday. Normal, that's what it was, something she hadn't believed she would ever experience again. But every day, it seemed, things were slowly getting back to normal. Different, but normal.

For as the heavens are higher than the earth, so are my ways higher than your ways, and my thoughts than your thoughts. Davina couldn't help smiling. They were down at the creek having their picnic and reading, or splashing in the water, and the joy they found in each other was as plain as the day was hot. It would be up to the Lord to bring Anna's Stanley back from the army, if that's what he wanted. She wished him a speedy return almost as much as she knew Anna did. *Rest in the Lord.*

A faint clatter from down the lane startled Davina. Pastor Blackwell wasn't expected. Could it be Winnie Johnson, who had said she'd get her husband, Preston, to drive her "one of these days"? Davina stood and went to the railing next to the steps, ready to extend a welcoming hand or enjoy a friendly embrace. She caught a glimpse through the trees of a pair of reddish-brown horses with white markings drawing a covered farm wagon she didn't recognize. Two riders followed the wagon up the lane, and just before the rig entered the farmyard, she saw the driver and was instantly chilled to the bone.

Davina hurried into the parlor for the scattergun that hung above the fireplace, but stopped short. The gun was missing. She looked around the room. It was nowhere in sight. Had Luke taken the gun and gone hunting? He had always told her when he was taking the gun.

She returned to the veranda and stood at the top of the steps, just as she had done during the slave trader's previous visit. LaVache turned the wagon around in the yard and pulled it to a halt in front of the doorway to the barn, also just as he had done before. The two riders, hard-looking men Davina had never seen before, drew their revolvers as they entered the yard. One stopped about twenty yards to Davina's left. The other continued slowly across the yard, passing directly in front of Davina and positioning himself about twenty yards to her right.

"I told you before," Davina yelled at LaVache. "I ain't selling any of my blacks. You mean to take them from me with guns drawn?"

Davina had no idea where Luke had been, but suddenly he was there, standing with arms crossed to her right on the veranda —and he appeared to be smiling. Willy, Ruthie, and Li'l Davy came running from behind the house and huddled beside her. And from the corner of her eye, Davina saw Min's dark head poke out of the larder door, then quickly disappear.

"Is it LaVache, Mama?" Willy asked, unable to see for himself.

"Yes, it is," she said, "and he's up to no good."

LaVache climbed down from the wagon and walked toward Davina until he stood in the center of the yard, his hands resting on the grips of his holstered revolvers. "I didn't come for one of your blacks, Mrs. Matthews. But I did hear some unsettling news."

"And what's that?"

"I heard you're thinking of freeing your blacks. Is that true, Mrs. Matthews?"

Davina looked sideways at Luke. It could only have been him. He would never disobey her, never betray her—or so she had thought until that moment. But it was the only explanation for this sudden invasion by that scoundrel LaVache, and the frozen smile on her son's face confirmed it.

"No, it's not true. But if I chose to do so, it would be my right by law," Davina said, trying hard to present herself certain and strong.

"Whose law? Only law here is me and Dill and Tyson," the slave trader said with a wave of his hand at the two riders. He took a few more steps toward Davina. "Mrs. Matthews, I said I'm not here for any of your blacks. The word in town is that you are still harboring a Yankee."

Luke! How could you do this to me? And to Anna?

"I'm a man of my word, Mrs. Matthews. You know that. So I take it most personally when someone lies to me." His words became terse and strident. "And you, Mrs. Matthews, lied to me.

You said that Yankee had gone back to his own kind, and now I know that Yankee never left at all."

So that's what this is about. Davina looked at Luke. The boy's eyes darted at LaVache, up the lane toward the creek, at the two riders, at the ground under his feet, and every so often, at her. Nervous as he was, she still saw only triumphant pride and cruel joy.

How could you do this thing? You've betrayed your own mother and sister. Don't you know this man's a devil?

"Luke!"

It was LaVache's voice, loud, hard, commanding.

"Come here, Luke."

Luke obeyed instantly—and with a smile. When was the last time he had obeyed her so quickly and without argument? In an instant the dark hole inside Davina yawned wide and threatened to swallow her completely. The rest and peace she had enjoyed moments before were gone. All of her hopes and wishes for Anna and Stanley were dashed, along with her wonder at how God had carried her through her dark night of trial.

"He's under my protection." Davina's throat ached from the tension. "If you must have blood, take mine."

"But I don't want you," LaVache said. "I want that Yankee. We can't have that Yankee changing the way we do things, and we sure can't have that Yankee taking up with a beautiful young southern lass like your daughter, can we?"

"No," the ruffian on the left yelled. "Ain't no Yankee gonna shame a fine Rebel girl. That's just silly." LaVache and his two riders all laughed, and much to Davina's dismay, Luke laughed, too.

Willy's voice rang out high above the racket. "He'll be gone tomorrow."

My blessed Willy. Maybe that man will listen to a child.

"What's that, boy?"

"Stanley's going back to the Yankees tomorrow," Willy said.

"Mrs. Matthews." LaVache's voice was heavy with disdain. "Now you have your little ones telling lies to protect that Yankee."

"It ain't so!" Willy said. "He ain't a Yankee no more. He's been good to me, and I don't want him to go, but he's going just the same. Tell him, Luke."

LaVache looked at Luke. "Is it true the Yankee's going back to the army?"

"Says he is," Luke said, "but like as not, he'll be back soon, maybe tomorrow night even."

LaVache looked at Davina, appearing to study her for a few long moments. "Well, Mrs. Matthews, this certainly is an interesting development."

"You mean you'll leave him be?"

"No, not at all, Mrs. Matthews. I came here for a Yankee, and I mean to leave with one."

Rage tore through Davina. "You will not have him!"

"Oh, but I will," LaVache said. "You will give up that Yankee, or—" In one smooth movement, he seized Luke by his mop of unruly hair with one hand, and with the other drew one of the revolvers and brought the muzzle up against the side of the boy's face. "Or I will take this one here."

"Mama!" Luke shrieked. The sudden terror in Luke's eyes was genuine, and Davina knew that Luke hadn't expected this trick of LaVache's. But he wouldn't dare harm Luke. Would he?

"Oh, yes, I will, Mrs. Matthews," LaVache said coldly, as if he could read her thoughts. "Maybe I'll shoot him right now. Or maybe, if you don't give me that damnable Yankee, I'll just take him. The army always needs drummer boys, seeing as how they're always getting killed. Or maybe I'll take him down to Mobile and sell him to some sea captain for a cabin boy. Either way, you'll never see your boy again."

"I know where he is!" Luke cried. "He's up—"

LaVache jammed the pistol into Luke's throat. "Hush, boy!

Your mama lied to me. Now she's going to tell me the truth." His voice rose to a shout. "Where is that Yankee, Mrs. Matthews?"

There was, Davina realized to her dismay, only one decision she could make. So much had been taken already, and now much more would be taken. Luke may have chosen the path of darkness, but she was still his mother—even though it had been many months since he had acted like the son she had borne. It was her job to turn him back to the path of light and life. He would reap what he had sown. He had chosen to dance with the devil, and now he had a gun to his head.

Lord Almighty, don't let this evil destroy my family. Turn my boy back to the light. Tell me what to say and do. Shame him and break him, if that's what it takes to make him a good man. And, Lord, please watch over Stanley. I pray he's one of yours.

"He's...Stanley's up the lane there to the creek with Anna," Davina said. "Don't you lay a hand on her." Anna would be destroyed, perhaps forever, by this. And what of Willy, who was now weeping openly and clinging desperately to her?

"How far is that?" LaVache asked Luke. He lifted the gun away from the boy's neck, but maintained the firm grip on his hair.

"A...a...a quarter mile maybe."

"Is he armed?"

"No, sir."

"Dill! Tyson! Ride on over that hill. Take that Yankee and hold him. I'll be right along with the wagon. Remember what I said, no shooting unless he gives you trouble. I don't want him dead, not yet anyway. I heard he's a big, strong fellow. That's what you have the rope for."

Dill and Tyson whooped in unison and galloped up the lane toward the cemetery, pistols drawn.

LaVache once again put the barrel of his gun against Luke's temple. Then he cocked the hammer slowly; its soft click carried clearly to Davina on the veranda. "I will have that Yankee, Mrs.

Matthews, or I'll have your boy. I didn't drive all the way out here for nothing."

He shoved Luke toward the wagon. "Get up there, boy. Don't give me any trouble if you want to make it back to your mama in one piece."

CHAPTER 47

"WOULD YOU READ THAT AGAIN, PLEASE?" STANLEY ASKED.
"The whole thing?" Anna asked.

"No, just the last few sentences." The two sat side by side again on the bank of the creek, Stanley's bare feet submerged in the cool water, Anna's not quite touching its surface. "I think it's right there," Stanley said, looking over her shoulder and pointing at the page.

"Oh, yeah, the one that's long enough for three sentences. 'I do not remember that I had, in all that time, one thought that so much as tended either to looking upwards towards God, or inwards towards a reflection upon my own ways; but a certain stupidity of soul, without desire of good, or conscience of evil, had entirely overwhelmed me; and I was all that the most hardened, unthinking, wicked creature among our common sailors can be supposed to be; not having the least sense, either of the fear of God in danger, or of thankfulness to God in deliverance.'"

"I was that man, Anna. I was just like Crusoe—'a certain stupidity of soul.'" Stanley took the book from Anna and read the words again as if to commit them to memory. "That was me, all of it, before your mama and Levi found me and brought me here."

Stanley's hair had fallen in front of his face when he bent his head to read. Anna brushed it back with her hand and turned his face toward hers. "Your tears come so easy, Stanley. It's your tender heart I—"

Hoofbeats, galloping fast and growing nearer, caused them to turn and look up the lane toward the cemetery. Two riders Anna didn't recognize, pistols at the ready, were coming fast. Her stomach knotted.

The two men pulled up just outside the tree line beside the creek and dismounted. They were of average size, their faces dark and weathered. One was an inch or two shorter and a few pounds heavier than the other. He waved his pistol at Stanley. "You the Yankee?" His voice matched his hard appearance.

Stanley nodded.

"Get up!" the man said.

They would have to do what the armed men said, at least for now. Anna jumped to her feet and offered her hand to Stanley. He reached for his thick hickory walking stick and struggled to his feet.

"Take that cane, girlie," the man said to Anna.

"But he can't walk without it."

The man laughed a little. "Guess he won't be running off, then. Bring the rope, Tyson."

"Rope?" The knot in Anna's stomach became wrenching terror. "You're going to—no! You can't."

"Yes, we can, girl," Tyson said. "But the boss said tie him. We'll string him up later, right, Dill?" Both men laughed.

Stanley handed his cane to Anna. Dill waved her aside with his pistol while Tyson bound Stanley's hands tightly in front of him.

The boss, the men had said. LaVache! It could only be him, Anna knew. That vile man would do whatever he wished to Stanley.

Her mind seized upon one frantic, desperate idea, and then another even more desperate, and another. But the men were armed, and what hope did a girl and a strong-but-injured man have against them? A dark covered wagon rattled over the crest of the hill and started down toward the creek. She stared at the driver—and at his passenger. Luke! This must all be his doing. Her worst fear had now become reality. Stanley would be taken from her, and there was no way she could stop it.

LaVache turned the wagon around. "Get down," he told Luke, and then climbed down himself.

"Aha!" LaVache called out when he spotted Stanley, bound and standing between Dill and Tyson. "You're right, boy," he said to Luke, "he's a big one. Now that I have him, you can go back to your mama."

Anna wished Luke would just run back over the hill and disappear. Instead, he moved only a few paces away from the wagon and leaned against a large ash tree to watch.

LaVache drew both of his pistols and leveled them at Stanley. "No trouble, or this pretty girl is going to see just what a gutless Yankee looks like on the inside, and we wouldn't want that, would we?"

"No sir," Stanley said. "No trouble."

LaVache ordered Tyson to untie Stanley's hands.

"Now," LaVache said, "get up in that wagon, boy."

It was dark inside the wagon, but the clanking of metal and the rattling of chains told Anna exactly what was happening. LaVache was chaining her Stanley just as he had chained slaves in that same wagon. His wrists and ankles were manacled. Then a thicker, heavier manacle was put around his neck, through which a strong chain was passed and locked securely to a heavy iron ring on the side of the wagon.

LaVache climbed into the driver's seat. Anna stepped closer to him, still holding Stanley's cane. "Are you going to kill Stanley?"

LaVache looked at her for a long moment. "I can't say, girl."

"Can't or won't?"

"Like I told your mother, I'm a man of my word. I can't tell you what I'm going to do with him, because I haven't made up my mind yet. But it doesn't matter. You'll never see him again."

Anna stifled a cry. The thought of Stanley's death tore at her insides, almost driving her to her knees. But there was no time for despair. Stanley wasn't dead yet, and until then...

Anna swallowed hard. She wiped her sleeve across her face and tried to quiet her trembling. Then she held the walking stick up toward LaVache, the thick, carved horse-head first. She fought to keep her words and her tone soft and respectful, empty of the hate and anger that raged inside her. "Please, sir, take his cane. He can't walk without it."

LaVache shook his head. "That's a good, stout stick. He could club me with it."

And I'll pray he gets the chance to. Anna lowered her voice to prevent Luke, who was still leaning against the tree on the other side of the wagon, from hearing. "He ain't that way. He's still a boy, sir, only sixteen, and he's got no hate in him. Almost killed at Shiloh, he was, and he's got no mama or papa, neither, and he's crippled like you seen yourself. He's a gentle boy, sir, and he's a hard worker. Real smart too. He can do most anything."

LaVache didn't look at Anna.

"Just look at the cane, Mr. LaVache. Ain't it beautiful? When's the last time you saw carving like that? I bet it would fetch you a fine price."

LaVache turned his head at last and gave her a calculating look. Then he grabbed the walking stick from her and threw it under the seat. "That's the first smart thing you've said, girl. He won't need it, you know, chained as he is."

"Did you say it don't matter to you if you kill him?"

LaVache nodded and picked up the reins.

"Then, since we won't never see him again in these parts, I beg you, sir, spare his life. 'Cause I don't see how killing a unarmed, crippled orphan would be a credit to you."

LaVache replied with a loud "Giddap."

Anna fell in directly behind the wagon. LaVache was in no hurry; he seemed to be drawing out the agony of the moment of parting. Anna held onto the tail end of the wagon, just as she had done when Aaron's coffin was carried to the cemetery. Anna glanced over her shoulder. Dill and Tyson followed a few paces behind, talking to each other, their pistols holstered now. Not that it mattered what Luke did, now or ever again, but he was trailing slowly along behind LaVache's two henchmen.

"You know what I told you, Anna." Stanley was just a few feet away; she could almost touch him, but to do so might make things go even harder for him.

"I know," Anna said. She kept a firm hold on the wagon and gazed at Stanley. The afternoon sunlight on the canvas top allowed her to see him now: his dark, wavy hair—he had allowed her to cut it—his pleasant, gentle face, those blue eyes that always lit up for her, his nose that turned down just a little at the tip. She studied every detail, committing his image to memory. "And you know what I told you, Stanley."

Stanley's eyes never left hers. He nodded and smiled. "The buttons say it all, Anna."

At the farmyard, LaVache stopped the wagon in the center of the yard. Dill and Tyson trotted their horses across the yard and positioned themselves on either side of the lane to the Chambers Store Road. "Say your good-byes, Yank," LaVache called.

Mama, her eyes red and her face streaked with tears, hurried toward the wagon.

"Stay where you are," LaVache ordered.

"Go ahead and shoot me, you devil," Mama cried, without slowing in the least. "I'm saying a proper good-bye to my boy."

She peered into the back of the wagon. Anna saw the shock on her face at seeing Stanley chained. "Oh, my poor boy. God go with you, Stanley. We'll pray for you every day."

"Good-bye, Mama," Stanley said, his own tears flowing again, "and thank you for—for all of it."

It took all of Anna's self-control to stay where she was, to not climb into the wagon to hug and kiss him. Luke appeared beside her and put his arm around her. Anna shrugged it off.

"Enough," yelled LaVache.

"Good-bye, Willy," Stanley called.

Willy sniffled. "Good-bye, brother."

A sharp crack of LaVache's whip started the wagon forward. "Half an hour, boys," he called to Dill and Tyson. "That's all I need. Make sure nobody leaves. Then you can head back to town."

Anna watched the wagon roll down the lane until it passed out of sight. It would be so easy to collapse in the dust of the yard as she had done when Aaron was brought home, to give in to the pain and hopelessness. But she didn't. Something was different in her now—something good and strong and decent had come alive within her, and his name was Stanley Mitchell.

She turned toward the house. Luke was still standing to her left, grinning from ear to ear. He raised his hand high and waved happily at the quickly vanishing cloud of dust, the last visible trace of the boy from Ohio. "Good riddance, Yank."

With all the force of her anguish and fury behind it, Anna's tightly clenched right fist caught her brother flush in the face and sent him sprawling in the dust. She looked down at him for a moment as he rocked from side to side, clutching his broken and bleeding nose with both hands.

Anna stood over her brother and shook a scolding finger at him, like she had seen her mother do many times before. "It's God that brung Stanley here," she said, her voice low and trembling with anger, "and God will bring him back. You just wait and see."

Then she stepped over him and walked toward the house, her stride long and purposeful.

If You Enjoyed This Book, Please Consider Sharing the Message with Others

❑ Mention *Until Shiloh Comes* on Twitter or Pinterest, or in a Facebook post or blog post.

❑ Recommend this book to your friends, discussion group, book club, or classmates.

❑ Like my Facebook page: facebook.com/karl.bacon.7 and post a comment about what you enjoyed most about the book.

❑ Visit my website: kbacon.com

❑ Email me: kb@kbacon.com

❑ Give a copy of this book to someone who might enjoy and be encouraged by it.

❑ Write a review on amazon.com, bn.com, goodreads.com, or cbd.com.

ABOUT THE AUTHOR

From youth, Karl A. Bacon has been a serious student of the Civil War. Countless hours of detailed research supply the foundation for each novel, including copious amounts of reading and Internet research as well as personal visits to battlefields and historic sites. This research provides depth and realism to make the novels as historically accurate and believable as possible. Karl's first novel, *An Eye for Glory*, was a *Publishers Weekly* Top Pick for Spring/Summer 2011 and a Christy Award Finalist for First Novel in 2012. Karl lives with his wife, Jackie, in Connecticut.

J-18